'Travis Hol... t very rare
book, a ... rical" and
remember ... fact - the
archivist P... any of us,

[illegible]

'[illegible] a [illegible] novel ... The writing is [illegible] the man-made madness of the Soviet Union' *The Times*

'[illegible] novel and a profoundly moving one' *Metro*

'[illegible] the cultural [illegible]' *[illegible] Review*

'[illegible] of Stalin's Soviet Union' *Sunday Times Magazine*

'[illegible] *Literary Review*

'This powerful debut about the extinction of memory in Stalin's Soviet Union [illegible]' *[illegible]*

'[illegible] *[illegible]*

# THE ARCHIVIST'S STORY

TRAVIS HOLLAND

BLOOMSBURY

Portions of this book appeared in a slightly different form in the *Michigan Quarterly Review*.

Translation of excerpts from the poetry of Osip Mandelstam, copyright © 2004 by Clarence Brown and W.S. Merwin, permission of Clarence Brown and the Wylie Agency.

First published in Great Britain 2007
This paperback edition published 2008



ISBN 978 0 7475 9320 1

A CIP record of this book is available from the British Library

Printed in Great Britain by Clays Limited, St Ives plc

All papers used by Bloomsbury Publishing are natural, recyclable products made from wood grown in well-managed forests. The manufacturing process conform to the environmental regulations of the country of origin

www.bloomsbury.com

*For Amy*

*You took away all the oceans and all the room.*
*You gave me my shoe-size in earth with bars around it.*
*Where did it get you? Nowhere.*
*You left me my lips, and they shape words, even in silence.*
—Osip Mandelstam

*I have only one request:*
*that I be allowed to complete my last work . . .*
—Isaac Babel
Final statement before NKVD Military Tribunal
January 26, 1940

# I

It is a small matter that brings them together. A story, untitled, unsigned, and by all appearances incomplete, which the arresting officers in their haste have neglected to record in the evidence manifest. A year ago, when the Lubyanka thrummed with activity, when all of Moscow seemed to hold its breath at night and every morning brought a new consignment of confiscated manuscripts to Pavel's desk, such a discovery would have hardly warranted a second look, let alone this face-to-face meeting the archivist frankly dreads. Babel has confessed: One story will not change that, nor will it save him. Still, Kutyrev has insisted the matter be formally resolved, and since Pavel must now answer to the ambitious young lieutenant, the question of authorship is to be settled, if only for the record. Already an empty office upstairs has been reserved for the purpose. In due course the appointed morning comes. Just as the first heavy drops of rain are beginning to fall onto the dreary courtyard below, a guard raps once on the door. Babel enters.

"I was about to make tea," Pavel offers. On the bureau beside the window sit an electric samovar, a serving tray, tea glasses and spoons, a darkly tarnished tin, all left behind by the office's previous occupant, absent now. Behind the desk, where a row of pictures once hung, the plaster is noticeably lighter; only nails remain. "Would you like to sit down?"

After a moment, as if Pavel's voice has only now reached him, Babel nods, then sits. He is unshaven. A bruise is fading under his right eye, and a faint film, like dried salt, coats his lips. The wilted wings of his shirt collar lie crookedly across the lapels of his wrinkled coat. And this finally, which Pavel finds most disturbing: The writer's glasses are gone. Somehow he had expected Babel to appear as he once did in his dust-jacket pictures.

Pavel lifts the empty teapot from the samovar. "I'll just get this filled."

At first the young guard standing watch outside merely stares dully at the teapot, as if he has never laid eyes on one before. He is at most twenty, with the sleepy eyes of a peasant. Some displaced farmer's son, perhaps, come to Moscow to better himself. Whatever he is, the expression on his face is familiar enough. "Water," Pavel sighs, handing the teapot over. He might as well be back at Kirov Academy, standing in front of a classroom of boys hardly younger than this guard, reading aloud lines from Tolstoy. *Ivan Ilych's life had been most simple and most ordinary and therefore most terrible.* Sons of want and privilege alike, born in revolution's shadow: It is his former students' generation now joining the numberless ranks already marching under the banner of collective progress, while their former teachers reconcile themselves to silence. In the two and a half years since his appointment to the special archives, where until Kutyrev's arrival this past May he was alone, Pavel has become painfully aware of just how fortunate he once was, how blessed. He would give anything to be standing before his students again, book in hand.

With the rain has come a kind of false twilight. All week the weather has been like this. Sitting, Pavel pulls the brass chain of the desk lamp, which clatters softly against the green glass shade. "I keep hoping we'll get a little sun soon," he says, trying to hide his nervousness. It is not every day one meets a writer of Babel's eminence. He asks, "Are you hungry? I'm sure I could have something sent up, if you'd like."

"Thank you. No."

A high, almost breathy voice: Babel will not even meet his eye. Pavel stares openly at the bruise on Babel's cheek, then looks away. The guard returns with the teapot.

At the window again Pavel fills the samovar. Next door a telephone rings once, is answered. A watery, pale light cups the rounded side of the warming samovar, spilling over Pavel's hands as he pries open the tin. Only a little tea remains, the blackish, powdery leavings like a kind of sand he tips into the waiting teapot. Tilting the tin toward the light, Pavel catches a glimpse of his own blurred reflection in it. Then he returns to the desk.

"Might I ask a question, Comrade Inspector?"

"I'm not an inspector," Pavel says quickly. "I work down in the archives." Leaning forward, he wipes the green cardboard of Babel's file folder with his fingers. A pink ribbon, neatly tied, holds the folder shut. "Actually," he adds, "I used to be a teacher, believe it or not. I taught your stories."

"My stories."

"From *Red Cavalry*." When one could teach them, Pavel thinks. When it was acceptable. Safe. "Some of your later work as well. 'Guy de Maupassant' is a personal favorite of mine." The opening lines of Babel's story, which he has never tired of reading, return to Pavel:

> In the winter of 1916 I found myself in St. Petersburg with a forged passport and not a cent to my name. Alexey

Kazantsev, a teacher of Russian literature, took me into his house.

A teacher of Russian literature—the irony stings now.

Babel squints at the green folder with an expression of dull, somewhat dazed perplexity, as if Pavel has conjured it up out of nothingness by some sleight of hand. Then his dark eyes empty again.

"May I ask," Babel says finally, "what day it is?"

"Tuesday."

"Is it still June?"

"July."

"Already—" At least that is what Pavel thinks he hears Babel murmur. *Already.* It has been barely two months since Babel's arrest, two months since the customary unmarked car carried him at dawn through the enormous black gate of the courtyard below. Has he lost his grip on time? Or perhaps, Pavel imagines, Babel is simply, quietly stunned: that he could be brought down so fast, so completely. That in only two months he could become the battered, cowed shell of a man now sitting in this all but abandoned office. Pavel remembers his own first months at the Lubyanka, themselves a stark revelation, though it is obscene to compare his experience with Babel's. He has not suffered one-tenth the torment Babel has likely had inflicted on him: days without sleep or food or water, threats, beatings.

Pavel says, "I've been asked—ordered—to clear up a discrepancy in your file. It's just a formality."

"What sort of discrepancy?"

"A manuscript my supervisor happened upon while reviewing your file. A story. Quite a remarkable story. There's no record of it in the evidence manifest, which means it can't be officially attributed to anyone, yourself included. Which means, officially speaking"—Pavel shrugs uncomfortably—"it doesn't exist. As I said, it's just a formality. If you could perhaps take a look, tell me if you recognize it. Can you read without your glasses?"

"Barely. I was told they would be returned to me," Babel says. "If I cooperated."

*Cooperated.* Confessed, he means—and in doing so, likely implicated others. Nowadays one cannot simply confess, one must also denounce. Acquaintances, colleagues, friends, even one's own family. Whom, if anyone, has Babel drawn into the net that has now fallen over his life? Eisenstein perhaps, Ehrenburg? Pasternak? A man of Babel's prominence would be expected to name others at least as well-known as himself.

*I spent my mornings hanging around the morgues and police stations.*

The line, another from "Guy de Maupassant," echoes through Pavel's brain as he walks once more to the window, where the samovar has begun to boil. Steam shimmers on the glass. "I'm afraid we'll have to make do without sugar," he apologizes, filling the teapot. A sedan is just then pulling into a parking space in the courtyard below, wipers briskly slapping away rain. The wipers cease, the driver's door swings open. An umbrella emerges, blooms: a black peony. Morgues and police stations, Pavel thinks—that is what this age will be remembered for, that is our legacy. "Sugar?" Babel asks. As if the word were new to him.

"For the tea."

Babel is silent.

"I could send for some," Pavel offers, though the prospect of facing the young guard again leaves him tired. No doubt it is also Kutyrev's dreadful, pointless errand that has left him disheartened. For months now the junior officer has seized upon practically every opportunity to drive home his authority over Pavel, like a dog lifting its leg on even the most neglected patch of garden, marking its territory. More than once Pavel has come close to telling Kutyrev that he needn't bother. He is welcome to the archives, right down to the last folder. Pavel hands Babel his tea glass. "Mind, it's hot."

Babel holds the steaming glass of watery tea near his chest. "You were a teacher," he says after a time.

"Of literature, yes."

"Literature." Spoken without irony, without bitterness. He straightens slightly in his chair. Perhaps, Pavel thinks, the tea has revived him. "Did you enjoy teaching?" Babel asks.

"Very much," says Pavel.

Rain taps at the window. Absently Pavel brushes back his hair, feels something hard. The partial husk of a seed comes away in his fingers: It must have fallen from one of the lindens near his building as he walked to the bus stop this morning. He lays it on the desktop.

"Your *Red Cavalry* stories," he tells Babel, "they were always quite popular with my students. Boys, you know. They tend to be drawn to war. Your stories fascinated them."

*Twenty-nine volumes of Maupassant stood on the shelf above the desk. The sun with its fingers of melting dissolution touched the morocco backs of the books—the magnificent grave of the human heart.*

He cannot get Babel's story out of his head. He notices that the fingers of Babel's right hand, spread on his thigh, are twitching ever so slightly, as if a faint current of electricity were coursing through them. Suddenly Pavel is struck by the realization that the very lines from the story floating in his brain once flowed from that hand, those fingers. He imagines that the lucky few train passengers who managed to catch a glimpse of Tolstoy, dying in that railroad stationhouse in Astapovo, must have felt a similar sense of mingled awe and disbelief.

From the corridor outside comes the faint rhythmic jingling

of keys. Regulation at the Lubyanka requires that guards with prisoners announce themselves—either in just this manner or by clicking their tongues—so that no two prisoners ever accidentally meet. An institution built brick by brick upon secrecy, a world unto itself. Still, try as he might to avoid them, the stories have nevertheless trickled down to Pavel, like water leaking from a poisoned well. Mandelstam, weakened by months of abuse, muttering fragments from his own poems to the guards who stormed his cell after he slashed his wrists with a razor. Pilnyak, sobbing like a child, slumping against the cold cellar wall when the executioner touched the pistol barrel to the back of his neck. *Wait, wait.*

Pavel asks, "Would you like more tea?" The writer's fingers, he notices, have stopped twitching.

"Yes."

As Pavel is filling the writer's glass, Babel says tentatively, "I was wondering if I might be permitted to write a letter. To my wife."

A little tea accidentally sloshes over the rim of the glass. "Sorry," Pavel says.

"Please. It would ease her mind."

"I don't think that's possible," Pavel says after a moment. The weariness that has dogged him all morning suddenly presses on his heart. "If it were permitted—" He sets the teapot down on the samovar with a clatter, nearly spilling more tea. "I'm sorry, comrade." The word—unforgivable, given the circumstances—is out of his mouth before Pavel can stop himself. *Comrade.* He adds nervously, "Understand, it's not a matter of whether or not I'd like to help you. I would. I'm married myself."

He breaks off, looking down at the skin of oil floating on the surface of his tea, which reminds him, quite inexplicably, of ice.

The river in spring, the dirty ice beneath Krymsky Bridge shearing off in chunks, carried away. He remembers that afternoon in January before his wife, Elena, left for Yalta, when they walked along the winter-black river beneath Lenin Hills. How she had told him she could not wait until April, when the ice would finally melt. "I'm so sick of winter. Sometimes I think how wonderful it would be to never have to come back here." At the station later, embracing, Elena had touched his ear with her lips and whispered, "Come with me, Pasha. Please." The rabbit collar of her coat brushed Pavel's neck, light as breath. Impossible, of course: They both understood that Pavel could not leave Moscow just then, not without permission from his supervisors. Still, she had asked, she had tried in her way.

Pavel feels Babel regarding him, waiting. "What I mean is, I was married," he tells Babel now. "My wife passed away last January."

Babel meets this with silence.

Pavel takes a deep breath, then unties the pink ribbon and opens Babel's folder. In it, faceup, lies a loose sheaf of unlined paper covered in tight, neat script: Babel's unfinished manuscript—if indeed he is its author, as Pavel has every reason to believe. Even incomplete, the writing here is as beautiful and vivid as anything Pavel has ever read. A treasure, perhaps among Babel's finest work. Pavel clears his throat. "I suppose we should get started," he says. When he looks up he sees that Babel has turned toward the window.

"Is it raining still?"

"A little, yes," Pavel says.

A silence settles over them, which Pavel finds himself unexpectedly reluctant to disturb. Then, almost tenderly, he asks Babel, "What is your wife's name?"

"Antonina."

Absently Babel lifts a finger to his mouth, thoughtfully rubs his lower lip. The light from the window lies like a dusting of snow on the shoulders of his coat, which doubtless he has slept in since his arrest. The full-lipped, almost sensuous mouth, those dark eyes, the high wide dome of a forehead with its single pronounced worry line: All at once Pavel is struck by the simple miracle of this moment, which nothing in his life could have prepared him for. The cooling samovar ticks like a metronome, roughly in time to the pulse Pavel can see beating faintly in Babel's throat.

"I promised her we would see each other again," Babel says. "Will they let her visit me, do you think?"

"I don't know."

"I wouldn't want my last words to her to be a lie."

"Of course not." *Come with me, Pasha. Please.* To which Pavel had replied: *I will see you soon.* His last words to Elena. The memory is enough to drive Pavel from his chair—he cannot face Babel. At the bureau he sets down his tea glass, then thinks, I wish I had gotten on that train.

As if picking up on this, Babel asks, "How did your wife die?"

"She was on her way to Yalta. The train derailed."

"An accident."

"The police suspect it may have been sabotage. Something laid across the tracks." Pavel must gather himself before continuing. "From what I was told, she was thrown from the carriage when it broke apart." A pumpkin, Pavel thinks: The image has stayed with him all these long terrible months, the line of wrecked carriages split innocently open like pumpkins on the snow. It is easier to envision this than to confront the images Pavel has repeatedly driven from his mind. Elena spilled out in that field; Elena in the back of a truck, wrapped in a sheet; Elena at the mouth of the crematorium, the tray beneath her trembling on its casters as the morgue attendant pushed her into the fire.

"I can't imagine people intentionally doing that," he says. "Can you?"

Babel stares bleakly down into his glass. "You've read my stories," he says finally, looking up at Pavel. "Your colleagues, when they came to arrest me at my dacha, they dragged my wife along. Did you know that? They made her knock on the door. In case I resisted. Can you imagine how she must have felt, to have to do that?" An edge of bitterness has crept into Babel's voice. "You are not the only one who has lost his wife."

Pavel turns away. A sob rises in his throat and is out before he can stifle it. For a moment he is overcome with a desire to sweep the samovar onto the floor, to knock his empty tea glass and the tin flying—the temptation is so strong Pavel must clutch his hands together, forcing them down.

"They shouldn't have taken your glasses," he says quietly.

*I read the book to the end and got out of bed. The fog came close to the window, the world was hidden from me. My heart contracted as the foreboding of some essential truth touched me with light fingers.*

The hidden world, Pavel thinks absently. This office, this prison. He wishes he had never stumbled upon it. Picking up the sheaf of unlined paper from the desk, he asks Babel, "Did you write this?" He holds the manuscript out, moving toward Babel until their knees touch.

"Mine," Babel says finally. His whole body seems to sag. "It's mine."

This close, Pavel can hear the writer breathing: another simple miracle, witnessed only by himself. Tolstoy, dying in wintry Astapovo, onto which for a time all of Russia, all the world, turned its gaze—that is what Pavel cannot help but compare this moment to and find it wanting. He has read accounts of how railroad engineers held back their whistles out of deference to the dying man, so as not to disturb him. The village's only telegraph office was commandeered in order to send out hourly reports of Tolstoy's temperature and pulse. Trains, packed with journalists, emissaries, priests, factory owners, plainclothes officers, peasants, slowed to a crawl several hundred meters from the platform and crept silently into the station. In the carriages a reverent hush fell as the passengers, the curious and faithful alike, crowded the windows. *I am still composing,* Tolstoy told his son Sergey between gasps for breath, even as death approached. *I am writing.*

# 2

Fourth Section's literary archives occupy a single room just below street level. Once a repository for janitorial supplies and discarded office equipment, its many rows of tall black metal shelves now bend beneath the weight of countless green folders and cardboard boxes, stacked floor to ceiling. Novels, stories, poems, plays, film scenarios—it is Fourth Section's duty to swim through this ocean of words, just as it is Pavel's duty to archive every box and bound folder that arrives on his desk, which sits, alongside Kutyrev's desk, squarely in the shadow of the stacks. Beneath the sharp, slightly sweetish scent of moldering paper another smell lingers, leftover of decades past when the Lubyanka served as national headquarters for the Rossiya Insurance Company. "Bleach," Pavel's predecessor, Omry Alexeyevich Denegin, had grunted by way of greeting that January morning two and a half years ago when they first met. "They used to keep barrels of it down here, you know. For cleaning."

"I suppose," Pavel had replied, "you get used to it. The smell."

"One would suppose."

A difficult old man, Denegin. He was in his late sixties, compact, with an impressive head of wiry thick hair, white as salt. A full week passed before he had warmed sufficiently to Pavel's presence to divulge the workings of the place, slipshod as they were. "Simple enough," he explained, smoothing down an eyebrow. "File comes in, you check whatever's in it against the evidence manifest—the arresting officers supply that—make sure they match up." After that the job simply consisted of loading the bulging folders and boxes onto a handcart and finding room for them back in the crowded hive of stacks. As far as any filing system went, there was none. A particular author's file might take days, even weeks, to locate, Pavel soon discovered. "We're mostly left to ourselves down here," Denegin told him. Pavel noticed he had an absent way of addressing people without quite looking at them, the way a distracted priest or professor might. In fact, Pavel later learned, the old man had once taught Russian literature at universities in Leningrad and Bonn and Berlin.

"Do you ever read any of them?" Pavel asked one day. He meant the manuscripts, of course.

"A line or two sometimes. I try not to. It's a door I'd prefer stay closed. You'll find that here."

"Find what?"

Denegin, Pavel remembers, had regarded him strangely. "Doors you don't want to open," he said.

At his desk now, Pavel unwraps his lunch, only to discover he has no appetite after his meeting. The hunk of cold sausage and black bread he has brought from home turn his stomach. He is still sitting there with his lunch uneaten before him when Kutyrev returns from the cafeteria.

"How did everything go?"

"It's done," Pavel says.

Kutyrev nods noncommittally, sits. From the pocket of his pressed uniform the junior lieutenant produces a cigarette, factory-rolled, which he promptly proceeds to shred, as is his ritual. In the two months he has been here Kutyrev has never once smoked. He is an apparent devotee of the cult of rigorous, self-congratulatory asceticism currently so popular in Soviet Russia. Every morning before dawn, whatever the weather, the young officer swims the length of a lake near his flat, then crosses Moscow by crowded bus. By the time Pavel arrives Kutyrev is generally already at his desk, heavy cheeks blooming in vivid patches like tea roses, green tunic dark with water where his thinning black hair has dripped. At six, regular as clockwork, the young officer switches off his lamp, crosses the city once more by bus to the communal flat that he and his wife, Valentina, whose unflattering picture adorns Kutyrev's desk, share with another couple. He is visibly proud of his wife's simple ugliness, proud of the equally ugly children he will one day sire, who will themselves in their turn dutifully bear their crust of daily hardship.

After the ritual of the shredded cigarette, Kutyrev turns his attention to Babel's file. "You've read him before, right? Is he any good?"

Pavel stares. "You've never read Babel?"

"No." Kutyrev thumbs through the pile of manuscripts. "What is all this, anyway?"

"Stories." Pavel is horrified by the young officer's ignorance, his indifference. "They're stories."

"For children?"

"No," Pavel tells him, "not for children."

Poor Denegin. He had such faith in the dusty fortress of letters he'd erected around himself, even as the storm—the public trials and secret military troikas, the spiraling purges: that mania of collective, inexhaustible bloodletting—raged at its walls. He believed he was safe here, unnoticed, invisible. For three months they worked side by side, and yet Denegin never once spoke of the thousands of manuscripts that filled the stacks in front of their desks, or of the writers, silenced now in one way or another, that each box, each folder represented. Even the subject of their past lives as teachers was scrupulously avoided, for which Pavel was thankful. Only once did Denegin allow that buried part of his history to surface, one snowy afternoon in late March just before he disappeared. They were both putting on their coats, getting ready to leave, when a lightbulb back among the shelves had winked out in its wire cage, leaving the narrow aisle in darkness. " 'The resurrection of the dead, brother,' " Denegin had recited, staring penetratingly into the stacks. " 'First in memory and in spirit.' " He turned. "Andrei Bely, you know. A personal favorite of mine. Have you read *The Silver Dove*?"

"No."

"Hardly anyone does anymore. He was an archivist, too. And a teacher. For a time." He smiled slightly. "Like us."

A joke, Pavel understood, or as close to one as Denegin would allow himself: There was no one like them.

Kutyrev announces, "By the way, the incinerator's working. You better get down there before it breaks again." He nudges the box beside his desk with his boot. "This one can go."

The incinerator. Until Kutyrev's arrival, another side of the Lubyanka Pavel has avoided. Now, once every few weeks, it is Pavel's duty to dispose of whichever files the young officer has culled from the archives. Old cases, investigations closed and forgotten years ago. *Weeding,* as Kutyrev blithely calls it. As if the archives were a garden too long ignored. Reluctantly Pavel lifts the box of manuscripts onto the cart, makes his way down to the service elevator at the end of the corridor, descends.

Outside the incinerator room, which lies at a corner of the subbasement, a line already stretches. Secretaries, junior officers, archivists: Pavel counts almost a dozen men and women, all minor functionaries like himself, over which a grim silence hangs. Only the officers, lazily imperious in their uniforms, their high black boots, exchange small talk and dark jokes among themselves, slyly eyeing the women.

There are two incinerators, both massive oil-burners. The old incinerator, which is constantly breaking down, dates from the turn of the century. The new unit, installed only a year ago, has yet to be lit—at least that is what the elderly engineer who is constantly replacing some valve or another has told Pavel. As Pavel stands waiting with his cart, the engineer emerges from the incinerator room, wiping at his pock-ravaged face with a filthy rag.

"Any day now, comrades," he announces cheerfully.

"That's what you always say," complains one of the young officers. "We should toss you into that fucking stinking thing. Old liar."

"Patience, patience."

Soon enough—too soon—Pavel's turn comes. The heat from the even rows of burners pours over him, the tongues of fire dance and flicker, throwing their light across the concrete floor. Immediately the smell of burning oil fills Pavel's nose, sickening him. It is so hot standing before the open incinerator that he must practically shield his face, and still his eyes feel as if they are shrinking in their sockets. Inside the box he discovers half a dozen folders—the manifest has been removed by Kutyrev, forwarded upstairs to Fourth Section's main office for permanent keeping. As Pavel hurriedly throws one of the folders into the incinerator the pink ribbon binding it flies loose, spilling out paper, page after page—poems, Pavel sees, hundreds of them. On one of the pages, a sheet of onionskin through which the fire shows, sketches of tiny beautifully rendered birds crowd the margin. Pavel imagines the birds must have perched on a ledge outside the poet's window. The sheets curl, the fire races through them. In a moment everything—poet, poems, birds—is gone. Afterward, on the rattling service elevator going up, Pavel's hands shake.

"You smell like kerosene," Kutyrev tells him.

Pavel pushes the cart against the wall, sits.

"May I give you a little friendly advice?"

That is all Pavel needs: friendly advice from Kutyrev. "Why not?" he says.

"You should get out more, exercise. Work up a sweat every now and then. It would do you good. I noticed you didn't even eat your lunch."

"I'm not hungry."

"That's what I mean. A fellow as thin as yourself needs to eat. If you moved around a little more, it might help your appetite."

"Tell me, Comrade Lieutenant," says Pavel after a time, "I was just wondering. Now that we've talked about me. Do you read much?"

"You mean books?"

"Yes."

Kutyrev frowns. "A little. I like Gorky. To be honest, I'm not really much of a reader."

Is that why they sent you down here? Pavel wonders. Is it because none of this touches you? His gaze falls on Babel's folder, the found story, which the junior officer has yet to return to its box. Pavel imagines a morning when he will arrive at his desk and find Babel's entire file—the manuscripts, the notebooks—waiting for him.

Pavel says, "You asked me earlier what kind of writer I

thought Babel was. If I thought he was a good writer."

"Is he?"

"He is a great writer."

Kutyrev is unimpressed. "If that's true, then why haven't I heard more about him? They would have made us read his books in school, like they made us read Gorky. You've seen Babel's file. There's enough in there to give a fellow a hernia. All those stories. Why aren't they in some bookstore somewhere, some library, if he's so great?"

"He stopped publishing for the most part. Some years ago." Master of the genre of silence—isn't that what Babel once half-jokingly called himself?

"Obviously he kept writing."

"Yes," Pavel says. "Obviously."

"For who?"

*Whom,* Pavel corrects mechanically. "For himself, I imagine."

Pavel has never forgotten the fierce look in Denegin's eyes as he gazed into the darkened stacks that winter day—it seems a lifetime ago now. *The resurrection of the dead, brother. First in memory and in spirit.* The words—Bely's words—had all the austere force of an incantation, a prayer. Afterward, emerging together onto busy Dzerzhinsky Square, a dry, stinging snow pelted their faces. Denegin had turned away from Pavel without so much as a nod, the wind tearing at his collar, and slipped into the stream of pedestrians hurrying along the sidewalk. Then he was gone.

# 3

The metro, Pavel notices, is less crowded this evening. So is the ancient bus onto which he transfers outside Gorky Station. The rain has ended, the clouds have cleared away. The lights of Gorky Park glitter lushly on the river: its Ferris wheel, the parachute drop. A roller coaster climbs, then plummets silently into the trees. Outside the new cemetery at Donskoy Monastery, where Pavel is the only passenger to exit, the flower vendors are packing up for the night. From there it is only a block's walk to his building.

The manager stops him as he passes her office. "This came for you," Natalya says, handing Pavel a telegram. He tears open the stiff gray envelope—it is from the morgue clerk in charge of Elena's case. *Inquiries still proceeding. Hopeful. Yours. Simonov.*

*Hopeful*—how Pavel has grown to loathe the word. *Wait,* Simonov might as well be telling Pavel, who has done nothing but wait all these long months.

"You look like you could use a drink," offers Natalya. She is a tall woman, slender, handsome in her way, despite the long, pale scar that curves from one corner of her mouth almost to her ear.

An iridescent blue scarf holds her dark hair back. The hanging red-shaded lamp illuminating the tidy little office casts a fringe of light across her face. Since Elena's death she and Pavel have shared the occasional meal together, though their acquaintanceship has never gone beyond that.

"I have to meet a friend for dinner. Another time perhaps."

From the nearby stairwell a woman's voice carries, shaky with age, gently remonstrative. "Hurry, darling, hurry." Marfa Borisova and her pug, headed down for their evening walk. Natalya's left hand, Pavel notices now, is bandaged.

"What happened to your hand?"

"I was clearing a space in the basement and scraped my knuckles on the wall. It's nothing."

Upstairs, in his flat, Pavel stands by the window, watching Marfa Borisova and her dog in the little path-lined park below. Thrushes are whirling over Donskoy, darting in and out of the pink bell tower. The last of the vendors loads a bucket of flowers into a waiting truck, departs. In the past, on her way home from hospital, Elena would sometimes salvage a handful of flowers from the litter of discards now brightening the cracked pavement, trimming away the broken stalks.

He tosses the telegram onto the table. A simple mistake: That is the story Simonov has told him all these months. Not about the accident itself but what followed, when Elena was, in the official parlance, "misallocated." As far as Pavel has been able to decipher, a register identifying the cremated remains of the six passengers killed along with his wife was quickly discovered to be incorrect—something about the numbers assigned to each container of ashes not matching the register, or vice versa. In short, months of delays, paperwork filed and refiled, and exactly a dozen telegrams like this one, all of which have so far amounted to one inescapable fact: Elena's remains, along with her personal effects, have yet to be returned to Pavel. Instead in her place he has been given empty assurances. Until the issue is resolved, he must go on waiting.

In the bathroom, stripped to the waist, Pavel scrubs the stink of furnace oil from his hands, the water nearly hot enough to scald. Afterward, examining his reflection in the mirror, he is struck by his appearance: his bony shoulders, the deep lines around his mouth, the receding hair at his temples. The year—he is only thirty-two but feels much older—has left its mark on him. Elena's blue toothbrush still stands in the drinking cup on the sink, her dark blond hair still clings cloudlike to the bristles of her hairbrush. Nor has Pavel thrown away the bottles of perfume on the bedroom dresser, the dresses hanging in the wardrobe. At times, breathing in the ghost of their collective scent, which week by week grows fainter, Pavel almost expects to hear the soft click of footsteps in the doorway behind him, feel Elena's hand touch his neck. "You came back," he will whisper. *I never left you.* He has not given her up. If his wife were to walk into their flat tomorrow, she could go on with her life, and he his.

The shops along Shabolovka have opened their doors, as if to welcome in the warm evening. Couples stroll along, hand in hand, children call to one another in a courtyard playground, shrieking with laughter. The strains of music—a radio—carry in the open window of the tram, washing over Pavel. *Tell the soldier of Katyusha's love. Let him dream about their days together.* Outside the cinema, a crowd waits. As the tram shudders along, Pavel lets his mind drift.

The tram stops, Pavel steps down. A stray dog drinking from a puddle lifts its head to regard him steadily, then trots off, vanishing into an alley. Half the buildings along the street, holdovers from the last century, are boarded over, surrounded by high metal fences and scaffolding. Slated for demolition. A paradigm, as Pavel's old friend Semyon has sourly put it, of Soviet planning and execution. The broken windows, the crumbling facades and empty, grass-filled courtyards: For over a year now they have remained untouched. The park near Semyon's flat, once full of children and pensioners, has become a haven for drunks. Still, even as he passes along the park's pitted brick fence, Pavel feels his mood lifted somewhat at the sight of Semyon's building. Tonight especially he is eager for his friend's company.

"We were beginning to think you'd been kidnapped," jokes Semyon.

"Why would you think that?"

"Vera, you know. She's convinced the neighborhood has been taken over by bandits." The older man raps the floor once with his cane, then calls to his wife, "I told you he was all right." He is dressed, as always, neatly if decidedly out of fashion, in a coat and vest, a striped bow tie.

Vera appears. "Hello, Pasha," she says coolly. A pair of reading glasses dangles from a chain around her plump neck. In the dim foyer her soft white curls glow like a cap. Beyond the foyer the ancient upright piano on which she has for over a decade now instructed her students stands open, as if waiting for the next lesson. Once, years ago, she would have embraced him. Now she merely offers Pavel her hand.

"Good evening, Vera," replies Pavel politely. In her eyes he became something of a pariah after the pathetic business that marked his leaving Kirov Academy. A cautious woman, always—after her father, Semyon has said, a cavalry officer under the white banner of the tsar, shot from his horse by a mob of starving, mutinous Russian soldiers in 1916. Still, she had always been warm with him, had always treated Pavel as if he were not simply Semyon's friend but a blood relation, a nephew, and Pavel had been deeply hurt when all that changed. Sadly, the years since his resignation have only pushed them further apart. "How are you?"

"Well enough." To Semyon she says, "Promise me you won't stay out too late."

"You worry too much, darling," Semyon says. He is nearly a head taller than Vera, thin, stoop-shouldered. As he leans to kiss her, his trimmed beard with its touches of gray brushes her hair.

"Poor woman," he tells Pavel minutes later as they slowly descend the stairs. "She had the worst nightmare last night. Something about thieves making off with my leg."

"Your leg."

Semyon widens his eyes dramatically. "Don't you read the papers? There's a booming black market in Moscow these days for prosthetics. Mine's practically a collector's item." With every step the leg, which starts just below Semyon's left knee and is held in place with a welter of leather straps and buckles, creaks softly. When they reach the street he pauses briefly to catch his breath, gazing across at the ruined park. Beyond the gates the wide path is littered with fallen tree limbs, bottles.

From Semyon's building it is only a fifteen-minute walk to the restaurant, past the park and along a line of shops, all but a handful of which have been permanently shuttered. They turn down an alley, where the sweetish smell of dung from a high-fenced droshky stable hangs heavily. If it is not out with its master, the old horse will sometimes press its nose to the gapped fence boards to sniff them as they pass, breathing warmly onto their hands.

The restaurant lies one street over, off a little courtyard shaded by pear trees. Its owner, Dashenko, grasps their hands fiercely when they enter, as if they are rescuers come to save him. "My friends," he sighs, handing their hats off to his daughter-in-law. His smile appears loosely pasted on this evening, as though the slightest wind could peel it away. He leads them through a sea of empty tables, each with its own flickering candle.

"How's business?" asks Semyon.

"Always joking," Dashenko says hoarsely. With his battered, heavy face and round shaved head, he resembles an aging boxer more than a restaurateur. He pulls a folded letter from his pocket and waves it at them. "From Central Development, in answer to the petition I sponsored. Which, by the way, Semyon Borisovich, you promised me you would sign."

"And I did."

"You certainly did not." He looks round at Pavel. "And here he makes jokes at my expense."

"You shouldn't let him get to you," says Pavel.

Semyon asks, "So what does Central Development have to say for itself?"

"The same thing Central Development always says. They want me out of the building. They want me to stop bothering them with paperwork. My guess is they're hoping I'll just shut up and go away."

Dashenko's daughter-in-law approaches with glasses, wine, bread.

Dashenko adds glumly, "At this rate I'll be out of business soon. Bankrupt. Sleeping in that awful park like some bum. Which is fine now, but what happens this winter? If the cold doesn't kill me some hooligan will slit my throat for my coat and shoes and dump me in the river."

"God help the thief who tries," Semyon murmurs.

"Go help Vanya in the kitchen," says Dashenko's daughter-in-law, patting Dashenko on the arm.

Semyon smiles at her. "Ah, wine," he sighs. He has become mildly infatuated with her, Pavel knows, this pale, pretty girl who is young enough to be one of his students, whom he has never seen except by candlelight. Later Semyon will leave an exorbitant tip, money he can little afford on the meager salary Moscow University pays him. *Offering up,* Semyon calls it, as if she were some religious icon into which he might pour his secret hopes.

After Dashenko slips away, Semyon asks her, "How are your studies going? Please tell me you've given up on this engineering nonsense."

"The country needs good engineers. Metroproject has been to our department twice this semester, recruiting. They're constantly expanding the metro lines."

"Shame on them."

She walks their orders to the kitchen. "Poor kitten," Semyon says. "When I think about her working her youth away in some cold damp tunnel, it breaks my heart. A generation of cave dwellers, hammering away in darkness."

A car passes slowly on the street. At her tiny table just off the kitchen, Dashenko's daughter-in-law leans over her open textbook, taking notes.

Semyon asks Pavel, "By the way, I've been wanting to ask. How's your mother?"

"She's doing fine."

"'Fine' meaning 'good,' or 'fine' as in you don't particularly feel like talking about her?"

"As in she seemed all right, last time we spoke."

"When was that?"

"About a week ago. I was thinking of taking the train out to visit her this weekend."

"She'll like that." Semyon smiles faintly. He spreads his napkin in his lap. "I worry about her, you know, Pasha. Being alone."

"She's not alone, Semyon. She has Victor and Olga to look after her. And their children. Alone is the last thing my mother is."

"I still worry."

Pavel knows what is behind Semyon's concern. In March, on a morning when the temperatures dipped well below freezing, his mother had left her flat wearing a light housedress and slippers, only to return two hours later with no memory of where she'd been. It was his mother's flatmate who phoned Pavel afterward. "She's safe now, that's the important thing," Olga said. By the time Pavel arrived, a doctor had already examined his mother and determined she'd had a blackout of some sort. Even now Pavel finds it difficult to believe—though the doctor, when Pavel pulled him aside, appeared sanguine enough. "Could have been low blood sugar, anxiety. If your mother were older, or a drinker, I might be concerned." He shrugged. "Look, if it happens again, then we'll worry, all right?" And in fact Pavel's mother had seemed perfectly normal, perfectly herself.

"I worry about you too, Pasha," Semyon says. "Frankly I can't understand why you don't have her come live with you."

"I've told you. She likes it where she is. You know how stubborn my mother can be."

Semyon lifts his hands, letting the issue go. "It's funny. Just the other day I was remembering that dreadful little room off Roschin you and your mother shared with all those families. God, what a hole that was. How old were you? Eleven, twelve?"

"Thirteen," Pavel says.

Another life, he thinks. Sheets, hung from hooks in the flaking ceiling, had divided the drafty room into three sections, each of which was claimed by a family. At night the noise—snores, coughs, the muffled groans of lovemaking—went on ceaselessly. Beside the straw mattress on which Pavel and his mother slept, a glittering white frost coated the wall on the coldest mornings. Had it not been for Semyon, who knows what would have happened to them? He remembers the afternoon Semyon first found them there, the dragging footsteps on the stairs, the cautious joy in his mother's face as she opened the door: All autumn, as the war collapsed into stalemate, she had waited for Pavel's father to return from Poland, into which he had vanished without a trace, as if the earth had swallowed him. Since August no letters had arrived, no word of his whereabouts had reached them. Only instead of Pavel's father there stood Semyon, sickly, haggard in his tattered service uniform and salt-whitened boots, leaning on a cane. "I was friends with your husband, Vasily," he said. Under one arm he carried a dented metal cartridge box, which he awkwardly presented to Pavel's mother. "I thought you would want his things." "Whose things?" asked Pavel's mother. The months of waiting, the hardship of constant worry and hunger, had whittled her down to a gaunt, hollow-eyed scarecrow. "Where's Vasily?" Of course the look on Semyon's face was answer enough—she was merely delaying the blow, Pavel knew. When it came, it was like a string had been cut in her—she collapsed into Semyon's arms, nearly dragging him down: with her grief, her terror. When the metal box tumbled to the floor, Pavel stooped to pick it up. That same day Semyon returned with a sack of food—bread, potted meat, a little butter—which the three of them shared in silence. Months later, after he found work tutoring, Semyon moved them into his room—a larger room, another hanging sheet, with a warm stove and a writing desk and an entire wall lined with books. "You're welcome to read whatever you like," he told Pavel. "That's what they're for, you know." When Pavel asked what he should read first, Semyon plucked a volume down. "Here. Gogol's a good enough beginning, I think." It was not long after this that Pavel's mother slipped quietly from their bed one night and crossed to Semyon's half of the room, only to return hours later, before dawn.

Their dinners arrive, small boiled red potatoes in weak butter, thin steaks curled at their corners like leaves. Poor fare, Pavel would admit. Even so, it is better than nothing. At any rate it is not the food he comes for, but Semyon's company.

Dashenko returns from the kitchen.

"How are your meals, gentlemen? May I bring you anything?"

"A bottle of vodka," says Pavel.

Dashenko's eyes brighten. "Ah." He taps two fingers against his throat slyly. "I have just the thing." He hurries off to the kitchen.

"Bad day?" asks Semyon.

"Another telegram from Simonov."

He does not mention Babel. That part of his life—his work at the Lubyanka—they have more or less tacitly agreed never to discuss. It is a testament to Semyon's loyalty that he has not shunned Pavel completely.

Semyon asks, "And?"

"And nothing. They're still trying to sort things out. Waiting for someone up the chain to move."

Semyon sighs, brushing away the bread crumbs beside his plate. "I'm sorry, Pasha. I mean, good Lord. After all this time, you'd think by now they would have—" He falls silent.

Dashenko returns, cradling a bottle like a baby on one arm. "You will not be disappointed, gentlemen, I promise. This vodka, it's almost impossible to come by. An old friend of mine gets it for me through a connection." With a flourish he cracks the seal on the gold metal cap.

"In that case, will you join us for a drink?" asks Pavel.

Dashenko calls to his daughter-in-law to bring another glass. Once their glasses are filled to the brim, Pavel asks if Dashenko would care to propose a toast. "You flatter me," the proprietor says.

"Please."

"All right." Dashenko lifts his glass. "A toast, comrades. To Stalin. And life getting better."

Even here, it would seem, in the crumbling heart of the city, one is incapable of escaping Stalin. Grimly Pavel drains his glass. The vodka has an astringent, oily aftertaste.

"Wonderful, isn't it?" asks Dashenko proudly.

Semyon turns the empty glass in his hand, then touches his mouth tentatively, as if feeling for blood. " 'Wonderful' doesn't even begin to describe this vodka."

"What did I tell you? The fellow I get it from, it's all he drinks."

"Really? Is he blind yet?"

Dashenko's smile falters.

"Speaking of our dear Stalin," says Semyon. "I have a new joke." He sets down his glass. "A commission of Party bosses is inspecting a madhouse. All week long the staff has been preparing for their arrival. The wards have been swept and scrubbed, the gardens weeded. Finally the big day has come. The commission arrives. All two hundred patients leap to their feet as one and shout: 'Life is getting better! Life is getting happier!' "

In the street the same black sedan that passed earlier again appears, rolling to a stop. From here Pavel can make out only the silhouettes of its occupants—two men, he guesses.

"Are you listening, Pasha?" says Semyon.

"Yes, Semyon." Dashenko's smile, Pavel cannot help noticing, has melted away altogether.

"So," continues Semyon. "The shout goes up. Only one of the

Party bosses has noticed a rather glum-looking fellow standing off by himself who has not joined in. Poor wretch, he thinks. To be cut off from the world like that. He approaches the man and asks, 'Tell me, comrade, why did you not shout our dear leader's words with the others?' 'Oh that,' the man says. 'I just work here. I'm not insane.' "

Outside the car's headlights suddenly come on, painting the potholed street with light; with a low murmur the sedan pulls away. The flickering candle blooms perceptibly brighter in the window as night comes on. Across the empty room Dashenko's daughter-in-law has nodded off over her book.

"Another drink?" Semyon asks Dashenko.

"No. Thank you, no." The proprietor appears stunned. "Excuse me."

After he has gone Semyon picks up the vodka, turning its label to the light to read. "Truly abominable," he says placidly, then pours himself another glass.

They finish their food in silence. Afterward, at the door, Dashenko hands them their hats. "Gentlemen," he says gravely. At her little table Dashenko's daughter-in-law jerks awake, then rises sleepily and begins going from table to table, blowing out candles.

Outside the warm air smells of damp cinders, as if the rain has only just passed. The last of the light has drained from the sky. They turn into the alley, pass the stable fence. "He could denounce you," Pavel says finally.

"And lose his best customer?"

"All it takes is one phone call, one letter. You saw the look on his face, Semyon."

They emerge into the street. The moon shines down, illuminating the faded posters plastered onto a locked kiosk half in shadow. Film advertisements, anti-Fascist posters. A young soldier gazes out coldly, rifle ready. *If Tomorrow Brings War, If the Campaign Begins, Be Prepared for the Battle Today!* On another poster a leering, ratlike Hitler appears to reach out, bloody hands hooked into claws. A dog lopes from the shadows, stops; head lifted, the animal sniffs the air warily. The stray from earlier, Pavel notes. Suddenly a second dog joins it. They are close enough for Pavel to see the moonlight shining in their black eyes. "Comrades," murmurs Semyon. As he and Pavel approach, the dogs turn and slip away.

"I nearly forgot to tell you. I'm to be censured on Monday," Semyon says lightly. "By my good colleagues. Publicly excoriated. For derogatory comments attributed to me—again by my good colleagues—regarding Nina Boyarska's latest critical masterpiece."

It is troubling news. This is not the first time Semyon has crossed Boyarska, who has headed Semyon's department since orchestrating the removal of the prior chairperson just over a year ago. Last winter, after Boyarska published a chapbook of light verse, her first foray into poetry, Semyon wrote a savage review of the book for a second-rate literary magazine, the entire text of which was promptly reprinted in a satirical student-run journal called *The Broken Axe.* In retaliation, Boyarska cut Semyon's course load from three classes to just one. A month later *The Broken Axe* was permanently shut down.

"What did you say this time?" asks Pavel.

"Oh, a good number of things, I'm sure. It's hard to remember everything, you know. I did call her a bitch."

"Semyon."

Semyon shrugs. "Well, she is, Pasha. The woman has an ice pick for a tongue. Personally I think she's a sadist. She's also a dreadful teacher. And, I might add, an absolutely terrible writer. Do you want to know who her latest literary hero is?" Semyon pauses for effect. "Dzhabaev. That talentless bootlick. He and Madame Boyarska are made for each other."

"What do you think she'll do?"

"Suspend me, I suppose. If she can. That or have me shuttled off into some lovely little administrative posting. Second Assistant to Director of Toilets. Anyway, I only teach the one class now," Semyon points out. "It's not like they're exiling me from the kingdom of heaven, Pasha."

"You have to be careful, Semyon," Pavel says. "You can't just go around insulting people like Boyarska whenever you feel like it. The woman has pull—you know that. Not to mention your little joke tonight." He reaches for Semyon's arm, stopping him. They have arrived at the edge of the park. "Listen to me. Whatever you have against Boyarska, please, let it go."

"Make nice, you mean."

"Yes. Apologize, if you have to. If not for your sake, then for Vera's."

Semyon is silent. "I'll think about it."

Pavel can only hope he will. "Thank you," he says.

They continue walking.

"Anyway," Semyon says, "if I do lose my job, we could always come live with you, Pasha. It would be like old times."

Pavel cannot help but smile. His friend—and in many ways he thinks of Semyon more as a father than as a friend—has always had a gift for lifting Pavel out of his pessimism.

"I'm not sure Vera would like that too much."

"She might. She hates where we are now. She might see it as a step up."

They are nearing Semyon's building. "Does she know?" asks

Pavel. "About this business Monday with Boyarska. Have you told her yet?"

"No. To be honest, I haven't figured out how. When you resigned from the academy, how did you break the news to Elena?"

"I said it could be a new beginning for us."

Even now the words embarrass Pavel. Although in a way it was a new beginning, since even the lowest periods in one's life must begin somewhere. He remembers the day he told Elena, how at first she'd simply sat on the edge of their bed without speaking, plucking at the yellow bedspread with her fine long fingers, then smoothing it down, as if she needed time to let this awful truth—their new lives—sink into her bones. Finally she said, "You'll find another position. Moscow's a big city. There are plenty of other schools." He wanted to believe her, just as Elena's disfigured patients wanted to believe her when she told them she would give them back their lives, she would make them whole again.

Not long before her accident, on one of those rare blessed Sundays when the morning seemed to unfurl like a level path, they had made love. Afterward, as they lay in bed, Elena rolled onto her side to study his face. "Have we changed so much, Pasha?" Her eyes, blue, calm, held him. Pavel noticed, not for the first time but nevertheless with the shock of surprise, the net of fine wrinkles around them. He had always found her beautiful; now, unexpectedly, even more so. "Not so much," Pavel said. "Do you think we have?" Elena did not answer right away. Then: "I know I love you. That's never changed." Pavel felt for her hand, held it. After a moment, gently, Elena pulled away.

# 4

On Sunday Pavel visits his mother. It is only a half hour ride by train to her neighborhood of newly erected flats in Birulevo, which, like so many of the vast complexes that ring Moscow's far suburbs, look north across low hills and swaths of birch forest, back toward the pale shimmering towers of the city. Near the station a number of locals have set up a sort of impromptu market, purely second-rate: smallish, shriveled tomatoes, beets and cucumbers in cloudy brine, jars of milk, lumpy butter in wax paper. The salty stink of dried fish and offal fills the air, smoke trickles from sizzling braziers. One elderly woman, wrapped in rags like a beggar and seated on an upturned tin bucket, sells fish her son has caught in the little lake just beyond the railroad tracks. As Pavel barters with the old woman, the son clomps up, torn green coveralls caked with mud to the knees, carrying a string of small fish. Dark circles of sweat spread under his arms.

"What kind of fish are these?" Pavel asks him.

The son stares. "The eating kind," the old woman answers.

At his mother's, Olga answers the door. She and her husband, Victor, along with their young sons, Andrei and Misha, have shared the two-room flat with Pavel's mother for nearly three years now. They are kind enough people, friendly, affectionate with his mother, the boys especially. In many ways they are more family to her now than he is.

"I brought dinner." He hands the newspaper-wrapped fish to Olga, who smiles and thanks him. She is a small, sturdy young woman with a mouthful of steel-capped teeth; already Pavel sees in her the stout little grandmother she will no doubt one day become. Her thick black hair, curly as a Gypsy's, tumbles past her shoulders.

Pavel pulls a pair of chocolate bars from his shirt pocket. "For the boys."

"You spoil them, Pavel."

"Actually it's my mother who spoils them. If I didn't bring something, she'd disown me."

In the tiny kitchen two pots of carrots and potatoes boil furiously on the stove. Through the open window a strip of hard yellow sunlight falls crookedly across the table like a runner.

"Where's Victor?" asks Pavel.

"Off with the boys. Trying to wear them out before supper, you know."

"Is my mother with them?"

"She's having a nap. She wanted to rest a little before you got here." Olga glances at her watch. "I should probably wake her soon."

"Can I help with anything?"

"You could clean these, if you'd like."

Pavel regards the dead fish warily.

"Don't worry," laughs Olga. "I'm just teasing. Would you like something to drink?"

"A beer would be nice."

Minutes later Victor and the boys return. Flushed from their play, the boys rush into the kitchen, jabbering like crows. Andrei, Victor's older son, has a red handkerchief tied about his neck in the manner of a Young Pioneer. "Did you bring us anything, Pavel Vasilievich?" he asks.

"Is that the hello I get?"

Victor appears. "I thought I heard a friendly voice." He reaches to shake Pavel's hand. "It's good to see you."

"He's our prisoner," little Misha announces proudly, grabbing Victor's leg. He is just five, dark like his mother, fierce. "I should shoot you for running away, spy," he tells his father.

"Please don't."

"With my gun," says Misha. He presses his mouth to his father's thigh, as if addressing it. "Where do you want me to shoot you, traitor?" he breathes. When he pulls away the imprint of his wet mouth dampens his father's trousers like a dark kiss.

"Why don't you let me have a little beer with our guest first," Victor says. "Then you can shoot me."

They sit in the living room with their beers. A fan rattles faintly on a table in the corner, pushing the thick summer air. Victor plucks up a pile of architectural journals the boys have knocked onto the floor—"My competitors," he tells Pavel ruefully—and sets them out of the way. A sheen of sweat shines high on his freckled forehead, where his blond hair has thinned and receded. Otherwise he appears unaffected by the heat.

"Building anything interesting these days?" asks Pavel.

Victor shakes his head. "Factory dormitories, apartments. You know: four walls and a roof. Every Russian's dream. So I'm told."

Andrei sidles over and smiles shyly at Pavel. "You did bring us something, didn't you, Pavel Vasilievich?" He has Victor's blond hair, his fair skin. He will be tall like his father, too.

"Maybe." Pavel winks.

"You are corrupting my sons, citizen," Victor announces.

"They're good boys. I wouldn't worry."

And they are good boys, despite their terrible game. But then, thinks Pavel, Andrei and Misha's fascination with spies and traitors is merely a symptom of the times, the air they have breathed all their lives. Pavlik Morozov, the martyred boy hero of every Young Pioneer, who informed on his father and was then murdered by his grandfather and uncle. The songs and poems have been pounded into the hearts of millions of Russia's children. *But his great glory will outlive everything!* Pavel remembers how he and Elena would sometimes bring up the prospect of having children, how he'd always wished for girls. For her part Elena desired only that her babies, whatever their sex, be born healthy, whole. Her work as a surgeon had taught her that much.

From the kitchen Olga calls, "Victor, would you wake Anna Mikhailovna, please?"

Pavel puts down his beer. "I'll do it."

The door to her room is shut. He raps on it softly. "Mother?" He knocks again, then enters.

The shades are drawn. His mother is lying on the bed, on top of the blanket, dressed in a long skirt and silky cream-colored blouse. Pavel is touched by the sight—she has worn her best for his visit. Except for a few keepsakes—photographs of Pavel and Elena, of the children, a tiny wooden jewelry box inlaid with ivory, a gift from Pavel's father—the room could be any woman's room. Slippers on the floor. The smell of lavender soap. Small luxuries. What cannot be packed away in a suitcase, whatever his mother cannot herself easily carry, she has no use for. She has lived like this ever since his father's death, drifting from one flat to another, from job to job. The three years she has been here with Victor and his family is the longest she has allowed herself to settle down in over a decade. Perhaps whatever compulsion it was last March that sent his mother out to wander in the snow is somehow tied to this restlessness. He lays a hand lightly on her shoulder. His mother opens her eyes.

"Pasha," she says softly, then sits up, fumbling for her glasses on the nightstand. "How long have you been here?" She has put on weight, he is happy to see.

"Not long." He touches her hair, which his mother has always hennaed. Another surprise: The roots are growing out gray. "What's this?" he asks before he can stop himself.

"Do I look too old?"

"You look perfect."

But his mother senses his hesitation. It is as if, in the three weeks since Pavel last saw her, she has begun to become an old woman. She looks away, embarrassed.

"Your hair looks very nice, Mama. Really."

"I could color it again."

"Don't. You're perfect just as you are. I was surprised, is all."

His mother nods, but clearly she is still hurt. She reaches out and pats Pavel's hand, as though, strangely enough, to comfort him. "I'm glad you're here. I've missed you, Pasha."

"I've missed you, too," Pavel tells her.

They eat in the small dining area just off the living room. Victor and his wife must slide into their seats by the open window, smiling good-naturedly, bumping the wall with their chairs. "Eat your fish," Olga tells Misha, who is pushing his food around his plate with his fork. "Pavel Vasilievich was nice enough to bring it for us."

"I don't like it."

"Eat," orders Victor.

But the boy is right. The fish is bad—bony, dry as paper. The others notice too, Pavel sees, though they are at pains not to show it. "I'm sorry," he says, putting down his fork. "I should have known better than to trust that old woman at the market."

"It's fine," says Victor.

Afterward, while the women wash dishes, Pavel and Victor take the boys out again. Clear of the buildings, Andrei and Misha race each other for the enormous playing field that sits beside the complex. "I'd drop dead if I tried that," Victor murmurs reflectively, drawing on a cigarette. "Isn't that sad? I'm only thirty, for God's sake. I'm supposed to be in the prime of my life, and I just get fatter and fatter." He lays a hand across his stomach, which hangs visibly over his belt.

"You all seem to be doing well."

Victor turns his head, pretends to spit. "Wouldn't want to tempt fate."

But he is pleased, Pavel sees. Content. And why not? He has Olga, he has his sons. He is young, he is prospering. A closet full of fitted suits, linen trousers like the ones he is wearing now, perhaps one day a car. And it will only get better for him. What is there in my own life, wonders Pavel suddenly, that even approaches this? Is he envious of Victor? Should he be? He has no wife, no children. If he were to disappear tomorrow, his mother would go on living as she has always lived, by her wits.

They leave the sidewalk to stand in the shade of a plum tree. Across the field Victor's sons have reached the edge of the woods. "Watch for snakes," Victor calls. Andrei turns and waves. Victor raises a hand. Over them the plum tree stirs, leaves rustling.

"How has my mother been?"

Victor lets his hand fall. "She's fine."

"You said the same thing about the fish."

Victor dips his head. "Well, that fellow she works for at the pharmacy—that shit Golovkin—he's been giving her a difficult time."

"About what?"

"You know Golovkin. Whatever he can find." Victor falls silent a moment. He lays a knuckle against the trunk of the tree. "Anyway, apparently there was some sort of mix-up. Your mother—I don't know—not following up on some orders. Nothing big. It's just that Golovkin's the kind of nasty little troll who enjoys it when people make mistakes, so he can rub their noses in it. He won't push it too far."

"She told you all this?"

Victor nods. "Your mother's okay, Pavel. Really."

Just then Misha begins screaming. By the time they reach him his upper lip has begun to swell like a sausage. "A wasp," Andrei tells them breathlessly, awed by his brother's hysterics. "He was trying to hit it with a stick and it stung him." He points to a brown wasp circling in a column of sunlight. The wasp dips menacingly toward them, then vanishes into the trees.

Back at the flat, Olga rocks Misha in her arms, cooing under her breath while Pavel's mother quickly sprinkles baking soda onto a wet cloth. She hands it to Olga, who presses the cloth against the crying child's swollen lip. Later, when things have settled, Pavel asks his mother if he might lie down.

"Are you feeling all right?"

"I'm just tired," Pavel says. And he is, quite suddenly: the crushing heat, the food and beer, heavy in his stomach. A dull pain has begun to beat behind his eyes. "It's just a little headache. Will you wake me?"

"Of course."

A widow's bed, Pavel thinks, lying down. In the kitchen Misha's howls have dwindled to a whimper, the muffled voices go on. He does not sleep so much as slip along in a kind of fitful half-sleep, just beneath the gray ice of consciousness. The voices recede, melt into one another, return. In the hallway outside, whispers. "Come away from there now," he hears his mother say. The thump of tripping footsteps, like books knocked from a table, then laughter. When Pavel opens his eyes again, his mother is sitting by the bed, studying his face. "What time is it?" he asks.

"Nearly seven. How's your head?"

"Better, thanks."

He sits up, rubs his face. The light has deepened. "It's going to rain," his mother says. "You better take my umbrella, Pasha. What time is your train?"

"Seven-thirty."

"Would you like me to make you some tea? Do you have time?"

He shakes his head. "I heard about Golovkin," he says. "Has he been bothering you?"

"It's nothing."

"Are you sure?"

His mother nods. She is studying him still, as though searching his face.

Pavel asks, "What is it?"

"A car came round the other night." His mother turns away. Her knee bumps the table beside her bed, nearly knocking over the little reading lamp with its dull bead-encrusted shade. "I was just lying here, and I heard the car. A little later I heard them bringing someone down. I know I shouldn't have, but I wanted to see who it was." Her hand jerks toward the lamp, as if she needs it on now, as if the light will help her find the words for what must be said, but then she seems to change her mind. "It was Mr. Stern, from 406. When they passed under the lamp outside—" His mother's voice breaks. "I saw his face."

Pavel reaches for her hand, as much to stop his mother from speaking as to calm her.

"They've never made you do anything like that, have they, Pasha? Take someone away like that?"

"No. Of course not, no."

"I would never blame you. You're a good man. I know that."

"Stop. Please, Mama. Just stop."

"I would never love you any less, Pasha. No matter what."

He squeezes her hand at those words: *No matter what.* Not out of gratitude or love, but grief, because he has brought this pain into their lives.

He bids Victor's family good-bye before going. "I thought you already left," says Misha. He is sitting cross-legged in his underwear on the living-room carpet, rapidly flipping through an old book of fairy tales. Apparently he has already forgotten his swollen lip, which has turned bright red, shiny. The book, Pavel recognizes, is from his own childhood. "I've been saving it," his mother tells him, then falls silent, watching Misha. *For your children,* she does not say. "I'll get my umbrella for you." At the door, when Pavel embraces her, pressing his lips to her dry cheek, his mother shivers.

# 5

For days that parting shiver haunts Pavel, troubling his sleep. From bed he lies looking out on the black power lines stretched like tightropes just outside his second-floor window. He rises and crosses the room to stand at the window. Past the little park dividing the narrow lane in front of his flat from the larger street that stretches along the north face of Donskoy, the tiered bell tower looms—like the walled monastery itself, massive, silent. Near its western corner, beyond the high pink wall, the squat crematory stack of the newer cemetery glows faintly like a guttering candle, coughing sparks. Once, perhaps twice a week now, a rusted truck will trundle in through the black steel gate. He remembers a time when, not so long ago—last year, the year before—the trucks would arrive two or three at a time, every night. Bound from Butyrka Prison, Lefortovo, the Lubyanka. Some mornings Pavel would find the sidewalk and hedges filmed in a fine white ash like snow.

Pavel remembers nights when it was Elena who could not sleep, when he would sense her absence even before he opened his eyes. Occasionally she would be at this window where he now stands, arms crossed, waist silhouetted through her nightgown in low orange light. Late one night last summer she had told him, "You know what's always scared me? It's that I'd get used to those trucks. That I'd stop noticing them."

"But you haven't."

"But I could, I think. It's just human nature, isn't it? It's what we do best. Adapt. What if those trucks never stop coming? What if one day I don't care anymore?"

Now, in the dark, Pavel dresses. It is just after four. He walks to the kitchen, heats water for tea, which he carries into the living room. A loose floorboard creaks like packed snow. He plucks a book from the bookshelf—Chekhov—reads:

> While you are young, strong, confident, be not weary in well-doing! There is no happiness, and there ought not to be; but if there is a meaning and an object in life, that meaning and object is not our happiness, but something greater and more rational. Do good!

*Do good!* Simpler times, Pavel thinks. To ask as much now from one's readers is to ask them to risk everything. He wonders what the good doctor would make of this new age. Perhaps more important, how would a writer like Chekhov be received today, in Stalin's Russia? There is enough here in this one simple heartfelt passage, from Chekhov's luminous story "Gooseberries," to twist into a crime. *No happiness! Who are you to make such a claim, citizen? A pessimist! Defeatist!*

He returns the book to its shelf. Kneeling, Pavel rifles through a stack of old literary journals, until he finds the one he is looking for.

> I stood there clutching the watch, alone; and suddenly,

> with a distinctness such as I had never before experienced, I saw the columns of the Municipal Building soaring up into the heights, the gas-lit foliage of the boulevard, Pushkin's bronze head touched by the dim gleam of the moon; saw for the first time the things surrounding me as they really were: frozen in silence and ineffably beautiful.

He remembers the first time he read these lines—Babel's lines, Babel's story "Di Grasso." How, afterward, every detail his eye fell upon seemed likewise sharpened, distinct, as in the story. That same evening, walking with Elena under the linden trees along Shabolovka, Pavel reached up, letting the leaves brush across his fingers. Elena's hand, when he lifted it to his lips and kissed it, smelled cleanly of soap.

If "Di Grasso" had never made it into this journal, if it had passed into his hands as Babel's other stories have, would he burn it? Would he have any choice?

Pavel sits reading until it is time to go. On his way out, he meets two of his neighbors on the stairs. By Pavel's reckoning there are at least six young men crammed into the single flat across the corridor, all machinists; these two work the night shift. The harsh chemicals and shrieking equipment they must handle, the long hours without sunlight—their labor has left them hollow-eyed, pale as ghosts.

A different city, Pavel thinks, stepping outside: Moscow in early morning, in darkness. The little park in front of his building is silent, no birds whirl about the bell tower over Donskoy. At his stop he alone waits; it is hours still before the flower vendors arrive. The wide, once-teeming boulevards stand vacant, desolate. On the bus later, passing Gorky Park, Pavel catches sight of the tall white parachute drop towering like a monument among the trees. Then down the long steep stairway of the metro, where trains howl, where the hot air blowing in the high window vents smells sharply of ashes, old fires; then up again and out onto Dzerzhinsky Square. Another morning. Taxis circle, an empty droshky clops past, its driver half-asleep. Across the square, the Lubyanka, every window is ablaze with light. And there with the dawn, almost as tall as the seven-story blank yellow facade of the Lubyanka, stands Felix Dzerzhinsky himself, folded cap in hand, the massive bronze statue nearly black with age. Our sword and our shield, thinks Pavel drearily. "Iron Felix." First master of secrets.

On Tuesday he telephones Semyon.

"How was your hearing?"

"Not so terrible, as public lashings go. I've been officially reprimanded by the university. At least they didn't suspend me. I'm still meeting my class. So I suppose I should be thankful," says Semyon. "They could have beaten me with copies of one of Boyarska's magnificent books. Speaking of atrocities, what do you suppose was in that vodka we drank the other night, Pasha? I felt absolutely terrible the next morning. How did you manage?"

"Not badly. Bit of a headache."

"That's because you're young. Your bones are still pliable. Wait till you're my age."

"Have you had a chance to speak to Boyarska?"

"You make it sound almost pleasant, Pasha. Two colleagues sitting down for a comfortable chat over tea."

"All right, then," Pavel says. "Have you apologized to her?"

"I'm just picking my moment."

Pavel sighs. That moment, he thinks, has long since come and gone. "Were you at least able to make a statement at your hearing? Please tell me you didn't say anything—" He hesitates.

"Idiotic?"

"Imprudent."

"Give me a little credit, Pasha. After all, I've been with the department, what, nearly sixteen years now? I've managed to get along just fine so far. Well, moderately fine," Semyon adds. "A few scrapes here and there. Comes with the territory. Anyway, my students still put up with me."

"They're young. Their bones are pliable."

Semyon laughs.

"If there's anything you need," Pavel says, "let me know."

"You could burn a candle for me."

"If I thought it would help, I would. In the meantime, try and make things right with Boyarska."

He hears Semyon exhale on his end. *Easier said than done.*

"Do you ever think you'll go back to teaching one day, Pasha?"

The question is one Pavel has often asked himself. Not that there is any possibility of his returning to Kirov Academy, where his presence would be an affront to his former colleagues. Still, a little school somewhere, perhaps in the country, away from Moscow, might be willing to overlook his past. Unbidden, an image rises to his mind: a folder, fallen open, spilling out not paper, not some poor soul's forsaken manuscript, but birds, hundreds of birds beating their wings furiously, desperate to find their way out of the incinerator, bursting into flames.

"I'd like to think so," Pavel says.

"I've always hoped you would. There are so few truly good teachers—it's a waste when one gets away."

"This spat with Boyarska will blow over eventually. You'll see. By this time next year no one will remember it."

"A year can be a long time."

"I know."

"Yes. You do, don't you," says Semyon.

That Friday, through Kutyrev, the order comes down from Fourth Section: They are to organize the archives. "We'll start a stack behind our desks," Kutyrev tells Pavel. He waves a hand at the back wall. "The *A*'s can go on this end."

Pavel regards the rows of metal shelves, each of which holds hundreds, perhaps thousands of files, some dating back half a decade or more. It will take months to sift through all of them. "You can't be serious."

"Unless you have a better idea."

All morning they work, carrying boxes and armfuls of dusty folders out of the stacks. The folders still bear the dull red wax stamps on their covers with which they were sealed. Touching them, feeling their solid weight, Pavel again cannot help but wonder what has become of the writers for whom these manuscripts, now hauled around like so much trash, once meant everything. Klyuev. Mirsky. Even Mandelstam, as far as Pavel knows, is still back here somewhere, lost among these stacks, though Pavel has yet to come across the poet's file. In his exile in barren, hellish Kolyma, does Mandelstam still remember poems he put to paper years ago? Do his words haunt him as they haunt Pavel now:

*Don't say a word to a soul.*
*Forget all you've seen,*
*Bird, old woman, cage,*
*And the rest.*

"Shameful," Kutyrev announces when they finally take a break. His undershirt—he has stripped off his uniform tunic—is streaked with grime, soaked through with sweat. A cobweb, caught in his black hair, flutters limply when he lifts his heavy arms and stretches.

"What is?"

"This mess. There are files down here from 1934. They should have been destroyed years ago. But we can't do that until we find them. Even then that's no guarantee it's the right file, since half of them aren't even properly labeled. Which means we'll have to go through them. Which could take—" Kutyrev shrugs.

"Months," Pavel says.

"No wonder you can't find anything around this goddamn place. It's total chaos. Do you have any idea what kind of backlog this creates? They've got whole filing cabinets upstairs full of closed cases, waiting to be processed. Waiting for us. I tell you, this should have been fixed a long time ago."

Pavel lifts the tail of his shirt, bending forward a little to wipe the dust and sweat from his eyes. A stabbing pain flares in his lower back, subsides. He is in no mood for Kutyrev's complaints.

"This chaos, comrade, is one I inherited. As far as I know, it's always been like this down here."

"That's no excuse."

Pavel is suddenly, powerfully sick to his core: of Kutyrev and his grinding, mindless ambition, of these deadening metal stacks and their dust, which Pavel can all but feel sticking in his lungs. Mostly, though, he is sick of himself. Exactly what sort of order did Kutyrev expect to find here? How in this day and age can one believe in order?

Later, as six o'clock nears, Kutyrev says brusquely, "I'll need you to come in tomorrow. Unless you're willing to work late tonight." He is sulking, Pavel sees. This is his way of making Pavel suffer for his earlier pique.

"I'll stay."

"Suit yourself."

After Kutyrev has gone, as Pavel is carrying yet another box of manuscripts to the wall, a thought stops him cold. If, as Kutyrev claims, they are waiting upstairs for the archives to be put into order, then what will become of the archives once that has been achieved? He sees now that he has allowed himself to be lulled into believing that this fortress of letters Denegin built would never entirely fall, despite all Kutyrev's frustrated hammering.

Back among the shelves, Pavel wonders: How long would it take to destroy all of this? Every file, every folder, down to the last story, the last poem. He lays a hand against one of the boxes, feels the manuscripts in it shift when he pushes against the cardboard, as if something living lay inside, asleep, dreaming. He moves on to another box, then another, letting his hand rest a moment on each of them. *The magnificent grave of the human heart.*

And here he is, the master himself. Babel. A single box, twenty-seven green folders. Pavel sets the heavy cardboard box onto the concrete floor. In the topmost folder lies Babel's unsigned, unfinished, beautiful story. Kneeling under the bare lightbulb in its wire cage, he reads it straight through. Afterward, when he returns to his desk, Pavel is almost surprised to discover that he is still holding the story in his hands. After that, what follows is surprisingly simple. The story, a mere eleven pages long, folded and tucked tightly under his belt, brushes the small of his back. His shirt and coat conceal the tiny bulge entirely. Upstairs, the guard posted at the main entrance of the Lubyanka barely glances at his identification card. But then the entrance guards are not really concerned with those leaving the building, only those coming in. In all Pavel's time here, no prisoner has ever escaped. Nor has he ever been searched. Today is no different.

That night he slips Babel's manuscript under the mattress of his bed. Tomorrow he will find a better place.

# 6

August nears. The days shorten, the heat lifts. For three days rain falls—a slow, desultory drizzle that lies like a mist over the black river and in the trees along Lenin Hills. Finally late one afternoon, as the first swallows are turning over Donskoy, the rain dies away.

A week passes, then another. And still he does not move Babel's story. For the moment he is safe. Germany—that is where everyone's attention has turned, that is what is on everyone's mind these days. What to do about Hitler? In Friday's *Pravda* a visit by British and French military missions to Moscow is announced, presumably to discuss this very question.

Not that anything will come of their discussion, Pavel fears. Still, he cannot help but cling to hope as he walks home that evening. He notices his neighbor Marfa Borisova in the park beside Donskoy, talking to a woman—even from behind the woman looks familiar, though at first his mind does not make the connection. Then with a shock he realizes it is his mother. "Here he is, love," calls Marfa Borisova, seeing Pavel. "Here's your son." She is a stout, large woman, well into her sixties, stubbornly blond, with the bright if brittle cheeriness of someone who has only herself and a little dog to look after. Elena, perhaps sensing this loneliness, always made a point of stopping and chatting with Marfa Borisova whenever she happened to meet her.

"Mama?"

His mother's face fills with relief. He has still not gotten used to her gray hair—perhaps that is why he did not recognize her. For a moment Pavel is sure his mother is going to weep, but the moment passes. "She just got a little turned around, is all." Marfa Borisova pats his mother's arm. Her brindle pug paws a bare spot in the path, grunting softly.

Pavel ushers his mother past the flower beds. He is alarmed by her appearance: Her shoes are badly scuffed, one of the buttons on her dress dangles by a string. But what worries him more is her stunned, blinking expression, as if she has been in an accident. "You're limping. Are you hurt?"

"Just blisters." His mother's hand tightens on his forearm. "I'll be fine once I get off my feet." As they reach his building tears begin rolling down her cheeks. "I lost my purse, Pasha."

"How did you get here?"

"I took a taxi from the station."

"Is that where you left your purse, do you think?"

"I don't know."

Slowly he helps her up the stairs to his flat. In the kitchen, kneeling, Pavel removes her battered pumps. Both of her heels are badly blistered, oozing watery blood. He fetches a bowl of warm water, a rag, iodine, soap, a clean towel, washes first one foot, then the other, wringing the sopping rag. Afterward he dabs the broken blisters with the iodine, and his mother hisses through her teeth.

"Why didn't you tell me you were coming? I could have met you at the station. Is this your idea of surprising me?" He is trying to keep his tone light, even playful.

"No."

"What happened to your shoes? Where were you walking?"

His mother tugs her foot from his hand. No more questions. Pavel knows better than to keep pressing her, at least for now. As long as he can remember his mother has had this way of shutting down whenever it suited her, especially under duress. If he pushes too hard, she will only shut him out. "I need to use your bathroom," she tells Pavel.

"Help yourself. I'll just run downstairs and check my mail. I'll only be a moment."

A lie, but well meant. Pavel does not want to upset his mother any more than she has already upset herself. Downstairs he knocks on Natalya's door and asks if he might use her telephone. He does not want his mother overhearing his conversation. A woman picks up the public line at Victor's building. Minutes later Olga is there. "I've been trying to reach you," she says worriedly. "Golovkin called. Your mother didn't return to work after lunch."

"She's here."

"Oh, thank God. Is she all right?"

"She seems a little rattled. Beyond that, I don't really know. I think she got lost. I'm going to have her stay with me tonight." A silence falls. Olga wants more, Pavel understands; she is waiting for some explanation as to where his mother has been all afternoon. But he is himself in the dark. "I'll bring her back home tomorrow."

He spreads a blanket on the sofa for himself. "I don't feel right taking your bed, Pasha," his mother tells him.

"I'll be perfectly fine."

"I feel like an intruder. Like I'm pushing you out of your own room."

"You're not pushing me anywhere." Pavel studies her face. She seems calmed, more herself again. "Mama, what happened to you today?"

"I just got a little confused, that's all."

"In the taxi?"

"At work. I was supposed to telephone a customer about an order. But I couldn't remember where I'd put the number. Golovkin kept needling me about it all morning, and I had to keep putting him off. I thought if I took a walk it might help me remember." She glances down at her feet—Pavel has given her his slippers to wear.

"That still doesn't explain how you ended up here."

"I don't know, Pasha." A frown passes over her face, like wind ruffling water. "I remember leaving the pharmacy. I do remember that."

Pavel can feel himself tensing, as if before a blow. It is an effort to keep his voice neutral. "Then what?"

"The train. Sitting on the train." She turns and gazes into the bedroom. "There was a man outside the station, this blind man, singing. For money. He was standing on a little wooden box. He had medals pinned to his jacket. For some reason I thought of your father, how old he would be now." She trails off. "I must have had my purse with me still, because I gave that man all my change. Then I took a taxi here, which means I must have had it then, too. For the fare."

"Yes."

"But then you weren't here. I knocked on your door. When you didn't answer—" She shakes her head, as if to expel some unpleasant thought.

"What, Mama?"

"I got scared."

"Of what?"

"I don't know," his mother says.

The next morning, while his mother sleeps, Pavel telephones a former colleague of Elena's, Timofey Alexandrov, who refers him to an old medical-school classmate now specializing in neurological disorders. "I'll give him a call, see if he can fit you in this morning." Ten minutes later Timofey Alexandrov telephones back to tell Pavel everything has been arranged.

What will his mother do when she discovers he has gone behind her back? Will she be furious? Pavel wonders. In the past that would have been his prediction, but now he is not so sure. Later, after his mother wakes, he has his answer.

"You should have asked, Pasha," his mother tells him. They are eating breakfast: boiled eggs, toast and tea. She appears more depressed than angry. Her hair is mussed; there are dark pouches under her eyes.

"You were asleep. I wanted to make sure I could get an appointment. By the way, how did you sleep?"

A shrug. "I'm used to more noise. Between Andrei and Misha, one of them is always waking up. Lately Misha's been getting up practically every night, yelling about nightmares. Really all he wants is to get in bed with Olga and Victor. You did the same thing when you were little. You used to curl up next to your father. You'd lay your head on his chest."

He remembers those nights, the steady, comforting sound of his father breathing in sleep, the deep beating of his heart against Pavel's ear. Sometimes his father would lay his hand on Pavel's head, its palm thick with calluses, and it seemed as if nothing could hurt them.

They arrive fifteen minutes before their ten o'clock appointment. The brightly lit waiting room is crowded with families—mothers, fathers, grandparents, children, all crammed into a room little larger than the bus Pavel rides to work each morning. Every chair is taken, the sick and infirm spill out into the corridor. Here he and his mother must stand waiting.

"My mouth hurts," an old woman announces. Her teeth, Pavel sees, are gone, her wet mouth gapes blackly. Her pale freckled scalp shows through her thin white hair. A look of confusion flutters across her gaunt face. The young woman beside her, wearily pretty in a once-purple headscarf that has been washed so often it is nearly translucent, takes her hand. "Do I know you?" she asks the young woman.

"I'm Nina, Mama. Your daughter."

"I have a daughter?"

"You have three daughters."

"I had babies?"

"Three babies, Mama. We're all grown up now."

The old woman begins to weep. "I don't like this place," she whispers hoarsely. Her daughter rubs her rounded shoulders and back as though she were a child. A moment later, soothed, settled, the old woman is smiling toothlessly: at Pavel, at his mother, who has slipped minute by minute into a deeply somber silence. The old woman's curled hand absently caresses her right breast: Perhaps, Pavel surmises, her body has retained a flicker of memory, of the babies she once suckled, the life—*lives*: hers, her daughters', grown to womanhood—lost to her now. "I know you," she tells her daughter.

"Of course you do," the daughter replies.

After half an hour a nurse leads Pavel and his mother into an examination room, where another twenty minutes pass before Dr. Hirsch appears. He is a lean, gray-haired, gravely handsome man tipping respectably toward late middle age. Holding his mother's chin steady, he peers into her eyes. "Lovely, lovely." He has the soft, comfortably forceful manner and somewhat ravaged good looks of a longtime seducer of women. And indeed there is something almost intimate in his ministrations.

"How have you been sleeping lately?"

"Fine," his mother says.

"Good. Any headaches?"

"Occasionally."

"Once a month? Once a week?"

"Maybe two or three a month. Nothing serious."

"On a scale of one to ten, how bad would you rate them? In terms of pain."

"Five. Sometimes six."

"Five or six. And how long do these headaches of yours usually last?"

"Not long. A few hours."

"Now tell me, how old are you, Mrs. Dubrova?"

"Fifty-eight."

"And your son here? How old is he? Can you tell me?"

"Thirty-two."

"Have you any other children?"

"No. Just Pasha."

"I see you're wearing a wedding ring. May I ask your husband's name?"

"I'm a widow," his mother says. "His name was Vasily."

"How long ago did your husband die?"

"Nineteen twenty."

"Under what circumstances?"

"He was killed in Poland. A shell exploded near him."

*Obliterated* would be a more apt way to describe his father's death. The shell reportedly landed almost on top of him. *Painless,*

woman who couldn't remember her own daughter. Only these people aren't characters conjured from imagination, their stories do not end when the reader closes the book and shuts off the lamp. He is unable to prevent himself from imagining a morning years from now when his mother will no longer remember him, when she will turn to him and ask, *Do I know you?*

And Pavel will tell her, *I am your son.*

# 7

At home a telegram from Simonov awaits him. "Good news?" asks Natalya. More of the same, Pavel tells her. "If I were a cynic, I might think this fellow Simonov is enjoying all this. Batting me about." He crumples the telegram into a ball. Natalya suggests he file a complaint with Simonov's superiors in Tamoy.

"I thought you said everything was being worked out," his mother says. "You told me they were making progress."

"They are. It's just taking longer than I expected."

Natalya meets his eyes. "I was just putting some water on for tea. Would you two like to join me?"

Pavel hesitates, glancing at his mother. "Tea would be nice," his mother says.

"Are you sure you don't want to lie down?"

"Yes, Pasha, I'm sure."

And it would appear, almost miraculously, that the morning has left no trace on her. In no time the women are chatting amicably, laughing over their biscuits and tea. But then his mother has always had this mystifying gift for quickly making friends, for putting people at ease. He remembers the afternoon he brought Elena to meet her for the first time, how his mother had embraced her warmly. "What a lovely girl. And so brilliant, Pasha tells me." With anyone else Elena might have balked, shy as she was, but she had warmed immediately to his mother. The two had become good friends.

"You must be kept terribly busy looking after the building," his mother says. They are in Natalya's cramped kitchen, one corner of which is crowded with stacks of battered cardboard boxes. "People knocking on your door at all hours." Her gaze slips curiously over the boxes, which are stamped *Pulp* in heavy red ink. "How long have you lived here?"

"In this building? Eight years."

His mother reaches for another biscuit. "All these boxes," she says airily.

"They're magazines," Natalya tells her. "Would you like to see?" From one of the boxes she pulls a copy of *Sport Life,* dated February of last year; the cover is slightly scratched, covered with a collage of athletes: skiers, gymnasts, footballers. Heroes of the age. "It's not exactly current, but the pictures are still good." She flips through the pages. "A friend of mine sets them aside for me."

"What do you do with them?"

"Save them. For other friends."

"Trade them, you mean."

Natalya shrugs, smiling. Pavel's mother smiles back at her.

"Your accent. You're not from Moscow."

"No, I'm from the east. Near Vladivostok. My father worked in a lumber mill."

Through the open window drifts the sound of a child singing. *The night comes rolling in, it reels and it spins.* Natalya tilts her head a little, following it. And for a moment, as he has found himself doing on past occasions, Pavel imagines what her former life was like. The weathered wooden huts leaning like pickets against the long pitiless winters, the constant whine of the mill. Was it there that she sharpened her talent for speculation, trading whatever fell into her hands for those small luxuries the camp offered? A box of bone buttons, postcards, cheap perfume. Proof of another, brighter world beyond those woods. The scar on her face—did she get it there? Pavel wonders.

"I've always thought," his mother says, "Vladivostok must be such an interesting place to live. With the water, the ocean. So far from everything. Exotic."

"It wasn't," Natalya tells her.

Upstairs, with her feet soaking in a pan of warm salt water, his mother says, "It's a pity about her face." She closes her eyes. "All those magazines. She should open a kiosk."

"I'm sure she does better this way. No one looking over her shoulder."

She has been dancing around the subject of his friendship with Natalya, holding back. Now at last it comes.

"Do you know her well, Pasha?"

"Not really."

"She was pretty—you can tell. Maybe not a beauty, but pretty."

His mother is herself still a handsome woman, though not the dark petite beauty she once was, and remains, if only in old photographs, in memory. *A wonder,* Pavel remembers his father joking, *your mother ever settled for a half-literate peasant like me.* However humble his beginnings, Pavel's father had dragged himself up, from oiler to machinist to, finally, senior draftsman, Simsky and Sons Manufacturing and Construction, Moscow. Only to give everything up for the revolution, rare true believer that he was.

"What happened to her? Do you know?"

"It's never come up," Pavel says. "I'm certainly not going to ask her."

"Of course not. I just thought she might have told you. You being friends and all."

Is that what they are, he and Natalya? He is not a man who makes friends easily. As a boy, in school and later university, it was easier to dedicate himself to his studies, to books. Others, outcasts like himself into whose lopsided social circles he was thrown by circumstance, eventually cultivated their various small eccentricities, channeling them into clubs, organizations, lives of a sort. They grew beards, became painters, actors, studied physics or law or dialectics, devoted themselves to the Party, to poetry. Moved on. Pavel had no eccentricities to cultivate. He was not odd but awkward, not unique but simply shy, and therefore often lonely. Being different would have offered him a peg on which to hang his identity.

He throws together a late lunch: cold chicken, bread, sliced apples and cheese. But his mother barely touches the food on her plate. She is still wearing the same wrinkled dress she wore yesterday, with its dangling button. "How are your feet?"

"They hurt, Pasha," his mother answers. She has been mostly quiet since their visit earlier with Natalya. He in turn tiptoes around her, waiting for whatever's next.

"I don't like that doctor," she says finally.

"Dr. Hirsch? Why do you say that?"

"He was rude. Making us wait all that time. Asking ridiculous questions. What year it is. What is that? Like I'm some drooling idiot. Like I'm insane."

"He has to ask those sorts of questions. It's what doctors do."

"Head doctors."

"Yes."

"What did you two talk about when you left the room? Did you talk about me?"

"That's why we were there. For you. Yes, Mama. What would you expect us to talk about?"

His mother's mouth tightens. "You saw those people. You saw that old woman next to us. Is that what you think I am?"

"Of course not."

"There's nothing wrong with me. That's what your doctor said, right? It's what he told me."

"He didn't say there was nothing wrong with you and you know it. He said he couldn't find anything conclusive. Which means he doesn't know why you blacked out." Pavel stops. *Blacked out*—it is the first time he has spoken the words. "Which is precisely why he asked you to come back for more tests."

"I know what 'conclusive' means, Pasha. I'm not a child. I'm not one of your students."

Pavel puts down his fork, exasperated. "Please, Mama. I don't want to argue."

"There's no argument, Pasha. Believe what you want. But there's nothing wrong with me."

Pavel carries their dishes into the kitchen to wash. From the window he watches Marfa Borisova and her pug—she is shooing the little dog from one of the flower beds, where it has been digging. She is dressed as if for an engagement, an evening on the town: smart burgundy suit and matching hat, wide black belt, black pumps. The sight strikes Pavel as terribly sad. But then who is he to pity poor Marfa Borisova? Who is he to pity anyone?

His mother shuffles in, wearing his slippers. "What are you looking at?"

"My neighbor. Marfa Borisova. You were talking to her yesterday."

"She's a nice woman." His mother's anger, it would seem, has passed. She is no longer in the mood for arguing. "That dog. Have you ever seen anything so ugly in all your life?"

"She's actually quite proud of the thing. She once told me the Chinese bred pugs to be foot warmers for emperors. Apparently Napoleon's wife, Josephine, had one. I believe it bit him."

His mother sighs. Clearly these last two days have weighed heavily on her. "I don't mean to be difficult, Pasha. I really don't. I'm sorry."

"It's a lot to take in, I'm sure."

They wash the dishes together, side by side at the sink, elbows brushing. Pavel washes and rinses, while his mother dries the glasses and plates with a hand towel.

"This one's chipped," his mother says. She rubs her thumb along the rim of a glass, from which a crack curves. "You should throw it out."

"Just put it aside. I'll throw it out," he tells her.

His mother nods. Then she covers her mouth with her hand. Shoulders heaving, she begins to weep. "I was just thinking of Elena," she says, sobbing.

"It's all right."

"I had so much hope for you." Her voice steadies, then hardens. "The people who did this. Sometimes I want them to suffer like we've suffered. Let them lose someone they love. I know it's terrible, Pasha—I do—but I don't care."

"We don't know what happened. It could have been an accident."

"Trains don't fly off their tracks for no reason."

Pavel says, "That doesn't mean it was malicious. People make mistakes. What if some engineer simply pulled the wrong handle, or some factory worker didn't tighten a bolt? Should they suffer, too?"

"Yes."

"You don't mean that," Pavel says.

"But I do," his mother says.

Pavel watches the water swirl down the drain. For every wreck, he thinks bleakly, a wrecker.

Over an hour remains before his mother's departure. They sit together beside the high arched windows overlooking the long platform of Kiev Station, under the old clock. On impulse, his mother has borrowed Pavel's copy of Chekhov's stories to read on the train.

"Which one should I read first?" she asks.

"Try 'Gooseberries.'"

The story has long held a special place in Pavel's heart. Ivan Ivanovitch, Burkin the high-school teacher—two old friends out on a walking tour on the countryside, stopping for a night at Alehin's estate. The servant girl Pelagea, so beautiful both men cannot help but stare at her, stunned by her loveliness. The rain-darkened millpond covered with white lilies, into which Ivan Ivanovitch flings himself with such unrestrained delight, the lilies bobbing around him. Later he tells Burkin and Alehin a story about his brother, a government clerk who long dreamed of one day owning a patch of farmland thick with gooseberries. How his brother's every waking moment became consumed with this vision of contentment and happiness, for which he willingly sacrificed everything: money, his youth, even a wife, who pined away to her death with hardly a whimper. Until finally the day came when the brother was able to purchase a farm and his gooseberry bushes and thus become a country gentleman—"Your Honor" to the peasants who bowed before him. *Nikolay Ivanovitch, who at one time in the government office was afraid to have any views of his own, now could say nothing that was not gospel truth, and uttered such truths in the tone of a prime minister.* When Ivan Ivanovitch finally visited him, he himself tasted the gooseberries his brother had so long coveted, which his brother greedily ate with triumph, and which Ivan Ivanovitch sadly discovered were sour and unripe. Carried away by his own story, Ivan Ivanovitch rushes over to his host, Alehin, and implores him to dedicate himself to helping others. *Do good!* Afterward the two old friends retire to their room with its big comfortable beds and clean linens, which Pelagea has prepared for them. There, long after Ivan Ivanovitch has drifted off to sleep, the high-school teacher Burkin lies awake, oppressed by the smell of stale tobacco from Ivan Ivanovitch's pipe lying nearby. *The rain was pattering on the windowpanes all night.*

His mother nods, then closes the book with a little sigh.

"You look disappointed," says Pavel.

"It's just that I feel sorry for him. The brother."

"Why him?"

"I don't know. Because it couldn't last, I suppose. His happiness. Isn't that what Ivan Ivanovitch says? I kept thinking, what happens when his brother realizes the gooseberries aren't sweet?"

"But he won't. That's Chekhov's point, I think."

"He will. Something bad will happen to him. Then he'll know." His mother rises a little to look out the window at the platform, then checks the clock above their heads. "I liked the servant girl. The way she seemed to float in and out of the story. Like an angel."

"Lovely Pelagea."

His mother smiles. "You remembered."

Together they walk down the long concrete platform, weaving through the crowd. Vendors hawking little baskets of spotty fruit and windup tin toys cry out hoarsely, beckoning. The air, sharp with diesel fumes and cinders, thrums with scraps of conversation, shouts of joy, bawling infants, laughter. A sickly brown pall hangs over the switchyard just beyond the platform, where a dense skein of tracks spreads like a tangled net beneath the lowering sun. Soldiers, boyish in baggy uniforms, pose drunkenly for photographs: They appear nothing like the broad-shouldered, steely-eyed soldiers in anti-German propaganda. Yet if war erupts, it will be these very boys standing between Russia and Hitler, Pavel knows.

He asks his mother, "Do you need money?"

"Why? Do you think Golovkin's going to fire me?"

"You tell me."

His mother shrugs. "We'll see what happens. I'm not worried, Pasha. If he does, I'll find another job."

True, his mother has always managed to find work. But then that was before her blackouts. He must learn to think of her in this new light. Which may inevitably entail her coming to live with him, once she can no longer support herself. Eventually, somehow, they will both have to find their footing.

"Are you sure you don't want me to go with you?"

His mother shakes her head. She is watching the soldiers.

"Do you remember when we saw your father off for Kiev?"

"Barely," Pavel says. "I remember wanting to hold his gun, but he wouldn't let me." The soldiers are shouldering their rucksacks, readying themselves. Would I recognize my father now? he wonders. For that matter, would he recognize us? The son grown into manhood, the once-beautiful wife now fast approaching old age, besieged by illness. Ghosts of another life.

"So pointless," his mother says. "Running off like that. At his age. You couldn't stop him, though. You were there. You saw how I tried."

The arguments and long silences, the simmering anger between his parents—Pavel remembers all of it. In those first years after his father's death, as hardship piled upon hardship, his mother would bitterly recount every word of those fights to him. How, finally, she had begged his father to stay. With time her tirades became less frequent, lost their heat, until finally, around when Pavel began university, they ceased altogether.

"Do you blame him anymore?" asks Pavel.

"For what—dying?"

"For what happened to us. How our lives turned out."

His mother shakes her head. She is holding the book of stories still. "Whatever anger I had for your father, it went away a long time ago, Pasha. Takes too much effort, staying angry at someone."

"Do you still love him?"

"I suppose so," his mother says after a while. "It's more pity than love now, really. Sadness."

"Because he died so young?"

"Because he lost everything. Dying."

His mother reaches out and touches Pavel's face tenderly. Then she glances down at the book under her arm, rubs her fingers along the worn spine. Down the platform the conductor is calling for the passengers to board. "Gooseberries," his mother says. "That's what your father wanted, in his own way. And what he got."

# 8

The shoulders of Kutyrev's uniform are dark with lake water where his hair has dripped. He has been swimming.

"You had a visitor," he informs Pavel.

"Who?"

"Sevarov."

Pavel goes cold. Sevarov, personal assistant to the newly appointed director of Fourth Section, is a figure around whom ghastly rumors have long swarmed—among them, that it was Sevarov himself who fired the bullet that hurried the former director Dmitry Maximov from this world. Among the graying, war-hardened old guard NKVD functionaries to have climbed the ranks, only Sevarov and a handful of others still stalk the corridors of the Lubyanka. The rest, like the ruthless masters they faithfully served—Yagoda, Yezhov—have been decimated by internal purges as bloody as those waged on the citizenry at large. Through all of it Sevarov has somehow remained untouched. Yet he is in fact quite mild in appearance, flabby though not fat, with slightly protuberant eyes and a neatly trimmed black moustache, like someone's harmless aging uncle. Still, the deeply unnerving impression Pavel has always come away with is of leaning over a dark well, feeling its cold emptiness on your face.

"What did he want?"

Kutyrev shrugs. "I assumed you would know." A muddy, faintly metallic smell of lake floats off him, like flowers left too long in their water. "He asked when you'd be back. I told him today."

From there the morning slows to a crawl. Repeatedly Pavel's thoughts return to Babel's story. If it is discovered, if he is even suspected, he is finished. It will be him they drag through the corridors of the Lubyanka, rattling their keys.

Kutyrev announces blandly, "This box can go." He has culled yet another file from the stacks. *Kutikov, Lev Nikitich.* When Pavel does not move he adds, "Now. If it's not too much trouble."

The line at the incinerator room appears longer today. Waiting, Pavel surreptitiously studies the face of the junior officer beside him—a boyish, pleasant face, still chapped raw from the morning razor. Every so often the young officer rocks forward on his toes a little, like a runner eager to be on his way. Someday soon it could be this boy ordering him to face the cellar wall, this boy's pistol pressing into the back of his neck. Would there be time to speak? Even if there was, what would Pavel say? *I lived.* He thinks: What did Lev Nikitich Kutikov say before they murdered him? And what did he leave behind? A single massively sprawling novel—nearly three thousand handwritten pages—which Pavel can all but hear whispering to him now, even as its last minutes tick away.

Six-twenty. Kutyrev drops the last of the day's boxes onto the stack behind their desks and stretches, the bones in his neck cracking noisily. He opens his desk drawer, produces a cigarette, which he crumbles slowly between his fingers.

"Looks like Sevarov forgot about you."

Pavel can only hope.

That night he removes Babel's manuscript from beneath the mattress. Down in the basement of his building, where each flat is allotted a space for storage, he ducks under exposed pipes, listening for rats. His space lies beyond the enormous boiler, cold now with summer. The string of lightbulbs barely keeps the darkness at bay. Pavel crouches by the wall, feels the mortared bricks with his hand until finally one slips loose. Behind it the wall is hollow. He slides Babel's story into the hole, then replaces the brick. As he is wiping his hands on his pants he hears the basement door creak.

"Someone down here?" calls Natalya.

"It's only me." Heart pounding, Pavel steps out from behind the boiler. "I was just looking for a box of clothes." He forces himself to smile.

"Any luck?"

"No."

Natalya glances past him.

"I wanted to thank you," Pavel quickly adds, in the hope of distracting her. "For the tea the other afternoon. It was very considerate of you."

"How's your mother doing?"

"Better. She's home, at least. Settled. She'll be able to rest."

Natalya nods.

"Would you like a drink?" Pavel asks. He is anxious to get her out of the basement, away from Babel's story. "I picked up a bottle of whiskey the other day. I could bring it down."

"All right." She looks at Pavel, then reaches and wipes at his cheek with her fingers. "You had dust on your face."

Sitting in her kitchen later, Pavel pours them each a glass of whiskey while Natalya expertly rolls a cigarette from a page of one of her latest acquisitions: a box of misprinted cookbooks. Finished, she holds up her cigarette, peering at a line of blocky black print as if to read it, then pops the cigarette into her mouth. The first match she strikes fizzles out, as does the second.

"I tell you, if we'd had matches this shitty when Napoleon invaded, Moscow never would have burned. Who needs another ball-bearing factory when a person can't buy a box of decent matches?"

"I don't think matches were used to burn Moscow," Pavel says. "I think they were still using flint and tinder in 1812."

"Says who?"

"Tolstoy."

"Clever you," murmurs Natalya.

Tolstoy. Among the writers Pavel once taught at Kirov Academy, only Gorky was as unassailable, as officially sanctioned, safe—one could hardly worry about taking a misstep when teaching Gorky, whose work Pavel always privately considered inferior, at its worst emotionally fraudulent. Not that he ever told his students, in whose eyes Gorky had long since assumed the aspect of a minor god. Stalin's muse. Tolstoy, irascible as he may have been in life, was, in death, considerably more tractable: One could bend his ideas around the rim of the Party. In the end the old man was perhaps simply too monumental to suppress, whereas other, lesser writers, living or dead, could be excised from the canon without difficulty. Even Chekhov, although tolerated, had his detractors among Pavel's more vocal colleagues, always alert to shifting political winds, always quick to add yet another name to the list of undesirable writers. Too apolitical, they called him; too ideologically soft.

"What were you planning on doing with all these cookbooks?"

"Why, are you interested in a trade?" Natalya asks with feigned slyness. "You get me a bottle of this wonderful whiskey, I'll give you the whole lot."

"I've got a better idea. Keep your cookbooks. You could use them."

"Are you saying I'm a bad cook?"

Pavel laughs. Remarkably he feels himself relaxing, the day loosening its grip on him, if only temporarily. "Actually I like your cooking," he tells Natalya. She is sitting back in her chair, thumb absently caressing the curved scar across her cheek, a gesture Pavel finds strangely arousing. The smoke from her tight little cigarette unrolls in a ribbon that twists on itself, rising.

She laughs. "You should get out more."

"You're one to talk. You're always here."

"Oh, I get out often enough," says Natalya mildly. "Anyway, this place would fall apart in a week if I weren't here. And then where would you be?"

"You tell me."

"Lost, my friend." Natalya lifts her glass, as if to toast Pavel, then takes a long savoring sip. "You'd be lost."

The next day Sevarov still does not appear.

So this is what it feels like to be pursued, thinks Pavel. To never know when or where the Sevarovs of the world will come for you. To bear the awful burden of waiting. In this way the Lubyanka is simply a microcosm of Moscow itself, where night by night the black sedans and unmarked prison trucks—*black ravens, black Marias*—slip down the darkened narrow lanes and alleyways, going about their terrible business.

"I can't help but wonder," muses Kutyrev, "what Sevarov would want with you." An unopened pack of cigarettes bulges in his breast pocket. "You wouldn't be going behind my back, would you, comrade? Reporting to the director?"

"About what exactly?"

Kutyrev shrugs. "About our progress on the reorganization. About me."

"No."

Kutyrev regards the file boxes stacked behind their desk, which now span the full length of the wall. "Maybe I'll ask around myself, see what I turn up. Pays to have friends here, you know. I've made a few. Maybe they'll shed some light on this business with you and Sevarov."

"Do whatever you want." Pavel speaks slowly to keep his voice from shaking. "Just leave me out of it."

At Dashenko's that night, over dinner, Semyon tells Pavel that he has a new joke for him. "Care to hear it?" From the kitchen radio floats the sound of a clarinet softly playing a jazz waltz, Shostakovich.

"Not really," says Pavel.

"A factory manager calls one of his workers into his office and demands to know why he was late coming in."

At his post by the door, watching the empty, littered street, Dashenko clasps and unclasps his hands like a man waiting for a train. All night he has kept his distance.

"So here stands our worker before his boss, head bowed. 'I'm sorry, Comrade Director,' he apologizes. 'I overslept.' 'That's no excuse,' shouts the manager. 'You could have just as easily slept here.' " Semyon pauses for effect. "You're not laughing."

"I'm not really in the mood for jokes tonight."

"So I see."

Semyon reaches for the wine, fills their glasses. The waltz goes on.

Semyon asks, "Is there anything I can do? Besides assaulting you with my hilarity."

"This is fine. What we're doing."

"What, eating bad food?"

"This." Pavel waves a hand vaguely: at their plates, the wine, the flickering candle, which is steadily melting away: at Semyon. In the kitchen the radio abruptly falls silent.

"And what exactly is this?"

"Not being alone," Pavel says.

Later, as Dashenko's daughter-in-law is collecting their plates, Semyon asks her what she is working on over at her table.

"It's nothing. An assignment for class. We're to come up with monument proposals for the Palace of Soviets."

"May I see?"

She returns with a sheet of drafting paper, on which is drawn a single massive plinth—"Of marble," she explains—aimed like a pike at the sky. Holding it at arm's length, tilting the picture toward the candlelight, Semyon examines the sketch gravely. "Interesting," he murmurs noncommittally. "What exactly is it supposed to commemorate?"

"The martyrs of the revolution."

Semyon passes the drawing to Pavel. "What do you think?"

"It's quite good," Pavel says politely. And it is, even if the subject repels him. "You're very talented."

"Only you'll have to make your monument bigger," Semyon suggests. "After all, we do have a great many martyrs, don't we?"

Dashenko's daughter-in-law nods uncertainly, as if she suspects Semyon is making fun of her. "The better proposals will get forwarded to the Palace of Soviets planning committee."

The Palace of Soviets. For a nearly a decade now that project, built on the grounds of the demolished Cathedral of Christ the Savior, has, like Semyon's neighborhood, gone nowhere. A story worthy of its own book, which, apocryphal or not, has persisted ever since: of the monks who wouldn't abandon the cathedral to its fate, who fled into its dark underground catacombs, and prayed, and were thus buried alive beneath the rubble. Semyon, Pavel notices, is no longer looking at the sketch but at him.

"I'm not very hopeful," admits Dashenko's daughter-in-law. "I never win anything. I'm only doing it because I have to."

"Then I will hope for you," says Semyon.

# 9

On Saturday, after Kutyrev has left, the summons finally comes. Sevarov appears. "Comrade Major Radlov would like a word with you." Instantly Pavel goes numb.

"Shall I bring my things?"

"As you like."

In the end Pavel takes only his coat. Part of him thinks he may need it later. He imagines Babel must have thought the same thing when they arrested him. Or this: a mistake. *It's all a mistake, I will be home again soon.* On the fifth floor an old woman in a headscarf is running a bulky electric vacuum cleaner over the deep crimson carpet. A fine sheen of sweat shines on her forehead and in the little black whiskers above her lip. A complicated fragrance fills the long corridor, wood oil and carbolic and, from the vacuum cleaner, an odor vaguely akin to burning hair. As they pass Pavel notices that the old woman's mouth is moving, as if in silent prayer.

In the anteroom Sevarov has him sit, then steps briefly into Radlov's office. When he emerges again Pavel immediately rises, but Sevarov waves him back down.

From the open window comes the steady faint sound of traffic below, like waves breaking at the base of a cliff. Sitting behind his heavy desk, Sevarov does nothing to break the tension—does not even make a show of busying himself. A picture of cold patience, mute as iron. Pavel has seen what men like Sevarov are capable of—prisoners beaten into a stupor, dragged moaning back to their cells. The simplest of languages—that is all Sevarov and his sort will tolerate: the language of the body. *I am hungry, I am afraid. I hurt.* Perhaps this is how he has survived so long here.

After what feels like an eternity the phone on Sevarov's desk rings. The officer picks it up, nods, then replaces the receiver.

"You may go in now."

A long green leather sofa with a single orange tasseled pillow, hollowed out where a head has recently rested, sits along the far wall of Radlov's office beside a low, crowded bookshelf. Nearby is a small round table, chairs. It is here, at the table, that Pavel finds Major Radlov, Director of Fourth Section. The new director, brought on only last April. Beria's man.

Smiling, Radlov waves him over, pushing out a chair with his boot. Even sitting, the officer somehow manages to retain an air of height and placid authority. With his wavy, flaxen hair, he could well be a matinee idol. Even those few defects his face possesses—the slightly crooked nose, the darkened lids under his eyes—only compliment the image. In another life the officer might have been discovered by some movie producer at Mosfilms and thrust onto the public, to be adored by millions precisely for these flaws. "Pavel Vasilievich, please," he calls in a voice of unexpected warmth, as if addressing an old friend. "You're just in time. I was about to have a bite to eat. Will you join me?"

Newspapers—*Pravda, Izvestia*—lie spread on the table. "Caught me shirking my work, I'm afraid." Radlov pushes the pile aside, clearing a space. Even in uniform, he has an air of slouching casualness about him that strikes Pavel as almost boyish, as though Radlov were a mere cadet playing at power. As if the desk across the room with its clutter of files, its bronze inkwell and pens and matching black telephones, were not his. "Sit."

Pavel sits.

"I'm sure you understand the compulsion," Radlov says. "Being a reader yourself."

"Compulsion?"

"For words." Radlov lightly raps the topmost newspaper with his knuckle. "Newspapers are by no means great literature, I know. Your basic black bread and kasha. Fills the belly, if not the soul. Still, it's my little way of escaping for a while."

There is a knock on the door. "Speaking of filling one's soul," Radlov murmurs theatrically as Sevarov enters, trailed by a beautiful, black-haired young woman carrying a silver serving tray. "Ah, dear Marina," the major sighs. "How are you today?" "Well, thank you, Comrade Major," the young woman whispers. From the open neck of her yellow blouse a light sunburn spreads across her collarbones. A blissful afternoon on the river or lakeside, with friends, a lover, a brief reprieve—that is what comes to mind. Her eyes, a startling milky green, never once lift to look upon them as she carefully sets out plates of cold cuts, potatoes in oil, olives, oranges, a basket of bread, butter, sugar, a silver pot of tea. When she leans down, her sleeve brushes Pavel's shoulder. A faint, sour smell, like ginkgo berries crushed underfoot, lingers briefly, fades. Her skin, her sweat? Fear? "Leave the tray," Radlov tells her.

"Yes, Comrade Major."

"Don't be shy," says Radlov after she has gone. He taps the table with the handle of a serving fork, as if calling a meeting to order. "It would be a sin to let all this good food go to waste. What would Marina think?"

*Soul. Sin.* The words, with their gloss of old-world, well-burnished religiosity, discards salvaged from the scrap pile of decades past, have no place here. Yet there is not the slightest note of irony or sarcasm in Radlov's tone. He is filling his plate and eating at once, as though famished. "Tell me," he says finally, spearing a potato wedge, "why are you here?"

Is this how it begins? Pavel wonders. Over tea and oranges. By a window bright with afternoon sunlight, with the thrumming square below. Calmly, cordially. With a question. The numbness in his chest dissolves, now he can feel himself tipping toward a rigid, dry-mouthed panic.

"Comrade Sevarov said you wanted to see me."

"Good man, Sevarov." A gold filling, perfectly round like a bird seed, flashes darkly deep in one corner of Radlov's mouth as he eats. "He was at Tannenberg, you know. Slaughtered God only knows how many Germans, from what I've heard. Not that he's the sort to go around bragging. Of course they did rout us." The major frowns. "You're not hungry?"

Cautiously Pavel picks up a slice of orange, bites into it. The sweet juice floods his mouth.

Radlov sits gazing at him, unblinking. Then his smile returns. "I understand you were a teacher."

"Yes."

"Wonderful profession. My father was a teacher. In Tomsk. As soon as I read your file I wanted to meet you."

In the anteroom a telephone rings. For a moment Sevarov's voice bores through the walls.

"You were at Kirov, yes?" asks Radlov.

"Yes, Comrade Major."

"Quite an institution. All those princes of the Party, all that potential. Like some great press stamping out gold coins. It must have been quite an experience for you. Quite a responsibility, as well."

"Yes."

Radlov regards him neutrally.

"I understand you were dismissed."

"I resigned, Comrade Major."

"After you were compelled to. Let's at least be accurate." Still smiling, Radlov leisurely butters a slice of bread. The warmth has not left his voice. Nonetheless there is something decidedly remote in his gaze.

"I'm curious, Pavel Vasilievich. What exactly was behind your dismissal. In your opinion."

He is baiting me, Pavel thinks. "I denounced a colleague. A teacher. There was a petition put forth for his dismissal. For remarks this man had reportedly made in front of his students."

"You authored this petition?"

"I was consulted about it."

"By this man Kudelin's students."

"Mikhail Kudelin. Yes." Why, Pavel wonders, bring up Kudelin now? He clears his throat—already his voice has begun to crack. He must fight off the impulse to whisper. "By his students. Some of whom were my students."

"These remarks"—Radlov picks at his teeth with the rounded tip of his knife—"what exactly were they? Your file's a bit sketchy on that account."

"He made an offhanded comment about collectivization and bread shortages during one of his lessons. He mentioned the famine."

Radlov apes mild astonishment. "What famine would that be, Pavel Vasilievich? I wasn't aware that we'd had any famines. At least under Soviet rule. Disruptions, yes, but then that is to be expected. But famine? That's taking things a bit far. Or am I mistaken?"

Pavel finds himself unable to reply. His heart contracts with fear. A trap—he has allowed himself to be lured into a trap. Soon Radlov will summon his assistant, and then the real interview will begin. Radlov refills his own teacup, then goes on eating.

"I misspoke," Pavel says.

Radlov nods. "Yes, well. I suppose we all make mistakes. Tell me. What did this Kudelin teach?"

"Math."

"Did you know him personally? Were you friends?"

"No."

"I imagine," says Radlov placidly, "that must have made slandering him that much easier. Isn't that what your colleagues later accused you of? Slander?"

"Yes," Pavel says.

A visit by the headmaster, not entirely unexpected. *A moment, Pavel.* To this day, what Pavel remembers most vividly is not the headmaster himself—portly, sorrowful Georgi Alexeyevich, pausing in the doorway of his classroom that afternoon in late December—instead, what remains is the memory of students, released once more to their lives, hurrying along the path outside, where the groundskeeper was raking away the last of the season's leaves. An afternoon, at least outwardly, no different from any other. Just like that afternoon five weeks earlier when one of his students, Peter, had appeared after class, boiling with youthful outrage.

"Do you have any idea what you're asking me to do?" Pavel had said, trying his best to mollify the boy. "The man is a colleague of mine, Peter. This petition—" He sighed. "These things have a way of taking on their own life. You don't want that."

"So you won't help me?"

"I am trying to help you, Peter. Please. Just let it go."

Peter's expression darkened. An eager boy, often the first to raise his hand whenever Pavel put some question before the class. Always so certain he had the right answer, even when he was wrong. "I know why you're protecting him," Peter said sullenly. Then, to make sure there was no mistaking his meaning, he added, "You agree with him, don't you?"

"I'm not protecting him," said Pavel carefully.

"That's not what people will think."

*What people will think.* Just like that, Pavel found himself at the precipice, where the same fate confronting Kudelin now confronted him. So that, seen in the cold, stark light of reason, what Pavel did next made perfect sense, even if he has never been able to forgive himself.

"And here you sit," Radlov says. "Redeemed. And once again you've been given an important responsibility."

"The reorganization."

"It's vital every process in this organization runs smoothly. Right now that isn't the case. But it will be. I'm relying on you."

Radlov studies him a long moment, then abruptly pushes back his chair, tossing his napkin onto the table. Standing, he is even taller than Pavel expected, even more strikingly handsome, a beautiful, austere pillar of a man.

"I want you to do something for me, Pavel Vasilievich," he says, staring down at Dzerzhinsky Square. "When you leave this evening, I want you to take a long look at the Lubyanka. My office is on the fifth floor. A sixth floor sits above me—an entire floor to which I must answer. From you to your superior to me to Beria himself, who answers directly to Stalin. Above Stalin there is only the revolution, to which we must all answer in one way or another. Whatever our particular gifts may be." Radlov turns. "Do you understand?"

"Yes," Pavel says.

Outside the first stars are beginning to appear over Moscow. "Everything flows upward," the major says. He tugs at the hem of his uniform tunic. "There is always someone to which we must answer. Always. Remember that." He lays the knuckles of his left hand against the glass and raps once, lightly, as upon a door. "It's good we had this chance to finally talk."

Pavel hesitates, then rises from his chair. The meeting, he realizes, is over.

"Be sure to take an orange with you," Radlov tells him.

# 10

Afterward, descending the long stairway of the Dzerzhinsky metro station, Pavel begins to tremble uncontrollably—hands, legs: his whole body. He must grip the handrail tightly to keep from falling, until the spell passes. A tomb, he thinks despairingly, looking down. He turns and pushes his way back up the stairs.

Outside again he breathes deeply, letting the air fill his lungs. Only now does Pavel ask himself where he is going. Even the thought of sitting for an hour or two over tea in some innocuous café near Red Square, surrounded by strangers, repels him. He has lost his taste for crowds; he has no wish to lose himself in the dazzling noise of shared anonymity: other people's happiness, other people's lives. And yet he does not want to be alone with his fear. Across the traffic-clotted square a handful of the Lubyanka's offices are already lit, as if in preparation for the evening's work ahead.

Pavel waves a taxi to the curb, climbs in. He tells the driver Semyon's address, then leans back against the seat.

"Nice neighborhood," the driver says sarcastically when they stop in front of Semyon's building.

"It used to be."

At Semyon's door Pavel listens for the piano, and hearing nothing, knocks. Almost immediately Vera answers. "I thought you were the police," she says.

Pavel stares at her.

"Well. Are you coming in or not?"

Pavel steps inside. From the little bathroom just off the foyer comes Semyon's voice, calling good-naturedly. "I'm afraid you're wasting your time, gentlemen. It's really nothing." He walks into the hallway in his undershirt, dabbing at his neck with a washcloth. "Pasha. What are you doing here?"

"Why are you expecting the police?"

"Ask him," Vera says irritably. "Some thug cuts his throat and what does he say? 'Oh well, just a scratch. No harm done. No need to complicate things by calling the police.' "Vera tugs angrily at the thin gray sweater she is wearing, the cuffs of which are frayed, unraveling. "As if there were anything complicated about this."

The *regular* police, Pavel understands now, relieved. Traffic tickets, drunken brawls, thefts, murders over money and love—so-called low crimes the NKVD has no role in prosecuting, and thus ignores.

Semyon sighs. "It *is* just a scratch, Vera. Don't be overdramatic."

"Let me see," Pavel says.

"Yes." Vera's eyes are suddenly shiny—she is close to tears, Pavel realizes. "Show Pasha your little scratch." He is tempted to reach for her hand, to comfort her, as he might have once done. But he and Vera are well past that point in their relationship, whatever their relationship is now. When she walks away he and Semyon face each other soberly.

"May I see your neck?" Pavel asks.

Reluctantly Semyon pulls away the washcloth, which is spotted with blood. A neat, shallow cut, clean as a surgeon's incision, gapes just under his left ear. Pavel is too stunned at first to react.

"Who did this to you? What happened?"

"I was just taking a little walk through the park. And these two fellows, they stop me, ask for money. I didn't have a kopeck—and I told them as much. So they asked again. More insistently, you might say." Semyon presses the washcloth to his throat. "The uglier fellow, the one who nicked me with his knife, he was so scared I believe he pissed himself. Which is what I'll tell the police if they ask for a description. If they ever arrive. 'Gentlemen, follow the smell of piss.' Although to be perfectly honest I'd just as soon put the whole unpleasant business behind me."

"You're not serious. And what? Let these two simply walk away?"

"Walk, run. Yes. That's the sum of it."

"Semyon, these men attacked you. With a knife. You're acting as though it were all some sort of farce." But Pavel can see that his words are having no effect. "Tell me," he asks, "what if you run into them again?"

"I suppose I better have some money on me."

He steps back into the bathroom. Pavel follows.

"What if it's Vera they stop next time? Have you considered that?"

Semyon stands at the sink, tilting his head to one side in order to examine the wound on his neck. A tuft of gray hair pokes from the top of his undershirt. "God pity them if they do." He smiles wanly. "See? No more blood." He drops the washcloth into the sink.

Pavel asks, "What were you thinking, walking in that park by yourself? You know how dangerous that place has become."

"I wasn't thinking anything, Pasha. That's the point of walking, isn't it? You're not required to think. Anyway, I wasn't entirely alone. I did have my cane. Do you suppose I should have hit these hooligans with my cane? Struck a blow for order?"

Semyon pulls with the tips of his fingers at the puffy dark skin beneath his eyes. "Good Lord, what an ugly old cripple I've become. How did that happen?"

He turns on the cold tap, the faucet head clouding with condensation. A thin ribbon of blood seeps from the washcloth and waves like an unraveling pennant of pinkish smoke in the clear shimmering water. How quickly one's fear shifts—that is what Pavel is thinking. A moment ago he could think of nothing but himself. Now it is Semyon he is afraid for.

After a time, in a lower voice, Semyon says, "There was this moment, when I looked up and saw those two coming toward me." He watches the water filling the sink.

"What?"

"This feeling came over me. This fear. Suddenly it was as though we were in the middle of nowhere, just us three. And I was absolutely terrified. Believe it or not, Pasha, I even considered running. Wooden leg and all. But then I thought, They'll catch me. The second I try, the very instant, they'll be on me. Because I'm weak." He meets Pavel's gaze in the mirror, eyes haunted by the memory. "And they picked up on that. On how afraid I was, like dogs picking up a scent. Until that moment I don't think they even intended to rob me."

Pavel, thinking back to his meeting with Radlov, remembering his own terror, is quiet.

"You were right not to run," he says finally. "If you'd run it might have come out worse for you."

"You're missing my point, Pasha."

"All right, then. Tell me."

"If they thought that about me—thought I was weak—it was because I thought so too. And I never have before. Even in the war, after my leg was shot off, I never felt helpless. If I'd been blinded, if I'd had my prick blown off, it might have been different. But a leg? Believe it or not, I was grateful. I've always been grateful, Pasha. Because I was alive and so many good men weren't. Men like your father. The moment you realize what a miracle of luck simply being alive is, you can't help but be grateful."

A clean shirt hangs on the corner of the open door. Semyon reaches for it now, slips it on. The gesture, so simple, seems intended to end their discussion. But then Semyon speaks.

"The oddest thing happened after class yesterday," he says, almost lightly. "I ran into an old acquaintance of mine—he's a visiting lecturer now, an expert in agricultural economics. Which of course makes him insufferably important. Knows everybody, has his hand in every jar from here to Kazakhstan." Semyon pauses, tilting his head toward the open door, listening. For Vera, Pavel senses. "Push that shut, would you?" he tells Pavel softly.

Pavel closes the door.

"He said he'd heard I'd been arrested." In the mirror Semyon's eyes once more meet Pavel's.

"Why would he say that?"

"Who knows? He was probably half-drunk—he always was when I knew him. Besides, the man's a certifiable moron. I think he's been kicked one too many times in the head by cows."

"This is no joke. If this acquaintance of yours is as connected as you say he is." From the other room comes the sound of the piano, a string of notes, a fragment of some song, softly played. Nonetheless Pavel lowers his voice even more. "Listen to me, Semyon. There's no telling who he's been talking to. What if one of these connections let something slip?"

"Then again, what if it's simply a rumor? One of ten thousand currently making its way through the gut of Moscow academia."

"What if it isn't?"

"You're beginning to sound like Vera. Flying off into hysterics over a scratch."

"Are you going to mention this to her?"

"God no. And you're not either," Semyon adds. "The woman's worried enough as it is. This is between us, Pasha. Promise me that."

"I won't say anything."

"Thank you. Now be a good soul and help me with these buttons."

In the living room, over a tin of stale biscuits and weak tea, they wait for the police to arrive. The sun casts its dying glow across the wooded park, the overgrown paths, the long brick wall. Shadows fill the empty street: an entire district, cut off from the surrounding city. Occasionally a car or truck passes by below, and Vera hurriedly crosses to the open window, cupping her elbows in her hands. Watching her, Pavel cannot help but remember other evenings, happier evenings, years ago in this same flat, with Elena, when Vera would entertain them on the piano. Schumann, Bach, Schubert. At her most playful she would slip in the occasional American ragtime number, Joplin's "Maple Leaf Rag," Joseph Lamb. Once, one rare night, she even sang for them, though the name of the song escapes Pavel now: He remembers only that her voice possessed an unexpected, rather simple loveliness. The sun sinks behind the trees, vanishes. A dog barks and is answered blocks away by another dog. The limp curtains stir as the evening breeze touches them.

"Maybe they got lost," Semyon tells Vera, turning on the reading lamp beside his chair.

"I don't see how they could. The officer I spoke to on the telephone, I made him repeat our address back twice, just to be sure."

"You never know. They could have forgotten about us."

"They haven't forgotten us," says Vera. "They're just incompetent."

For a few minutes no one speaks. The glass panels of Semyon's old cluttered bookcase gleam warmly, like the windows of a dollhouse. There are books all over the room: on tables and chairs and desktop, on the floor and atop the stout black upright piano.

" 'O twilight! Mercy of the world dawn once again upon me,' " Semyon recites in his sonorous, slightly hoarse lecturer's voice. With his fingers he caresses the slender brass neck of the lamp beside him, as if absently petting a sleeping cat.

"Balmont?" Pavel guesses.

"Close. Bryusov. Our dutiful doomed Bolshevik." Semyon says, "I remember once, when the heat went out in our department, one of my colleagues went around for days chanting Bryusov. And Balmont, for that matter. All the Symbolists. Said it kept him warm." He smiles ruefully. "Poor Glebnikov. He was so hapless. A true eccentric. He used to break down crying in front of his students, reading some poem or another. They loved him for it. He was so gentle, so vulnerable—after class you'd see them brushing the lint from his sweater, helping him with his coat. Like he was a child."

*Was.* He is referring to his colleague Glebnikov in the past tense, the way one speaks of the dead. A door, Pavel understands, better left unopened.

"How are your students?" Pavel asks Vera, changing the subject.

"They're good—those I have left anyway. Those who haven't moved away."

"Nonsense," Semyon says. "Their parents drag them halfway across Moscow, just so they can keep up with their lessons," he tells Pavel. "They're absolutely loyal to Vera. It's quite touching."

"I'm not sure the children enjoy spending all their time on buses," Vera says. "Anyway, I worry about them. They're too young to be running around like that. It was much easier when they could just walk here." She glances at the piano. "I miss seeing them around the neighborhood."

"They'll be back," Semyon says. "You'll see, love. Once our betters finish restoring the neighborhood to its former glory, you'll be up to your elbows in children."

Vera waves the suggestion away.

"Play something for us," Semyon urges.

Vera clears her throat, then rises from the sofa and crosses the room. Seated at the piano, she presses each creaking pedal, as if the piano is some temperamental machine she must coax slowly to life. Satisfied, she commences playing—one of Chopin's nocturnes. Her plump hands, spread over the yellowed keys, move with a grace and ease Pavel has always found miraculous. There is something deeply comforting in her playing, something profoundly beautiful and pure in this picture she and the piano make. Her worn sweater, the loose light cotton hem of her housedress trembling as her scuffed shoes lift and settle on the pedals. He has missed this more than he realized. Beside Vera, arrayed behind glass, the spines of Semyon's books gleam like artifacts in a museum. Each with its own distinct, irreplaceable life.

Later Pavel is awakened by the sound of Semyon closing the windows, one by one. He has nodded off on the sofa, head slumped sideways. It is colder, almost to the point of chilliness. Except for a tiny dollop of light down the hallway, the flat is dark. "Semyon?" Pavel is suddenly, inexplicably afraid. Then Semyon is there.

"Here," he tells Pavel quietly, "stretch out now."

"How long have I been asleep?"

Semyon gently tugs off his shoes, setting them on the floor. A moment later a blanket is pulled over Pavel. "Not long," says Semyon. "Just a few minutes." For a moment he lays his hand on Pavel's head, leaving it there, as if blessing him: A warmth spreads down through Pavel, a feeling of peace. As though he were a boy again. His father's hand resting on his head, its comforting weight, keeping him safe.

# II

Nearly a week later Pavel returns home from work to find an ambulance parked in front of his building. Crowded on the wide stone steps, a half dozen or so of Pavel's neighbors mill about, talking in low tones. He recognizes one of the factory workers from across the hall.

"What's happened?"

The young man shrugs. He has the broad, powerful-looking shoulders and somewhat blunted features one sees everywhere these days—in cigarette advertisements, in movie posters and anti-Fascist propaganda: the line-worker turned soldier, resolute in the face of the German military machine now poised along Poland's border. In the soft twilight his chemical-scoured hands are as luminous as milk. "Somebody died."

"Who?"

"It's the old woman up on three," one of the other tenants says. "The one with that ugly little dog who's always shitting on the sidewalk."

"Marfa Borisova?"

"Whatever her name is. She had a heart attack or something. Natalya Arkadyevna found her."

"I heard she cut her wrists," the young man confides to them.

"Nonsense."

"It's what I heard."

They are both wrong. Marfa Borisova is not dead. Silent, slowly blinking as if stunned, she is carried from the building by a pair of attendants, her pink belted robe open over one pale slack thigh. An uneasy hush falls. "They'll fix you right up, dear," Natalya is saying, trailing behind them. When the attendants pause briefly to catch their breath, letting the upper half of the stretcher rest on the back lip of the ambulance, she hurriedly flips the robe back over Marfa Borisova's bare leg.

"What happened?" asks Pavel after the ambulance has driven away.

Natalya looks down at Borisova's pug, which has emerged from the building unnoticed. "She had a stroke, they think." The dog trots past them, claws clicking on the steps, headed for the park.

"Someone said you found her."

Natalya nods.

"How did you know?"

"She called me on the telephone." Natalya's mouth twists into a small bitter smile. "That's the second time that's happened. An old couple, the Bronsteins, used to live in 217. One morning the wife calls me. 'Can you come over, please? I need your help.' Calm as can be. I thought, all right, a leaky faucet. I get there, I find her husband in their bedroom, half hanging off the mattress. Dead."

"What did she expect you to do?"

"I don't know. She was completely in shock. I got him back on the bed, covered him with a sheet." Natalya stops, as if the memory is too disturbing to go on talking about. "Then I called for an ambulance."

The onlookers are melting away, returning to their flats.

"That must have been difficult."

"It was terrible. Seeing him like that. I felt ashamed." She takes a shaky breath before going on. "When I got up to Marfa's she seemed all right at first. She was just sitting in the kitchen. But then she started slurring her words, and she slumped over. All I could do was hold her hand. By the time the ambulance arrived she couldn't even speak." She reaches up and rubs her forehead, scrunching her eyes tightly. When she tips forward a little, as if overcome by dizziness, Pavel grabs her before she falls, gripping her arm. It is all catching up with her.

"Why don't you come up for a drink?"

Natalya gazes at Borisova's pug, which is squatting beside a bed of daffodils, contentedly scratching its neck. "I guess I should get him."

"I'll help."

They cross the street. Wrinkled ears flattened, the pug warily scampers away from them. Natalya calls after it, patting her thigh. For a moment the dog regards them soberly. Then it trots quickly back across the street and slips into the alleyway beside their building, and is gone.

"Little shit."

"He'll come back," Pavel says.

Upstairs, in Pavel's flat, they take their drinks into the living room, where Natalya crouches before the bookcase with her glass resting on her thigh. "I keep forgetting you were a teacher," she says. Pavel has never told her about the scandal that surrounded his leaving Kirov Academy—Kudelin's denunciation, the storm of accusations and counteraccusations that erupted afterward, after it became clear that an innocent man had been wrongly accused. How, when his colleagues discovered that Pavel had been consulted by the same students who, in their naive zeal, destroyed Kudelin's reputation, it was Pavel's head they demanded, and got. *You could have stopped this before it got out of control, Pavel Vasilievich, and yet you did nothing. Worse than nothing, you sent that boy on his way with that petition, which you yourself read. You knew what was coming. The moment that petition went public, Kudelin was finished.* With Natalya, Pavel has been assiduous in avoiding that chapter of his past. For all their friendliness there has always been a certain safe level of guardedness between them. Perhaps this as much as anything else has drawn them to each other.

"I forget too sometimes," Pavel jokes.

She smiles thoughtfully. "Did you enjoy it? Teaching."

"Very much."

"I bet you were good at it."

"Sometimes. I was certainly ambitious. Which is not always a virtue. I hope I was a good teacher."

Up until now they have always done their drinking at her flat. And perhaps the same thought has crossed Natalya's mind, perhaps she senses it as well. That something has changed, that by his simply inviting her here they have both crossed into new country.

"Poor Marfa." She has turned to the window. She looks down at the little park, the flower beds and sand paths sinking in shadow. "I'm sorry about your wife, Pavel," she says after a long silence. "I wish I'd known her better."

He nods. "Yes."

Natalya regards the row of photographs arrayed along the upper shelf of the bookcase. Yalta, years past. Elena in a long summer dress, hatless, blond hair blown across her eyes, standing by the seawall outside their hotel. Elena asleep on a beach chair under a parasol, *Anna Karenina* open across her lap. Then further back still, Elena standing next to him, smiling shyly in a little veil of lace flowers, with Red Square spread out at her back. That was the picture Pavel's mother had taken the day they married. Almost absently, Natalya's hand rises, fingers brushing Elena's face, wiping away the faint film of dust that coats the glass.

"I sometimes wonder," says Pavel, surprising himself, "whether it would be better if I just put her pictures away."

Natalya glances at him, and Pavel sees at once the question in her eyes. What is he telling her? That it is too painful to go on looking at Elena's pictures day after day, knowing he will never see her again? That would be the simple answer, the expected answer. How then to reconcile this with the sense of uneasiness that has grown up in him since his wife's death? Uneasiness, because Elena has slipped, ever so gradually, into abstraction. She has become these pictures. A handful of memories. Worse, she has become the imagined last moments of her life, which Pavel will likely never be able to let go.

But of course the questions never come. Instead Natalya says, "I hope Marfa's all right. I felt so useless. I wish I'd been able to help her."

"You did. You stayed with her."

"A lot of good that did."

Pavel wonders if Marfa Borisova has reached the hospital by now. When they carried her out earlier, did she feel the creaking stretcher sway under her, the sudden coolness of the evening air on her naked thigh? A splash of red and saffron yellow in the corner of her vision—the bright flower beds across the street. Did she recognize them? Did Natalya's voice reach her, was she comforted? Or did none of it touch her? Was she already, even at that moment, gone? He thinks: And Elena? What did she feel, dying in darkness in that field near Tamoy? Could she feel the snow under her, the cold spreading up through her? Could she hear the cries of the other passengers and the crunch of their footsteps as they stumbled through snowdrifts, calling ever more desperately for husbands, for wives, for their children? In some way she is still lying in that lonely field, waiting for Pavel to find her.

"Did you know that I had two daughters once?" asks Natalya after a time. She has turned again to look down at the park. Or perhaps she is looking past the park now, toward Donskoy, or even beyond the monastery and its lush, untidy cemetery, grown wild with summer, hidden behind that high pink wall. From outside comes the sudden, frantic flurry of beating wings—a pigeon, launching itself out from the lip of granite beneath the window.

"No," Pavel says. "I didn't know that."

"I'll have dreams about them sometimes, and when I wake up it's almost like losing them all over again. The pain." She touches the scar on her cheek, and again her gaze slips across the photographs on the shelf. "Is it like that for you with Elena?"

"Sometimes."

Natalya lets her hand fall. "I used to find myself wishing that they would go away. The dreams. So I could go on with my life. But I don't wish for that anymore. Now, if I dream about them, I'm thankful afterward. Even if it hurts. Because it hurts. Because it should." She drains her glass and sets it down on the windowsill. "Thank you for the drink."

"You're welcome."

His eyes drop to the dark half-moon the damp glass has left on her brown wool skirt. Pavel would like to lay his hand over it.

"I should go," says Natalya.

He walks her to the door, then stands listening to her footsteps on the stairs.

# 12

Later he telephones his mother. The man who picks up the public phone on her floor is so drunk Pavel can barely understand him. "Who do you want?" the man asks rudely, but before Pavel can speak the phone is dropped, perhaps on purpose—he can hear the man muttering curses as the handset thumps in his ear. The line goes dead. When the operator puts Pavel through a second time the same man answers, only now he is almost comically formal in his courtesy. "Yes? Who is calling, please?"

"I need to speak to Anna Dubrova in 310."

"Anna Dubrova . . ."

"In 310. Tell her her son is calling. And don't hang up on me again."

There is a silence. "Very well, comrade," the man says politely.

A moment later he hears the man knocking on a door, then the murmur of voices, footsteps. "Pavel?" It is Victor. "Is everything all right?"

"Yes, everything's fine. I was just hoping to talk to my mother."

"She and Olga took the boys to a movie. I needed to get

some work done. They should be back soon." Victor pauses, then adds, "We've missed you, you know. When are you going to come see us again?"

"I will soon," Pavel says. An image flashes across his mind: slack-mouthed Marfa Borisova, lolling as her stretcher was hoisted into the back of the ambulance. He remembers how her bare feet trembled as the stretcher was roughly slid into place and locked down. Inexplicably, that memory triggers another: of Babel, the fingers of his hand twitching on his leg. "How is my mother?" Pavel asks.

"She doesn't seem so anxious anymore. About work, about Andrei and Misha. For a while there, after your last visit—well, anyway, she didn't want to let them out of her sight. I tell you, Pavel, that doctor you took her to, whatever he did, apparently it worked."

"He didn't do anything," says Pavel.

"No?"

"He couldn't find anything wrong with her."

"Well, that's good news, then," Victor says. "Isn't it?"

"I don't know, Victor."

And he doesn't. Pavel would like to believe his mother has put these blackouts behind her, but he can't. When he thinks of her now he thinks of her sitting alone on the train to Moscow, lost in the fugue fallen over her consciousness. He sees his mother standing outside his empty flat, knocking on his door with increasing bewilderment and fear.

"You'd tell me if anything happened, wouldn't you?"

"You have to ask?" says Victor.

"I just want to make sure. I need to be sure."

Victor says gently, "I understand. Of course I would tell you." Then, "Are you all right? You sound a little . . ." Victor hesitates. "Not yourself tonight."

Is he himself? "It's just been a difficult day," Pavel says. Before Victor can reply he asks, "Will you tell my mother I called?"

"I'll tell her."

"Thank you."

He is too restless to sleep. Head on the pillow, Pavel lies listening to the drumbeat of his own pulse, the blood pounding softly in his ear. A truck, shuddering along in low gear, passes in the street. He listens for the cry of brakes, the low metallic rattle of the gate being pulled back—on certain clear, still nights the sound carries all the way from Donskoy. But the truck continues on its way. Pavel throws off the sheets, dresses.

In the kitchen he leaves the light off. The street lamps cast their glow across table and floor like a net flung into water. He fills the teapot, lights the hissing gas eye of the stove. As he reaches into the cupboard for a cup, Pavel thinks, Tomorrow I will load my cart with manuscripts, and the next day, and the day after that, I will load my cart again. He still has not come upon Mandelstam's confiscated poems. But soon enough even they will turn up, eventually the archives will no longer be able to hide Mandelstam, and his poems will be fed into the flames. Pavel turns off the gas burner, then stands listening to the stove tick as it cools.

*Masked ball. Wolfhound century.*
*Don't forget it.*
*Keep out of sight, a cap in a sleeve,*
*And God preserve you!*

Could one stay hidden forever? Pavel wonders. He finds his shoes, slips downstairs. At the basement door he feels for the light switch inside, fingers crawling over cool brick. When he locates it Pavel steps forward and quietly pulls shut the door behind him. In the darkness, a faint scratching sound reaches him, as if someone were drawing their fingernails across a door. But it is only a rat—the instant the string of lights flares overhead, the scratching ceases. Still, the image stays with him: hands clawing weakly at a door, a wall. Mandelstam, tracing his poems with a fingernail on the plaster wall of his cell. *Keep my words forever for their aftertaste of misfortune and smoke.* True or not, another rumor that has persisted at the Lubyanka.

Even as his hand touches the loose brick in the wall Pavel wonders if it is not too late to turn back. But how can he stop now? The close basement air with its sharp, earthy odor of decay, like leaves rotting along a garden wall, slips silently into his lungs: He can taste it, taste death. If he can save Babel's story, save some remnant of his work, perhaps he can redeem himself, if there is anything in him left to redeem. Perhaps it is not too late.

Pavel reaches down into the wall until he touches the sheaf of papers: Already they are dusty, coated with a fine grit like sand from the crumbled mortar. A thought pierces him: I am reaching into a grave. For a second he almost expects to feel a hand find his, there in the darkness. A shiver passes through him. Then, carefully, he draws the rolled manuscript from its hole and, in the shadow of the boiler, reads.

# 13

At the Lubyanka the next day Pavel steals another story from Babel's file. As with the first manuscript, the act by itself is no great feat—Kutyrev has taken the rare afternoon off to attend the enormous Aviation Day celebration at Tushino airfield, and Pavel has the archives to himself. Nevertheless his heart shudders in his chest as he slides the story under the waistband of his belted trousers, under his shirt, then slips on his coat. He is teetering on the abyss: One mistake, a single misstep, and he could tumble to his death.

He leaves at his regular time, six-thirty—the busiest time to leave and therefore the best. Even today, with so many off celebrating at Tushino, the elevators are packed, grindingly slow. At last an elevator with just enough space for him arrives, crowded with day-shift midlevel officers bleary-eyed with paperwork, secretaries silent after a day of telephones and typing. Pavel steps in.

Upstairs the lobby rings with brisk footsteps, voices, rough laughter: the anticipatory, almost electric end-of-day thrum, which greets Pavel the instant the elevator's door slides open. A cloud of blue smoke, fed by countless cigarettes, drifts under the high ceiling. The customarily fast-flowing entranceway is somewhat clogged with people today. Instead of the usual lone junior officer, a pair of guards has been posted, and they are taking their time with the identification cards, studying each thoroughly. Pavel is tempted to turn around, but then one of the guards, glancing over the waiting throng, catches his eye. Pavel forces himself to return the young guard's gaze with what he hopes passes for disinterest, boredom. Nevertheless a dizzying panic wells in his chest, which loosens only when the guard, whom Pavel now recognizes, finally looks away. It is the gangly, sleepy-eyed young guard who escorted Babel to their meeting in July. Pavel tries to aim himself for the other guard, but there is no line, only a mass of bodies moving slowly forward.

"Here." The young guard waves him over. Pavel hands him his identification.

"What's happening, comrade?"

"Orders," the young guard replies curtly. He is scrutinizing Pavel's photograph. "Have you been contacted recently by anyone unknown to you?" His voice is flat.

"No."

The young guard's eyes are blank. Hazel eyes, flecked with green. The folded story pressed against Pavel's back digs uncomfortably into his skin. Pavel is suddenly convinced that if he is to be caught, it will be now, by this boy.

"Have any individuals known or unknown to you attempted to engage you in conversation regarding your work here?" Again those eyes, that empty gaze.

"No."

Spies—they are hunting for spies, Pavel understands. Nazi infiltrators, agents provocateurs under the bed. Not a day goes by without some newspaper screaming about German agents med-

Semyon assured him when Pavel asked years ago. *Your father probably didn't even see the damn thing explode. Maybe a flash. Lucky that way, really.* If so, it was his father's only luck. A forty-year-old volunteer, no less, fighting a young man's war. Political Commissar Dubrov. A midmorning assault, a lumbering charge across a sweltering open field toward a Polish line bristling with Vickers machine guns. One moment his father was there, running, the next he was gone. *Just like my leg,* said Semyon. A burst from a Vickers had taken care of that.

"Can you tell me," the doctor asks Pavel's mother, "what year it is now?"

His mother frowns. "Nineteen thirty-nine."

"Excellent. And what city are we in, Mrs. Dubrova? This very moment."

His mother's frown deepens.

"I know—it's a silly question," the doctor says apologetically. "Please, indulge me."

"We're in Moscow."

"And your son. Can you tell me your son's name, please?"

"His name is Pavel. Pasha."

"Wonderful." Dr. Hirsch smiles warmly. "Now, I'd like to talk to Pavel outside for just a moment, if that's all right. In the meantime, just relax."

In the corridor the doctor gently pulls the door shut behind him.

"Does your mother drink? Heavily, I mean."

"No," Pavel says.

"You're certain?"

"Absolutely. These"—Pavel struggles for the word—"episodes—they just come out of nowhere. Without warning."

"She's had them before?"

"Once. Back in March. The doctor who examined her then

said she just needed to rest. He thought it might be anxiety. Poor diet perhaps."

"Has she had any other symptoms? Difficulty concentrating. Flashes of light or sound. Problems remembering things."

"She's had some issues with work, I understand. Not following up on tasks."

Dr. Hirsch nods. "All right, then. I still have a few things to run through with your mother. And I will want to see her again for a follow-up—say, in a month or so. Would you mind waiting outside? Shouldn't take more than fifteen minutes."

Pavel asks, "What's wrong with her, Doctor?"

"Right now, I honestly don't know. As you said—and I have no reason not to believe you—your mother's not a serious drinker, which all but eliminates polyneuritic psychosis. Korsakoff's syndrome. It's caused by thiamine deficiency. Essentially your short-term memory mortifies. You might remember moments from your childhood with perfect clarity but be unable to recall what you ate for breakfast. One more or less becomes unable to make new memories."

"Is it curable?"

"If one stops drinking, yes, usually. But your mother doesn't drink."

"So what do we do?"

"Our best, comrade. We do our best." He pats Pavel's shoulder encouragingly. "I'll send your mother out as soon as we're through."

In the waiting room a little boy weakly flails away on his mother's lap, paddling the air with his hands, as if struggling to wake from some dream of falling. The boy's eyes, beautifully blue, follow Pavel as he passes; the frank despair in them chills his heart. Is this what awaits him and his mother? Private miseries played out in public, as in the pages of a novel. Like that old dling in Danzig, in Warsaw—against the police, against Jews. *Individuals known or unknown*. The whole continent has become one vast powder keg: All that is needed now is the match.

The guard looks down once more at his photograph. "No teapot today?" he asks, a faint contempt threading his voice. He hands Pavel back his identification card.

"Not today."

Outside, the linden trees along the sidewalk pulse in the gusting wind, showing the pale silvery undersides of their leaves. Sweat trickles under Pavel's arms and down his back. Behind him the heavy wooden door swings open, one of the middle-aged secretaries from the elevator emerges and looks contentedly up at the sky. "Pretty day," she says. In an instant the long afternoon and all its demands have tumbled from her shoulders, Pavel sees. She is, for the time being, free. The shimmering trees, the immense blue sky softening toward evening, the breeze, unexpectedly cool, blowing into their faces: Summer will soon be over.

# 14

The train thunders through forests of birch and pine, sudden fields of wheat grass and brilliant yellow goldenrod grown waist-high after the long summer. Looking out, Pavel imagines other fields, other forests, buried under a blanket of snow, locked fast in winter, as they were when Elena passed them in January. She was so happy to put Moscow behind her—she'd always loved to travel, and in the weeks before she left had talked blissfully of the prospect of unfettered days of warmth and sun, with no patients to worry over, no one to put back together again. The long leisurely journey to Yalta was part of the reward she had promised herself.

At his mother's stop, old women with net bags stroll through the outdoor market among the rickety tables. As he passes by one stand a vendor calls out, waving him over. It is the old woman from whom he bought the fish when he visited his mother last month. She has traded her upturned bucket for a folding chair and table, branched out into produce, flowers. By the looks of things, she is prospering.

"Those fish you sold me were bad," Pavel tells her.

"Blame the lake, not me," the old woman says defensively. "Anyway, I never eat anything that comes out of that lake. Ask my son." Gasping a little, she struggles to her feet, pats the flowers spread on her plank table. "Have you ever seen such flowers? Aren't they lovely? Just came in on the train this morning."

She is lying, of course. They are only wildflowers, likely cut from some nearby field. Still, he buys a bunch from her for his mother, waiting while she wraps them in newspaper.

It is a short walk to the pharmacy where his mother works. He has not visited it in well over a year. Not that the place has changed in the least, Pavel sees: the same dim, dusty aisles, the same stinging sour smell of mustard plaster and carbolic and menthol, of long sickness. "I'm looking for Anna Mikhailovna," he tells the girl behind the cash register. "There's someone here for Anna Mikhailovna," the girl languidly calls to the back of the store, where a curtain divides the stockroom from the rest of the pharmacy. Golovkin appears, flushed, wiping the perspiration from his fleshy face with the hem of his dirty apron. He is a squat, heavy-browed, balding stub of a man, perpetually unhappy. "She's not here anymore."

"What do you mean?"

"I mean I fired her. What, two days ago? I couldn't rely on her anymore." He makes a show of washing his hands. "I've got enough worries without her piling on more shit. If you want my opinion, your mama needs her head examined." He taps a temple. "Her brain's going soft."

"Watch your mouth," Pavel says.

"I'll say whatever I want. This is my place." Golovkin's voice climbs. "If you don't like it, get out."

Two days ago. Thursday, the day Pavel spoke to Victor on the telephone and Victor assured him his mother was all right. What else, Pavel wonders angrily, has he not been told?

At his mother's flat there is no answer. The hollow sound of Pavel's knocking echoes back into the hallway: Each time his fist falls on the door the wildflowers rain tiny purple petals onto the carpet. Suddenly he is no longer angry but frightened. What will happen to his mother now?

Outside Pavel follows the paved path to the playing field, but it is empty today. A sheet of windblown newspaper, tumbling lazily in the air, snags on a clump of bushes at the woods' edge.

His mother has returned. "Misha and I were visiting with a friend of mine," she explains. She pulls Pavel to her, crushing the wildflowers between them. In the living room they are met by Misha.

"Who're you?" the boy asks suspiciously.

"Stop clowning. You know my Pasha."

Misha scowls. His black hair has gotten thicker. He kneels and begins to play with a wooden train, running it back and forth across the carpet, making soft chugging sounds.

"I went by the pharmacy," Pavel says.

His mother looks away. "I was going to tell you about that."

"When?"

"In my own time, Pasha. When I was ready." She reaches down, lets her hand rest a moment on Misha's head. "Don't look at me like that," she says evenly, though there is a touch of weariness in her expression. "Like I've been a naughty child."

"I'm just upset. How are you going to support yourself?"

"I'll get another job. My friend says she can get me one at the candy shop where she works."

But how long will that last? "Why didn't you tell me?" Pavel asks.

His mother frowns. "It was just a job, Pasha. Not even a very good one."

"A job from which you were fired because—" Pavel stops—he cannot bring himself to say what he is thinking.

"Because what?" His mother's voice tightens with anger. "Say it, Pasha. Because I'm going senile? Because I'm losing my mind?"

Because something terrible is at work in you, Pavel thinks despairingly. Because you are the one person who ties me to this world, this life, now that Elena is gone. If I lose you, I'll have nothing left. Yes, he thinks: because you are losing your mind. "I think we need to make another appointment for you with Dr. Hirsch."

"No."

"Just let him look at you, Mama. Please. How can that possibly hurt?"

For a moment his mother stares at him, then turns away and walks into the tiny kitchen, where she pulls a vase from the cabinet. "These flowers won't last three days," she says, not unkindly. "They're already dried out." She pinches a spray of petals and rolls them between her fingers.

"Maybe the water will help," Pavel says.

Through the doorway he watches Misha clamber onto the sofa with a book—his old picture book, Pavel sees, carried down through all these years like some remnant salvaged from his childhood. The boy opens the book, presses a finger to the page. "Ball," he says to himself softly, frowning: There is a concentrated, almost fierce resoluteness in his expression, as if it is up to him alone to name what his eye has fallen on.

Olga comes home. She is wheeling a little folding cart full of grocery sacks. "Hello, Pavel," she says breathlessly, tired from her climb up the stairs. When Misha rushes to her with his book, hugging her leg, she gently pries him loose and brushes the black hair from his brow. "What's that you're reading?"

"Ball," says Misha.

"No, baby. Book. You know that."

Pavel's mother rises from the sofa where she and Pavel have been drinking tea. "Let me help with those." She takes the cart from Olga, touches her arm. "Poor thing. You look exhausted. Why don't you sit down, love. I'll make you some tea." There is an ease, a simple kindness and intimacy to the gesture that Pavel finds touching. Olga smiles gratefully, and noticing the flowers on the dining table, asks, "Where did those come from?"

"Pasha brought them."

While Pavel is helping his mother put away the groceries, Victor stomps into the flat, carrying Andrei over his shoulder and a blueprint tube under his arm.

"Look who I caught!" he growls.

"Pick me up, pick me up!" shrieks Misha, pulling at his brother's legs.

"Oh, while I'm thinking of it," Pavel's mother says suddenly. "We're going to the country for the weekend in September. Victor's supervisor is letting us use the company dacha. Would you like to come?"

A weekend in the country. How long has it been since he allowed himself such a luxury?

"That would be nice," says Pavel.

Later, as his mother and Olga give Misha his bath, Pavel pulls Victor into the kitchen to talk.

"Why didn't you tell me my mother was fired?"

Victor is clearly stunned. "When did this happen?"

"Thursday. I just found out myself from Golovkin."

Victor runs a hand through his thinning hair. "That fat little bastard." He shakes his head. "I'm sorry about this, Pasha. They've had me so damn busy lately at work, my brain must be scrambled. I really had no idea about your mother."

"Neither did I," Pavel says. "Look, I can handle her expenses for now, as far as that goes. She said something about working with a friend of hers at a candy store. If that doesn't pan out, she can come live with me."

"We can work around the money, Pasha. That's not a concern. It's your mother I'm worried about. You know that, don't you?"

"I know," Pavel says.

His mother insists on walking him to the station. In the field beyond the railroad embankment sparrows suddenly shoot up, scattering like a handful of flung seed before disappearing again into the high grass. A pall of blue smoke from the cooking braziers hangs over the market. There are more people out now picking over the tables.

"Such a beautiful day," his mother says, taking his arm.

And it is, although he has not noticed until now. He feels a flush of inexplicable happiness, like an unexpected wind filling a sail. Together they climb the steps to the platform.

A handwritten sign taped to the inside of the ticket window reads, *Will Return in Ten Minutes*. The ticket agent, smoking nearby in her blue uniform smock, ignores them.

"It's all right if you have to get back," Pavel tells his mother.

"I don't."

To the north the Moscow skyline suddenly flares golden in the lowering sun.

In the distance a train horn bawls: It is the 8:45, right on time. Briskly tossing away her cigarette, the ticket agent returns to her booth and pulls down the sign. Pavel stands.

"I'll just be a minute."

At the sound of his voice his mother's shoulders jerk slightly, as if he has startled her from some deep reverie. For a few disconcerting seconds she stares blankly into Pavel's face. *She doesn't recognize me.* The thought sickens Pavel. Then the moment passes, his mother is utterly herself again. So much so that Pavel is left wondering whether he imagined it all.

From Kiev Station a taxi shuttles him home. An indulgence perhaps, but then he is too tired tonight to wait for the bus. He wants only to fall into bed and sleep.

On the steps of his building Pavel is met by Marfa Borisova's little dog. "What do you want?" he sighs, and when the pug scratches tentatively at the door, Pavel adds sharply, "I don't have anything for you."

But the dog will not go away. All week now Pavel has watched it from his flat, trotting along the sandy paths, pausing to briskly lift a hind leg, marking its territory. With the cooler mornings has come fog, which clings to the bushes and trees, blanketing the flower beds, so that the sturdy little dog, despite its purposeful air, seems to him adrift. Dutifully Natalya has set out a bowl of food every day, though the animal has otherwise avoided human contact.

When he opens the door the pug precedes him inside, then hurries ahead up the dark stairway. On the second floor, Pavel turns toward his own flat, then stops. Reluctantly he climbs to the landing above.

The pug is waiting outside Marfa Borisova's door. "She's not in there," Pavel says. "She's gone away." The little dog regards him steadily, until Pavel can no longer stand it. "Come on, then," he says. When he looks back, the pug is still watching him, head tilted curiously, as though debating what it will do now that it is alone.

# 15

A stunning picture appears on the front page of Thursday's *Pravda,* which only days earlier decried Hitler's merciless persecution of Jews in Czechoslovakia. Molotov, People's Commissar of Foreign Affairs, flanked by a lean, coolly smiling man Pavel has never seen before, whose trimly tailored black suit brings to mind an undertaker.

> **At 3:30 P.M. on August 23 a first conversation took place between V. M. Molotov and the Foreign Minister of Germany, Herr von Ribbentrop. The conversation took place in the presence of Comrade Stalin and the German Ambassador, Count von der Schulenburg. It lasted about three hours. After an interval the conversation was resumed at 10:00 P.M. and ended with the signing of the Non-Aggression Agreement of which the text follows.**

And indeed there stands Stalin, jovial in his pale buttoned tunic, the tips of his thick black moustache curled up like the corners of a sly smile. The same moustache Mandelstam, in a poem, once publicly mocked at a dinner party, calling it a cockroach. Thus signing his own death warrant.

Shocking as the story is, what disturbs Pavel even more is the public calm that follows. Madness, he thinks as the metro shrieks into Gorky Station. The world has been turned on its head, our enemy has become our closest ally, and yet no one will speak of it. On Monday he can barely work up the energy to drag himself to the Lubyanka.

"How long do you think before we finish?" he asks Kutyrev.

"Hard to say. At this rate, it shouldn't be too long."

"Weeks? Months?"

"Maybe a month. Six weeks."

They have been emptying the stacks all morning, adding to the wall of manuscripts, which already nearly reaches up to Pavel's waist. Occasionally an unlabeled box will be set aside so that it can be later sorted through, recatalogued.

Pavel says, "That soon?"

"It could take longer—there's a lot back there."

Kutyrev finds his pack of cigarettes, shakes one loose. Only instead of shredding it, today of all days the young officer has apparently decided to allow himself the small pleasure of tobacco—perhaps as a reward for his diligence. Cigarette lit, he sits on the corner of his desk.

"What will you do when we're finished?"

"Move on to something else," says Kutyrev.

Move up, he means. Advancement, promotion. A larger flat, perhaps even a car for himself and his ugly wife. Or does Kutyrev cast the net of his ambitions wider? Does he somehow see his work here contributing to the socialist revolution so long promised? The light at the end of the long tunnel, a life without suffering or uncertainty—not only for himself but all humanity? It is a dreadful testament to the times that Kutyrev and the millions like him can imagine the waterless path they are laboring along to be anything but what it is and will always be: a path of bones. "How old are you?" asks Pavel suddenly.

"I'll be twenty-six in December. Why?"

"Just curious."

Kutyrev flicks his cigarette ash onto the floor, then absently rubs it into the concrete with his shoe. "That's not too old to start building a career," he says defensively.

"What kind of work did you do before?"

"Different things. Painted houses with my brother-in-law for a while. Drove a moving truck."

"Why didn't you stick with that?"

"I wanted to do something with my life," says Kutyrev.

Pavel nearly laughs. "What, moving boxes around? Didn't you get enough of that before?"

Kutyrev glowers over his cigarette. "You have to start somewhere. Anyway, I've made some good connections. I won't be stuck down here forever." *Like you,* the look he gives Pavel says.

"You could have joined the army. They certainly need men."

Kutyrev shifts his bulk, the desk creaking under him. He smiles bitterly, showing his white, even, surprisingly small teeth. "At least I haven't given up."

"Is that what you think I've done? Given up?"

"Yes."

# 16

He stops by Natalya's office window. "Have you heard anything about Marfa Borisova?"

"Actually I went by the hospital this morning."

"How is she?"

"The same. She still can't talk. Her doctor thinks she may have had more than one stroke. He says now it's basically a matter of waiting to see if her brain will heal itself."

Waiting. For Elena to be found; for his mother's condition to further manifest itself; for Semyon's problems to go away. Now they must wait for Marfa Borisova's fate to be settled.

"How long did they let you stay?"

"For a few minutes. I don't think she knew I was there. They have her in one of the larger wards. I had to practically shout at her, it was so noisy." Natalya shakes her head. "Anyway, I told her you were looking after her dog for the time being. Just in case."

"In case what?"

"In case she could hear me. In case she was worried."

* * *

That night, after finishing their meals, Pavel walks Semyon home from Dashenko's restaurant.

"I heard the most interesting bit of news the other day," Semyon announces. "Stalin's pipe went missing."

Another joke. The sidewalk beside the park wall has collapsed into itself, leaving behind a gaping black hole like a toothless mouth. They step into the street and cross. The lamps here are out, the shops have been boarded over, abandoned. Still, it is a beautiful night.

"Aren't you going to ask me what happened?"

"No," Pavel says.

Semyon looks disappointed. "You're not curious?"

"What I am is tired, Semyon. I just want to go home, get in my bed, try to sleep. The same thing you should want."

Ahead of them Pavel makes out the figure of a man standing beside a lamppost. As they approach, the man's hand rises to his mouth: a bottle, glinting in the moonlight.

"You sound more angry than tired," Semyon says.

Pavel says nothing.

The man has seen them, he is staggering toward them now, listing as if into a strong wind. Despite it being August still, Pavel sees that he is wearing a long coat, the trailing hem of which swishes at his ankles like a monk's cassock. "Brothers—" Pavel can barely make out the word, the man is slurring so badly. A smell, rancid, powerful, reaches him, and Pavel recoils.

"Your brothers," Semyon tells the man, not unkindly, "are in that park over there, I'm afraid." He reaches a hand up to his neck, where the knife wound has left a small pink scar. "Here." From his vest pocket Semyon draws a handful of change. "To each according to their need. Or appetite."

"Bless you," the man says.

They walk on without speaking.

"I sometimes wonder," Semyon says after a time, "if I've done a single bit of good for my students. All my lecturing. How has it helped them? Or anyone? That fellow back there, you think he'd be where he is now if he'd ever read Bryusov or Balmont? Even if he had, you think his having once wept over a poem might be enough to keep some fellow from slitting his throat?" He looks at Pavel. "Perhaps you were right to leave teaching behind."

"I left teaching because I helped ruin a man's life."

"You didn't denounce Kudelin. His students did."

"After they came to me, Semyon. I should have refused to have anything to do with that petition. I should have tried harder to talk Peter out of writing it, but I was too worried about my own skin."

It occurs to Pavel now, as it has before while walking these streets, that the shops and rusting kiosks and tenantless flats they are passing—dark, shuttered, scrawled with graffiti—could well be portents of what awaits all of Russia. War, famine, apocalypse. The end of history. Then again he could be seeing the age as it already is, stripped to its essence. Russia's true, unadorned face: ravaged, bereft, eaten hollow with grief for its lost children. From the park comes a hoarse shout, celebratory, muffled through the trees, answered a moment later by another, more distant call.

"I'm sorry," Semyon says. "I should know better than to lecture you. I do know better."

"It's all right."

Semyon says, "What you said earlier—your being tired. It's true. One gets tired. Maybe that's my problem with Boyarska. I certainly used to be better about keeping my mouth shut. In fact I was exceptionally good at it."

The shadows along the street—the lampposts, kiosks, the long park wall—wink out. The wind has risen: An enormous cloud, its edges fringed in light, crosses over the moon.

"What happened to you, Pasha, that whole ugly affair at Kirov, that could just as well have been me. I've asked myself what I would have done in your place."

He stops suddenly, listening. Pavel feels Semyon's hand on his arm, staying him.

"What is it?"

"Do you remember that night I told you about my old colleague Glebnikov?" asks Semyon. "After he disappeared—do you know what I did? Absolutely nothing. I just went on giving my little lectures, counseling my students, grading their essays. All the while acting like poor Glebnikov never existed. As if I didn't see his ghost every time I turned around. And not just Glebnikov's ghost. Maybe that's my problem, too. Everywhere I go these days I find myself running into ghosts."

# 17

Already Marfa Borisova's little dog has settled into its new life. In the evenings, after Pavel has walked the pug in the park, after he has eaten dinner, he places a bowl of kibble on the floor, says quietly, "There you are," or simply, "Eat," and immediately the dog buries its head in the bowl. Afterward, sated, the animal trots into the living room and hops up onto the sofa. It has the oddest, almost fussy habit, Pavel has discovered, of pulling down the cushions with its paw in order to lie on them. Does even a flicker of memory of Marfa Borisova remain? "You should be ashamed of yourself," Pavel says. Still, it is impossible not to like the dog. "When all this is over, when you are back home again, you'll forget me, too, I'm sure." He scratches the pug behind its ears. Bulging eyes squeezed tight with pleasure, the dog grunts softly. Soon it is sleeping, dainty paws twitching against his arm.

"I was thinking I might go by and see Marfa tomorrow," Natalya tells him Tuesday morning as he and the dog are returning from an early walk. She has herself already been out, in all likelihood visiting her business connections. "Would you like to come along?"

"Do you think that's appropriate? I mean, I hardly know her."

"You know her dog. Considering the circumstances, I'd say that's enough." She takes off her hat, hanging it onto the rack beside her desk. "How are you and the little beast getting along?"

"Well enough." Pavel looks down at the pug, and the dog, as if aware that it has become the subject of their conversation, stares back steadily.

"He certainly is an ugly thing."

"He's not so ugly," Pavel says defensively. "He's actually pretty affectionate, once he warms up to you."

Natalya smiles. "Looks like you two are getting quite attached." Their eyes meet—Pavel has not forgotten that afternoon in his flat, the flare of desire he felt when he looked down at her skirt, the dark half-moon he wanted so badly to lay his hand upon. A new country. Neither, it would seem, has Natalya forgotten.

"Will you at least think about tomorrow?"

"Yes," says Pavel. "I'll think about it."

"Are you going down to Dynamo Stadium?" asks Kutyrev. Another mass celebration, in a month flush with them. The young officer has been infected by the unaccountably buoyant holiday atmosphere pervading Moscow, despite the recent pact with Germany, a truce that would have once seemed unthinkable. His uniform appears freshly pressed, his leather boots shine like black mirrors. His black hair is neatly if unevenly trimmed. Does his wife cut it? wonders Pavel. Perhaps in the kitchen, with a sheet spread under his chair to catch the falling hair. He remembers Elena cutting his hair just that way the year they married, in the kitchen of their old flat, her stomach lightly brushing against his shoulder, the whispery *snick-snick* of the scissors.

"I didn't know you were a soccer fan," Pavel says.

"The game's just part of it. There's to be a big parade afterward, speeches. You should go."

"Should I?" An edge of annoyance sharpens Pavel's voice. "And why is that?"

"It doesn't hurt to remind yourself from time to time what we're working for, comrade."

"Parades, you mean."

Kutyrev stares. "The people," he says.

What nonsense, Pavel thinks wearily. Are these the very people that have been pouring into the Lubyanka night after night these last two and a half years? Sheep to the slaughter. He would rather have drown himself in that lake Kutyrev so loves than be lectured to by a man whose highest moral aspirations can be summed up by an afternoon of soccer and mindless speeches.

"Or do you think you're better than the rest of us?" asks Kutyrev acidly, perhaps picking up on Pavel's thoughts. "Just like you think you're above all this."

"And what exactly would 'this' be?"

The junior officer waves a hand at the manuscripts stacked behind their desks. "Our work. *My* work. You couldn't care less about the reorganization."

"I do my work, comrade. Everything you've asked of me, I've done. What more do you want?"

"A little enthusiasm wouldn't hurt."

*Enthusiasm*: It is all Pavel can do to keep himself from spitting in Kutyrev's face. Of course Kutyrev would easily beat him senseless. Pavel sees—certainly not for the first time—the hard, ruthless outline of Kutyrev's convictions, sharp as the edge of an axe. The true believer, unburdened by doubt, a soldier of the revolution. He remembers Babel's awestruck description of the division commander Savitsky in "My First Goose," *the purple of his riding britches and the crimson of his little tilted cap and the decoration stuck on his chest cleaving the hut as a standard cleaves the sky.* In the face of such focused passion, such strength, what chance do these manuscripts have?

"I'd be careful if I were you," Kutyrev tells him.

Pavel's mouth goes dry. "What is that supposed to mean?"

"It means nothing's permanent here. Including yourself."

"You've been talking to someone about me."

Kutyrev shrugs slyly.

"Who?"

"You're so smart. Figure it out yourself, teacher."

After Kutyrev has left for Dynamo Stadium, Pavel remains at his desk. Has one of Kutyrev's connections told him something, or is he just bluffing? Pavel cannot help but remember the warnings and threats he once rained down on his more rebellious students, the enjoinders to work more diligently, to pay attention, to be quiet. Now it is the teacher who is taught his place.

More awaits him. That afternoon when Pavel returns from the incinerator he finds Sevarov sitting at his desk.

"You've been busy, I see."

Pavel, standing there with the cart, nods numbly. Finally Sevarov waves a hand at the cart, rises. "Leave it," he orders.

Later, in the elevator going up, Sevarov wrinkles his nose. "Is that you?" The cables creak above them, rattling in their dark well. The smell, the officer means. Pavel's clothes reek of fuel oil.

"It's from the incinerator."

The door slides open. They walk the long carpeted corridor without exchanging another word. In one office they pass, someone weeps softly; it is impossible for Pavel to tell if it is a man or a woman.

A book lies open on the table before Radlov, who appears mildly surprised to see Pavel. "Comrade," he says, closing the book. Plates of food are arranged at the table's center—sausages, fried potatoes, fat slices of tomato in vinegar—along with a decanter of vodka, a pot of steaming tea. "Have you had lunch?" Radlov asks after Sevarov has withdrawn.

"Yes, Comrade Major."

"Yes? Well. You won't mind if I eat something. Actually this is breakfast for me. Breakfast and lunch."

The table has been moved. Now it is closer to the window, so that, sitting, he is able to fully see the broad traffic-clotted square below. It is a bright temperate day outside—perfect holiday weather. Across the square pedestrians pour from the mouth of the metro station. So not everyone has put aside work for a day of soccer, parades, speeches.

"My wife," says Radlov, apropos of nothing. "The woman is constantly after me to eat, always slipping little notes into my pockets to remind me. I tell her, 'The problem isn't whether or not I remember to eat. It's whether I have time.' If only there were more hours in the day. Still, I suppose it's her duty to worry, just as it is my duty to worry her." He sighs. "So. How's the reorganization?"

"We're making progress, Comrade Major."

"Good." Radlov nods. He lifts one of the heavy, dripping sausages onto his plate and saws into it with his knife. For a few minutes, ignored, Pavel must sit listening to him eat.

"All those files," Radlov says finally. "It must be overwhelming at times. I can hardly keep my little library at home in order. But then I have my own system, you know." He taps his temple. Then he gestures to the book near his plate. An older copy of Gogol's collected stories, its worn, much-handled blue cloth cover stamped in flaking gold ink. "You've read Gogol, I assume.

I imagine you must have even taught his work at one time or another."

"On occasion, yes, Comrade Major."

"Let me ask you, then. As a former teacher of literature, you possess a certain—how should I put it?—sensitivity to language. Is that not so? You're able to see things others might miss. Penetrate the surface."

"Of books?"

"Books, stories, poems."

Pavel hesitates. "I would say I'm a fairly close reader, whatever that means. But how sensitive I am, I can't say, Comrade Major. I think I read a book the same way the next man does."

"Now you're being modest. Remember, Pavel Vasilievich, I've read your file. You were quite the rising young star at Kirov Academy. Respected by your peers. Admired by your students. That's no small feat."

Pavel shifts uncomfortably in his chair.

"I've been rereading 'The Overcoat,'" Radlov continues. "Marvelous story, don't you think? So funny, and yet so sad, too. Awful really. Poor Akaky Akakyevich. Of course I'm only able to read when I have time. Sometimes I'm only able to get a few lines in before the telephone starts ringing. But I keep at it. If nothing else, I'm persistent." The officer smiles. "He killed himself. Gogol. Do you know how?"

Pavel says, "He stopped eating."

Radlov's smile widens. The irony is not lost on him, Pavel sees: the plate-crowded table, the small feast set before them.

"Do you think," asks Radlov, "that because you've read his stories, you understand Gogol any better than those who knew him personally? His family, closest friends. After all, what did they really know about him? That he spouted religious rubbish? That he was unhappy? Here the man has been dead nearly a century and I understand perfectly well why he would want to starve himself to death." Radlov rubs a thumb over the book's cover, then examines it briefly. He wipes the gold ink that has flaked off on his finger onto the tablecloth.

Is this what he has been called here for? To discuss the inner life of Gogol? Pavel is suddenly struck by the thought that Radlov embodies everything Kutyrev dreams of becoming. Radlov has struggled up through the ranks, he has not gone unnoticed. Still, how many lives lie scattered in his wake? So that today, with merely a word, he might summon forth a feast fit for a boyar, just as he has summoned Pavel?

"Are you going to answer my question, comrade?"

"About Gogol?"

"About understanding a person solely from what they've written," says Radlov. "I assume that's why you and your predecessor were brought on. Although, to be perfectly honest, Pavel Vasilievich, no one's been able to give me a good answer as to why you're here." Radlov gazes curiously down at his hand holding the fork: The long tendon across the back of it has begun to twitch visibly. "What's your thinking on the matter?"

"I don't know why Comrade—" Pavel stops himself: To even speak of the disgraced dead is to risk joining them. He must choose his words carefully. "I never knew what your predecessor's exact motives were for bringing me here, Comrade Major. We never discussed them."

"His son was a student of yours, yes?"

"Yes. Peter Maximov."

"So this Peter Maximov—obviously he spoke to his father about your being asked to leave Kirov. Why?"

"I believe Peter felt personally responsible for what happened to me. My resigning. Because of the petition against Kudelin. He thought he was helping me."

"Is that what Major Maximov was up to? Helping you? So you think it was charity that brought you here?" The officer laughs dryly, covering his mouth with his napkin.

"I believe he brought me here because he needed to fill a position." A position, Pavel does not add, I had no choice of refusing. A position it would have been suicide to refuse. Maximov, summoning Pavel to this very office, had made that abundantly clear.

"*Your* predecessor's position."

"Yes," Pavel says.

"Which brings us full circle," says Radlov. "Tell me—putting aside the father for a moment—what was the son like? Your young savior. Was this Peter Maximov a good student?"

"He was one of my best students," Pavel says. "Very bright, very earnest." An idealist, Pavel does not add. "He had tremendous ambition."

"To do what? Follow in his father's footsteps? You know as well as I do where they led." Radlov makes a lazy spiraling gesture with his finger, pointing down.

"He wanted to be a writer."

The officer's eyes widen. "My God, that's hardly better." A small, teasing smile tugs at his lips. "Please tell me you didn't encourage him."

Over these last two and a half years Pavel has often found himself wondering what became of Peter Maximov, whom he has never blamed, and who would be nineteen now. What a terrible blow that must have been, watching his father's fall: the summary dismissal from Fourth Section, then his arrest. All that earnestness and idealism, shattered.

"I was supposed to encourage him," says Pavel.

"Of course you were." A shadow of disappointment crosses Radlov's face. "Shame on you." He reaches for his glass, drinks. All at once the humor has drained from his voice. "I suppose he admired you."

"Yes."

"Why, because you were his teacher?" When Pavel does not reply Radlov repeats: "Because you were his teacher." He is no longer asking now: It is a statement of fact, implacable, irrefutable.

"Because," Pavel says, "he needed someone to admire, I think."

Radlov rises and goes over to the bookshelf, where he plucks up a folder. Pavel can hear Sevarov on the telephone outside. Down on the square below a bus rumbles past, belching a brown plume of diesel smoke. The faces of the passengers packed inside gaze blankly out. All those lives, thinks Pavel suddenly. What do they see when they look up at the Lubyanka? Do they ever allow themselves to imagine—even for a moment—the men and women locked away here?

From the open folder Radlov now reads aloud, " 'With every word, every act and gesture, Mikhail Kudelin makes only more apparent his contempt for the values we cherish at Kirov Academy, and by association, his disregard for the Party itself. We the undersigned consider this disgraceful behavior both reckless and intolerable, and therefore recommend Mikhail Kudelin's immediate dismissal.' " Radlov pauses. " 'Reckless and intolerable.' 'With every word, every act and gesture . . .' Strong words. Did you come up with them yourself or did this boy Peter?"

"The boy did."

"Was this Kudelin fellow really so terrible?"

Snow was falling that afternoon in late November when he last saw Mikhail Kudelin. Glancing up from the essay he was grading, Pavel saw Kudelin, alone now, cautiously making his way across the empty courtyard, which only an hour ago had been thronged with students hurrying home. This was Kudelin's final day. At the open gate the instructor turned suddenly and looked back toward Kirov Academy, so that for a moment Pavel could see his face. Flakes of snow had collected in Kudelin's curly brown hair and on the shoulders of his belted coat. In the six years Pavel had been at Kirov he had had few occasions to speak to Kudelin, who had acquired a reputation for being rather standoffish. An aging bachelor, awkward around women, at times curt to the point of rudeness. In warmer weather he would mount his gleaming blue bicycle, briefcase dangling from the handlebar, and pedal home to the flat he shared with his elderly parents. For all Pavel knew, Kudelin had no life other than the life he had here, teaching. Now that was done. Sitting comfortably behind that window that afternoon, lapped in the light and warmth of his classroom, Pavel suddenly saw himself as Kudelin must have just then seen him: the man who possesses every happiness. His betrayer. How he must have despised me, Pavel thinks. And rightly so.

"The petition was wrong, in every sense," Pavel says now. He is suddenly angry with Radlov, sick of the officer's game. "As far as I know, Mikhail Kudelin was a decent man."

"So you helped slander him?"

"You have my file, Comrade Major. I admitted as much before the board at Kirov."

"What your file tells me, comrade, is everything except why. Why would you help one of your students destroy this poor fellow's reputation? What in the world did he ever do to you? You must feel a certain responsibility for what happened to him. I imagine your colleagues must have or they wouldn't have turned on you so quickly."

"I accepted full responsibility for my actions, Comrade Major."

"And Kudelin's actions?"

"What do you mean?"

"I mean, *comrade,* when he tied the rope to that rafter and hanged himself." Radlov regards him coldly. "Are you responsible for that as well?"

"Yes," Pavel says.

"Why?"

Because I was a coward, Pavel thinks. Because I kept silent. "I should have stopped Peter Maximov from distributing that petition. He was my student. He trusted me. I let him down."

Radlov's gaze remains fixed on him. "Let us suppose just for a moment," he says finally, his tone mellowing slightly, "that I am trying to figure out what to do with you. I've read what's been written about you, Pavel Vasilievich, and now I've met you personally. Which should I put my faith in, do you think?"

Without waiting for an answer Radlov drops Pavel's file back onto the bookshelf. Sitting again, the officer pulls back his sleeve to examine his watch, then picks up the copy of Gogol. He reads aloud:

> And the poor young man used to bury his face in his hands, and many a time in his life he would shudder when he perceived how much inhumanity there was in man, how much savage brutality there lurked beneath the most refined, cultured manners, and, dear Lord, even in the man the world regarded as upright and honorable . . .

With that Radlov lays the book down again beside his plate, on which the congealing sausage grease has begun to whiten. "'Upright and honorable,'" he says absently. A distance has entered the officer's gaze. "I told you my father was a teacher, yes?" He looks at Pavel.

"Yes."

"Strange. It was exactly the opposite with him. He *was* a good man. Straight through. The brutal ones, the true savages, were his neighbors. Do you know, after he was arrested, they broke into his flat and stripped the place clean, right down to the baseboards? Their children's teacher—some of them were even former students. And yet *they* denounce him? *They* are permitted to feel superior to him?"

Pavel can feel the muscle in his calf twitching. He has the urge to run from the office, to cover his ears. He does not want to hear what Radlov seems intent on telling him: the father, upright, honorable, flung into the grinding teeth of the machine while the son, loyal servant of that very machine, stood by. Because that is what happened. Had Radlov even been suspected of wavering in his cold devotion, he would not be where he is today, at this cluttered table overlooking Dzerzhinsky Square. His reward.

The window to Natalya's tiny office is closed, the red curtain drawn tight. From the basement he hears the sound of boxes being dragged across the floor. The door, slightly ajar, spills its seam of ugly light across the corridor.

"You're just in time," Natalya tells Pavel. She is stacking battered cardboard boxes—more of her discards rescued from the pulp mill. "Can you give me a hand with these?"

"What are they?"

"Calendars."

From a box that has ripped open Pavel removes one of the calendars. On the cover is a cheap watercolor print: a still life, white vase, a spray of orange and red flowers set against a blue tablecloth. Each month is represented by a different watercolor, all done in the same competent if doggedly uninspired style. "This calendar is two years old," says Pavel.

"Thus my getting them for next to nothing. They were just sitting in some warehouse gathering dust. I'm thinking of framing the pictures. What do you think of them?"

"Honestly?"

"That bad?" Natalya shrugs. "Well. At the very least I can use them to roll my cigarettes."

As they are finishing Pavel asks, "Were you still planning on going to see Marfa Borisova tomorrow?"

"Yes."

"I'd like to go with you."

Natalya looks at him. "All right." If she is wondering what has brought about this change of heart, in the end she keeps her curiosity to herself.

# 18

The hospital, just west of sprawling Yuzhny Port, is in a neighborhood of Moscow Pavel has not visited before. He and Natalya must transfer twice, from tram to shuddering tram, before walking the last half kilometer. Every fifty meters or so sits a flower kiosk, shutters thrown open as if in defiance of the rain clouds gathering over the city. "Should we pick up something for her?" asks Pavel, eyeing the people around them, many of whom are carrying bouquets of flowers, cakes. "If you like," says Natalya. The wind, which has been rising all day, lifts the round collar of the light blue dress she has worn, likely her best. The spray of tiny wooden berries pinned to her hat trembles; she must grip the hat in her hands in order not to lose it to the wind.

As he is paying for the flowers, Natalya asks, "What is that? I smelled it the last time I was here."

He sniffs the air: It is sweet, laden with sugar. "Maybe there's a bakery around."

"It's chocolate," explains the flower vendor, handing Pavel his change. "There's a candy factory just behind the hospital, on the next street." She leans across the wooden counter on one fat arm, points. "You get to where you don't even notice anymore."

The smell of chocolate only grows stronger as they approach the hospital, which has the look about it of a French manor now far along in its decline. Innumerable buildings just like this—leftovers from the last century—haunt Moscow. The gates have been removed, the enormous circular courtyard given over to a half dozen boxy ambulances in various stages of disrepair. A banner flaps in the wind high over the wide entrance steps. *The Health of The Nation Depends upon The Health of Its Workers.* The rope on one corner of the canvas banner has come loose, and the banner snaps loudly like a sail that has torn from its rigging. As they climb the steps the first fat drops of rain begin darkening the courtyard.

At the reception desk the nurse on duty consults her lists. "What was that name again?"

"Borisova. Marfa Borisova," explains Natalya patiently. Behind them the line of waiting visitors is growing longer as people hurry in from the courtyard, clothes dripping water.

"I'm sorry, but there's no one by that name here."

"I just visited her last week."

"Could you please check again?" asks Pavel.

An older nurse—a supervisor, no doubt—approaches. "Is there some problem?"

"She says we have a patient here, but I can't find the woman on our roster. I've already checked twice."

"Are you family?" asks the older nurse.

"She's my aunt." The lie falls from Natalya's lips without hesitation, surprising Pavel. "Now, I know she's here. I can show you exactly where her bed is, if you'd like."

The older nurse regards them coolly.

"Please. It will only take a few minutes."

"All right," the older nurse says finally.

In what was once likely the ballroom lie a hundred beds or more, all occupied, packed together so closely, Pavel thinks, one could cross the length of the room walking on them and never once touch the floor. Three chandeliers, tiered like upturned wedding cakes, hang from the ornate ceiling, which still bears the gaudy plaster fleur-de-lis of a bygone age. A pair of little boys, giggling wildly, chase each other into their path. "Mind your children," the older nurse scolds their mother, a mournful-looking young woman sitting at the bedside of a gaunt elderly man who gazes fiercely at Pavel. With a sigh the young mother calls her children to her.

At the far end of the ward Natalya stops, looking around as if confused.

"Are you certain this is the right ward?" Pavel asks her gently.

"Yes, I'm sure."

"She may have been discharged," the older nurse points out. "Or transferred to another hospital, depending on her status."

Pavel asks, "Is there any way to find out?"

"I could check with one of the ward nurses."

They wait within sight of the reception desk, by a window overlooking the courtyard. Outside the rain is falling steadily. A fan of rain, blown in the open door, shines on the marble floor.

Honking a tinny horn, one of the ambulances outside trundles from the courtyard, splashing through puddles, then turns into the street.

They are prepared to wait all evening, if it takes that. As it turns out the nurse returns after only fifteen minutes. "I'm very sorry," she tells Natalya. "Your aunt passed away two days ago. That's why she wasn't on our roster. I don't understand why you weren't notified."

Natalya nods dazedly.

"What happened?" asks Pavel.

"I wasn't on duty at the time, so I don't know the exact details. Apparently she died early Monday morning, during the night shift. Given the hour, I assume she simply passed away in her sleep. Quietly, I'm sure," the older nurse adds.

It is only after she has gone that Natalya finally speaks.

"I told her she would be home in a few weeks."

"You were comforting her."

Natalya shakes her head. "Do you know the entire time she was here I was the only person who came to see her? The building manager. No family, not a single friend. She might as well never have existed."

The rain beating at the windows has slackened somewhat, Pavel sees. "I feel like I'm going to be sick," Natalya announces weakly, holding a hand to her throat.

"Do you need to sit down?"

"I need to get out of here. It's this place, this fucking hospital—that's what's making me sick. I don't think I'll ever be able to eat another piece of chocolate again."

"We'll go," says Pavel.

Natalya looks down at the bouquet of flowers in his hand. "What should we do with those?"

"Here." Pavel lays the flowers down on the wide sill of the window. "Maybe someone else will find some use for them." A second later he regrets his words, cold as they sound. Natalya seems not to have noticed. From a nearby chair he plucks up a copy of yesterday's newspaper. "For the rain," Pavel says, handing it to her.

Outside the gutters are awash, streaming into the roadway. They hurry past the kiosk where earlier Pavel purchased the flowers, which has pulled tight its shutters. All along the street, people are taking shelter in doorways and under trees, huddling beneath dark dripping canopies of leaves. The wind-driven rain whitens on the pavement, lashing mercilessly at them. Pavel spots the empty entranceway of a darkened shop and steers them toward it.

They are both soaked. The sodden newspaper Natalya is holding has turned nearly translucent in her hands. "So much for that," she says, dropping it. In the window of the shop an assortment of radios sit silent. With trembling fingers, faintly blue-black with ink, Natalya brushes her wet hair from her face. Through her rain-darkened dress Pavel can see distinctly the flare of her wide collarbones, her breasts. In the washed-out, watery light the scar on her cheek appears etched into her face.

"We'll have to wait it out."

Natalya turns. "You're shivering."

"So are you," Pavel replies quietly. He wants to touch her mouth, her cheek, to feel the ridge of scar under his fingers. And perhaps she senses this, for her eyes all at once seem to darken, her gaze steadying on his face.

He touches her arm, lets his hand fall. A long moment passes when neither of them speaks. Finally the wind begins to weaken, the rain tapers off, ceases.

"We better go before it starts up again," Pavel suggests.

On the tram afterward they become separated. From time to time he looks for her hat with its bright spray of trembling wooden berries. The air is close and damp, the windows fogged from breathing. Getting off, Pavel finds Natalya waiting for him. "Does it feel late to you?" she asks. He looks up at the dark sky, nods. They walk the two blocks to their building without speaking, and climb the steps.

"I'll see you later, then."

"Good-bye," says Pavel.

Upstairs he tells himself, Better this way. He changes into dry clothes, then takes Marfa Borisova's pug—it is impossible to think of the dog as being his, even now—for a walk. When they reach the little park he unsnaps the lead, letting the dog roam freely. Immediately the pug wades into a dense yellow patch of flowers, only to emerge a minute later, a scattering of wet petals on its brindle coat. As he crouches to wipe the petals away, a sadness wells up in Pavel.

"I'm sorry," he says.

He has just filled the dog's water bowl when there is a knock at the door. Natalya. She says, "I never thanked you for coming with me today." She too has changed out of her wet clothes. "Will you come down for a drink?"

"Yes." Pavel is surprised by how calm he sounds, as if this were nothing new to him. Yet inside he is anything but calm. Nearly a decade has passed since he has been intimate with a woman other than Elena.

In Natalya's bedroom, in their clothes, even as Pavel lifts her dress to pull aside her underwear, and finds her with his fingers, he has the sensation of partially observing himself, of watching their lovemaking unfold. Where Elena was soft, full in the hips, Natalya is all hard bone: With every thrust he can feel himself colliding against her. It is all done without speaking; there is only the low rhythmic hammering of the bed frame against the wall, the rasp of their breathing. Pressing his mouth to her throat, feeling her pulse beat against his lips, Pavel wills himself to imagine that it is Elena under him, Elena's hands pulling him deep into her, needing him. And for a moment the illusion holds. Tamoy, the train split in two upon the snow: For a moment it is all wiped away. Elena is not lost.

Afterward, sitting on the edge of the bed, Natalya tugs her skirt back across her knees. The air in the little room is thick with their breathing.

"I could hear you the other night. Down in the basement."

Pavel freezes. "I was looking for a box of clothes."

She does not ask, *In the middle of the night?* "Like last time?"

"Yes." Slowly Pavel reaches for his shirt. "Like last time," he says evenly. "Why are you telling me this, Natalya? Is there something you want to ask?"

Natalya is quiet. "I don't know," she says. "It doesn't matter, Pavel. Whatever you were doing. I'm just—" He hears her stir. "It's been such a strange day, that's all."

"Yes," Pavel says.

Afterward, upstairs, from his living room, Pavel watches a crow cautiously pick at a piece of trash half-submerged in a puddle in the street below. In this light the object reminds him of a hat, rumpled, forgotten. For a moment he imagines a man suspended in the black water beneath it, as in some fairy tale: a man who has waited an eternity for a crow like this one to happen along and find him, and set him free.

# 19

When he stops by Natalya's office window the next evening, nothing between them has changed. There is no more nor no less warmth in her voice, no hint in her eyes of the intimacy, however brief, they have shared. Still, Pavel is unable to shake the feeling that she has stumbled upon his secret. If so, can he trust her not to denounce him? Has he any choice but to trust her?

Another telegram, she tells him, has arrived.

> NEW DEVELOPMENT. WILL CONTACT YOU TONIGHT BY TELEPHONE. SIMONOV.

"What do you think it could be?" asks Natalya.

"At this point I have no idea."

Upstairs Pavel anxiously awaits Simonov's call. He cannot sit. Shirtsleeves rolled past his elbows, he brushes out the rugs, sweeps and mops the floors. Like a shadow Marfa Borisova's pug trails behind him, always at his heels. At one point, pausing to glance down, he sees the window with its patch of blackened sky, even as a grave, reflected in the dog's bulging brown eyes. "I don't even know what to hope for anymore," Pavel murmurs. He is beginning to understand what it must be like for the little dog to be walked on its lead, always having someone tugging at you from behind.

From Simonov's telegrams Pavel has formed a mental picture of the morgue clerk, a picture to which he has unconsciously assigned a voice. The dry, emotionless voice of a man long grown accustomed to the company of the dead. Instead the voice in his ear now, the voice reaching out to him from what could well be another world, is surprisingly warm, if somewhat tentative.

"They've caught them."

"Caught—" Pavel stops, confused.

"The men responsible for the accident," Simonov explains. "Cousins, from one of the collective farms nearby. I've been going back and forth to the police station ever since I heard, trying to find out as much as I could. Supposedly one of them worked as a brakeman some years ago."

Pavel, still trying to make sense of Simonov's story, is quiet.

"They were trying to sell stolen goods. When the police searched their room they discovered a number of suitcases." Simonov clears his throat. "One of your wife's bags was among the items recovered. A blue handbag."

Pavel pinches the bridge of his nose. It is past eleven o'clock. Outside, over Donskoy, a slender finger of smoke points skyward.

"What happens now?"

"A trial, I imagine. The police are keeping the bag as evidence. But don't worry, the investigation shouldn't take long." For a few seconds Simonov is quiet. "Please understand. This accident has been hanging over everyone here. The night your wife's train derailed, half the village turned out to help."

Pavel says nothing.

"I'm not making excuses," says Simonov. "But I believe it's important you know that we tried our absolute best to handle the situation as well as we could. Given our limited resources."

"Comrade Simonov," Pavel says tiredly. "I appreciate your taking the time to call me—I do. But it's late. And to be perfectly blunt, I'd rather not talk about the accident right now. You say you've done your best to resolve this matter. Now may I explain my position?"

"Of course."

"Last January my wife, Elena, boarded a train for Yalta. We both know what happened to that train. Whether it was intentionally derailed or not isn't, for the moment, of particular interest to me. What is, what I am most concerned with, is that my wife's remains are returned to me. For eight months now—eight months—" Pavel repeats, "you have sent me telegrams, all of which so far add up to nothing. My wife is still missing. Now, after yet another telegram, you telephone me to say that the police believe they have the men responsible for my wife's death. What you have not told me yet is—again—what matters most to me." Pavel's voice falters. He must take a breath before continuing. "Until you find my wife, I want you to leave me alone. Please."

The line hums faintly. Simonov says, "I understand."

Pavel returns the phone to its hook.

Toward dawn Pavel is awakened by barking. The pug, hackles bristled into a ridge along its back, paces at the front door. Pavel sits up: He has fallen asleep on the sofa. His throat burns with thirst, the glass on the floor beside the sofa still holds a finger of whiskey. A knock comes, then another. "Just a moment," Pavel calls. Even as he rises and crosses the room, a single refrain beats in his skull like a siren. *They have come . . . they have come . . . they have come . . .*

"Who is it?"

"Natalya."

Has she betrayed him? Strangely Pavel feels no anger, only a dazed forlornness. Whatever happens next, it is beyond his control. He opens the door. Natalya stands there, alone. She is shaking visibly.

"Have you heard yet?"

She steps inside, closes the door behind her.

"Heard what? What's happened, Natalya?"

"Turn on your radio."

"Natalya—"

"The Germans. They've invaded Poland."

They must wait a few minutes for the wireless to warm up. From the storm of hissing static a voice gradually materializes, reaching out to them as though across a great wintry distance. ". . . German forces are returning fire on Polish positions. Reports so far suggest a massive and overwhelming response to the preemptive Polish attack, both by land and air." *Preemptive Polish attack.* "They're saying Poland attacked Germany first?" Pavel asks incredulously. "Why would the Poles do that? It's suicide." Natalya shakes her head gravely. *Lies,* the look in her gaze tells him. *They are lying to us.*

# 20

"I thought we might take a little stroll," says Semyon later that day. They slip on their coats. "I feel like walking tonight." Behind them, in his flat, a floorboard creaks: Vera, waiting for them to leave.

Outside the evening is waning. "That house there," Semyon abruptly remarks, pointing his cane at the blank face of a condemned mansion they are passing. "A student of mine used to share a room there with another fellow, an old sailor. Said the sailor kept an emperor penguin by his bed."

"Is this another joke?"

"It wasn't a live penguin, Pasha. It was stuffed. The sailor had shot it."

They turn down the alley. At the stable fence the old horse presses its nose against the boards until they creak, wet breath warm on their fingers. "There's a good fellow," Semyon says. "Would you like me to let you out of there?" For a moment the horse regards them placidly through a gap in the fence. Then it moves away. They walk on.

"Where are we going?"

"I thought we could walk down to the river," Semyon suggests.

The alley narrows. Then, from the avenue ahead, comes the steady, clear clop of hooves: a droshky, hood back, draws slowly by as they step from the alley, horse and driver alike nodding in rhythm. Just like that they are among crowds.

A couple carrying a small child overtakes them as they walk toward the river. "Tree . . . horse . . ." the little girl is chanting in her father's arms. In the doorway of a music shop a salesclerk in tie and vest stands idly plucking the strings of a guitar. They stop. "Beautiful, isn't it?" the salesclerk asks, holding the guitar by its neck like a goose at market offered up for the oven.

They continue walking. A packed tram trundles past, roof pole arcing tiny sparks. The tip of Semyon's cane, swinging forward, taps the sidewalk the very instant the lamps along the avenue leading down to the river break into light.

Outside a teahouse a handful of iron tables dots the sidewalk. A waiter in a white vest leans in the doorway.

"Do you mind if we stop for a cup?" asks Semyon.

"What about dinner?"

"To be honest, I don't think I have the stamina for Dashenko's tonight."

The waiter walks over when they sit down. "We have a very nice fruit plate tonight," he tells them.

"Just tea, thank you," Pavel says.

"I remember times," Semyon says after the waiter has gone, "when I would have killed that fellow there for a piece of fruit. Half a piece." Slowly he rolls the shaft of his cane against his leg.

The clear ringing of spoons on teacups floats on the air. The price of progress, Pavel thinks: bread for freedom. What is the old saying—*You can't make an omelet without breaking a few eggs.* As long as the egg broken is someone else, and the deed is done out of sight.

Pavel asks, "Have you ever read any of Isaac Babel's stories?"

"Of course." Semyon is quiet a moment. "I heard him give a reading once, you know, maybe eleven years ago, at a literary reception. A review I'd written had been printed in the same journal as a story of Babel's. Back when his star was still climbing. And mine, you might say. Academically. Which is to say a much, much smaller star." From another table comes a burst of laughter.

The waiter brings their tea over, and returns to his doorway.

"What did you think of him?" asks Pavel.

"The man or his work?"

"His stories."

"I think they're utterly exquisite. Take a story like 'Awakening,' or 'My First Goose.' Take 'Di Grasso.' Line for line they're as close to perfect as anything I've ever read. Which means I would rank some of them among the truly great stories."

"What about Babel himself? What was he like?"

"He was funny. Very funny, in fact. Which surprised me, since I'd pictured him as being so serious. Serious and rather sad. Like his stories. Although some of the humor I saw in Babel that night does occasionally come through in his stories." Semyon adds, "I've always thought it a shame he didn't publish more. But then I suppose he had his own reasons." Semyon's voice drops. "The nonsense that passes for literature these days," he says bitterly. "Socialist realism—all socialism and no reality. Fairy tales for grown-ups who should know better. I sometimes wonder what future generations will make of us. A bunch of idiotic drones, parading around shouting slogans about how happy our lives are."

"Maybe they won't make anything of us," Pavel says after a time. "Maybe we don't deserve to be remembered."

"Nonsense. I for one insist on being remembered. Why else would I make such a nuisance of myself?"

"Well, maybe just you, then."

"Good." Semyon smiles. "That's a start."

Afterward they continue on to the river. There, in the falling light, a crowd has gathered on the landing below to await the next ferry.

"I'm to be fired," Semyon announces.

"Are you sure?"

"Seems I've been summoned to appear before the university Party committee in two weeks. Regarding my membership. The following Monday I meet with the inestimable Boyarska. The math is simple enough."

"They're going to expel you from the Party."

Semyon lifts his shoulders slightly, lets them drop. "I expect they will."

"Do you know what this means?"

"It means," says Semyon evenly, "I am being cut out of the pack. Much to the delight of Madame Boyarska, no doubt."

First expulsion, then dismissal. Both men understand perfectly well what is likely to follow. Upriver the ferry appears, white against the dark water, slipping silently beneath the bridge.

"Is there anywhere you could go?" asks Pavel carefully. "You and Vera. Maybe get away from Moscow for a little while."

A faint smile appears on Semyon's face. "A holiday in the country?" He is looking down at the water, at the lilies floating along the wall, under which a single pale fish lazily swims.

"Call it whatever you want," Pavel says. As long as you're away from Moscow, he thinks. As long as you are not at your flat when they come looking for you.

"And when we return from our little holiday, what do you suppose I do then? Pick up where I left off?"

Pavel does not answer.

"Tell me, Pasha, what then? I want to know." Semyon turns. "When do we come back?"

When it is safe to come back. When there are no more manuscripts to burn, no more secrets to bury. Never, Pavel thinks. He remembers that summer after the war with Poland, after Semyon and his mother had become, for a time, lovers. Every few weeks, when he was not tutoring, Semyon would borrow a car and drive them out into the countryside for picnics. They always went to the same spot, a little clearing overlooking rye fields, past which a wide cold stream flowed. After the long drive in sweltering heat they would strip to their underclothes and wade out into the water, Semyon bracing a hand on Pavel's shoulder, hopping along on his good leg. Clouds of mayflies drifted over the stream, dragonflies lit on logs washed up in the shallows. Once they were deep enough out Semyon would let go and float on his back, carried away on the slow current while Pavel and his mother watched. Then he would swim back to them. A good swimmer, strong.

"I will give you money," he tells Semyon. "Everything I have. And I'll send more when I can."

"I won't need money if I don't go."

"Semyon, think about what you're saying."

Semyon looks upriver. "I've done nothing but think about it, Pasha. I've made up my mind." The throbbing growl of the ferry's engine carries across the water. The crowd assembled on the landing stirs in anticipation. Pavel catches sight of the little girl he saw earlier, still in her father's arms. For a moment he is too heartsick, too devastated, to speak.

"Why? Just tell me that."

"I'm tired of running. All those years I kept my mouth shut, kept my head down with the rest of the herd. You get to where you haven't the stomach to go on pretending the world is a better place because men like Glebnikov aren't in it anymore. I won't run from this."

"And what? You think that will matter to Boyarska?"

"Of course not. Don't you understand, Pasha? I couldn't care less if it meant anything to her. It matters to me."

They are both quiet.

"You're wrong, you know," Semyon says finally. "Everything deserves to be remembered, Pasha. Even us."

# 21

On Saturday Pavel accompanies his mother and Victor's family on their weekend retreat to the country. The car, an aging Opel on loan from a coworker of Victor's, bumps along the winding country road. Through the trees the sky is cloudless, a beautiful pale blue. They pass a village—a run-down petrol station and dark store, a collection of brightly painted ramshackle dachas behind fences built right next to the roadway—then turn onto a car path spangled with sunlight, into the woods.

When they reach the company compound, the elderly caretaker pulls back the high green fence, doffing his cap. "I feel like a boyar," Victor jokes. The white gravel lane, curving through trimmed box hedges, pops softly under the tires. A blue-shuttered caretaker's cottage, a garden shed. A pair of dachas, each at either end of the compound. Theirs, it would appear, is the larger dacha standing at the edge of a crumbling clay bluff over the river.

After unpacking, Pavel walks down the hallway to his mother's room. Misha and Andrei's shouts echo up from the empty fountain they have discovered out front. Even with the window open onto the warm bright morning the plaster walls retain a trace of last night's cold. A tall pile of folded sweaters sits on the end of the bed.

"You sure you brought enough sweaters?" Pavel jokes. "You have enough here for weeks."

His mother smiles. "Wouldn't that be nice?" She looks out the window. "It's so lovely, don't you think?"

"It is."

Downstairs, in the kitchen, Victor is cutting up a tinned ham for sandwiches. Here too the tall windows have been opened wide to let in the pine-sweet September air. "Hungry?" asks Pavel. "Starved," Victor sighs. "I suppose it'll take a while for all this to sink in."

"What's that?"

"This place." Victor waves the knife, then tosses a piece of ham to Marfa Borisova's pug. "It's like having an entire hotel to ourselves. Granted, a drafty old hotel, but a hotel all the same. Out of season."

A bumblebee beats softly at the screen door. From the foyer comes the dry, steady click of the tall grandfather clock. The afternoon stretches before them.

"It's good to get away," Pavel says.

*Away.* From Moscow, from the dark news coming out of Poland, scant as it has been. Rumblings of war. Less than a month ago, before Molotov's pact with Ribbentrop, the machinery of official righteousness would have by now been humming along at full capacity, furiously stamping out a steady stream of invective and outrage. In factory commissaries and public meeting halls across the Soviet Union there would be proclamations of solidarity with the Polish people, hastily written manifestos, letters published daily in *Pravda,* mass demonstrations. Instead, only this uneasy silence.

"I'm going for a walk."

Pavel follows the gravel car path, letting the pug wander. Past the caretaker's cottage the second, smaller dacha occupies the far corner of the compound. On the creaking porch Pavel peers in through the dusty windows, knocks once, and then, out of curiosity, enters. Empty, of course—Victor has already told him they are the only overnight guests this weekend. "Come on," he tells the pug, but the dog for some reason will go no farther than the threshold. Pavel explores the lower floor, then climbs the stairs. He pauses at the door of one of the rooms, then another. Each is identically furnished: bed, wardrobe, writing desk, chair. Across the desktops dance the blurred shadows of leaves. Later, when Pavel emerges once more onto the porch, he is grateful to see Marfa Borisova's pug waiting for him.

The next morning Pavel discovers that he is not the only one awake before dawn. His mother sits on the tiny concrete deck out back overlooking the river, a thick blanket across her lap. "Sleep well?" she asks him. "Well enough," Pavel says.

It has been years since he and his mother greeted the day together. Pavel can remember when he was a little boy, how she would wake him, pulling gently on his nose, calling him her puppy, her pet. Hers was the first face he saw in the morning, the last he saw at night. How distant his childhood seems this morning. For all his love for her, there are times now when it feels as if they are less mother and son than simply two people tied precariously together by shared history. Fellow passengers, departed from a city they will not ever see again. And if her half of that history were lost, if his mother's mind one day goes, what will there be left to tie her to him?

"Would you like to take a walk?" his mother asks.

"Now?"

"Why not? Just let me get my shoes."

She meets him on the front steps. Just over the treetops a flock of geese is passing, calling to one another. His mother looks up, following their progress. The stars are fading.

Outside the compound they turn onto the rutted car path, walking along the high fence. The dog waddles ahead.

"When I was a girl, when we used to spend our summers at your great-grandfather's estate, it was like this. Quiet. You forget what that feels like." She smiles. "Your father—you remember how he hated when I talked about my childhood? All those servants running around. Always embarrassed him."

Only a handful of stories have survived. Pavel's great-grandfather's estate outside Kolomna had once covered over two hundred acres of farmland and hardwood forest, encompassing an entire village. In the evenings the men returning from the hayfields in their bark-plaited shoes would bow to the old man as he rode past on his horse. Some of those men, Pavel has long assumed, were likely the sons and grandsons of serfs his great-grandfather once owned.

A dusty pink glow touches the clouds. The high fence falls away. Ahead of them the path curves into the forest.

"You never talk about your mother," Pavel says.

"There isn't much to talk about. I was only nine when she died. I always thought she was so pretty. And clever, too. She used to draw the most beautiful pictures. Charcoal sketches. Of me, my brothers. They were quite wonderful. I wish I'd held on to them."

A shadow: his grandmother, her world. To think a person could leave so little behind.

"I always thought you got your imagination from her, Pasha."

Pavel laughs. "What imagination? I'm as dull as they come."

"No, you're not, Pasha. You're sensitive. The way you took to books when you were little, like you were born to them."

Another story, part of the lore of Pavel's childhood that his mother to this day swears by. How a teacher had threatened to hold him back because he couldn't read with the rest of his classmates. How, every night for a week, his mother sat reading to him, her finger pointing out each letter on the page, and at the end of that week, to his teacher's astonishment, Pavel could read entirely by himself. *The most amazing thing she had ever seen,* his mother swore. Half recollection, half fairy tale—that is how he has come to think of it: a miracle of the everyday, savored on the tongue like some melting sweet confection, in which the blind child born in darkness suddenly sees.

Another compound, silent as the morning, materializes. The fence is unpainted, the boards fallen away in places. An iron gate hangs half-open in disrepair, spiky weeds grown along its base like the eyebrows of an old man. When Pavel pushes open the gate to peer into the compound, rust crumbles from the massive groaning hinges.

The gaping shell of an unfinished dacha confronts them. Around it the land is returning to wilderness: The row of plane trees have lost their shape, the grass is grown knee-high, a small oak tree lies on its side where some past storm likely blew it over, clotted roots like a nest of garden snakes. A pile of weathered lumber rots in the open air. A project halted in midstride.

"Perhaps they ran out of money," his mother suggests.

Or time, Pavel thinks. Even here, in this simple heaven, they are not immune.

After breakfast they hear the sound of a car approaching the house. Victor and the boys go out front to meet Victor's supervisor, Maxim Andrevich, who has come with his wife and young daughter to soak in the quiet luxury of country life, if only for an afternoon.

"Citizens, I bring good news," shouts Maxim Andrevich. He carries a cardboard box of liquor into the kitchen and drops it on the counter. He is a round-bellied man with a neatly trimmed ginger beard, a patch of sunburnt skin peeling away on his nose, and wears a light, cream-colored linen suit, loose at the shoulders. His blond wife, painfully slim in an expensive-looking sleeveless green silk dress and wide straw sunhat, regards the cluttered kitchen skeptically. A beautiful woman, with high, wide cheekbones, though Pavel can see how that beauty, which has already begun to harden, will abandon her completely in the coming years. Her daughter has stopped in the doorway, her large dark eyes solemn behind red-framed glasses.

"How was your ride out?" asks Pavel politely.

"Awful," the wife says.

"She thinks I ran a family of Gypsies off the road on purpose. She accuses me of hating Gypsies, which is a lie, of course. It's just that I'm not the best driver." Maxim Andrevich slaps the countertop. "Glasses, if you please," he tells Victor. "Well, where shall we start, gentlemen? Whiskey? Vodka?"

"Just beer for me," says Pavel.

"Good Lord, a pacifist. Victor, who is this Tolstoyan?"

Victor smiles uneasily. His boss has been drinking—Pavel can smell the alcohol on Maxim Andrevich's breath. He pities Victor, who is in an awkward position. Why not? Pavel thinks. As long as I'm here, I might as well play along.

"I'll have whiskey."

Maxim Andrevich grins. "Good man. Victor, where are those glasses? I'm wasting away here."

Later, on his way to the bathroom, Pavel happens upon Maxim Andrevich's daughter. She is in the sunroom, standing beside the plush, faded sofa, petting Marfa Borisova's pug. Spangles of sunlight, stirred by the trees outside, climb her outstretched arm.

"You've found a friend," Pavel says.

"I like dogs."

She will be a beauty herself one day, like her mother. The same thick blond hair and sculpted cheekbones. In ten years men on the street, on metros, will turn to stare at her. If the world has not torn itself to pieces by then, which could well happen. If we are all not dead, Pavel thinks. For now that life is as hidden away from her as it is from him. For now she is only an awkwardly shy girl in thick glasses.

"Well, you're certainly welcome to him," Pavel jokes. "He's looking for a good home."

"Mother won't let me have a dog. She's afraid of them."

"You could say he's a cat. He's hardly bigger than a cat."

"She doesn't like animals."

"Even cats?"

"Any animal," the girl says.

Maxim Andrevich insists they take a ride into the village in his car, a sleek gray ZIS sedan. At the little store he buys up all the cigarettes in the cracked glass display, flirting with the blue-eyed cashier, then nearly drives into a ditch on the way back, swerving to avoid an old man on a tractor. "Ah, country life," he sighs.

When they pass the compound gate ten minutes later Pavel says, "That was our stop, you know."

"Nonsense."

A low branch slaps the windshield.

"At least slow down, Maxim Andrevich," says Victor. "Please. I'd like to see my children again."

Maxim Andrevich snorts with laughter, then snaps on the radio—like the car itself, the rarest of luxuries. "Music!" he shouts. Only instead of music, there is news: of the expected record-shattering fall wheat harvest, of the upcoming Youth Day demonstrations in Moscow and Leningrad. Of Poland, writhing under Germany's heel, there is no mention whatsoever. Perhaps, thinks Pavel, he is wrong to imagine other countries existing beyond Russia's border. Maybe everything they have believed all their lives, every map that he has ever seen, is a fantasy, a fiction: the westward traveler, stepping across the border into Poland, stepping into a bottomless emptiness, the trains plummeting from their tracks into darkness without a sound. Maybe that is what happened to his father. Maybe he is still falling.

"My daughter, Lidia—did I tell you my wife is making her take dance classes?" Maxim Andrevich asks Victor. "Says she could lose a few pounds. To Lidia's face she says this." He catches Pavel's eye in the rearview mirror. "Could you imagine saying that to your own daughter?"

"No," Pavel says.

"She didn't even want to come here. The one day I get to relax a little, get my mind off work, and my dear wife would rather stay home and terrorize the housekeeper."

The long fence of the abandoned compound appears. Maxim Andrevich brakes hard.

"Pavel, be a good man and get the gate, would you?"

"You're not driving in there, are you?" asks Victor.

Maxim Andrevich smiles.

He pulls the ZIS right up to the steps of the ruined dacha. Inside, out of the sunlight, it is cooler, almost cold. A mat of dead leaves, blown in last fall or the fall before, litters the bare concrete. The plaster walls beside the empty window frames, once smooth as wedding cake, have begun to bulge and crack under the assault of time, the buckling stairs creak underfoot. As Pavel follows Victor and Maxim Andrevich upstairs he detects, beneath the smell of mold and damp, another much subtler odor, almost sweet: of long decay, like newly turned garden soil.

The roof in one of the larger rooms has collapsed, taking a good portion of the ceiling with it. Shattered roofing tiles lie scattered underfoot. By the window someone has left behind a crude pallet of sorts—a rotting blanket, an old coat rolled into a pillow in which the faint outline of a head still remains. Maxim Andrevich, urinating in a corner, sighs. He slumps forward heavily.

"My one day," he murmurs.

Victor turns away, looking out the window.

Maxim Andrevich finishes, then struggles to tuck in his shirt. "I think I pissed on my shoe." He slips over the broken tiles. "I should be more careful. A man of my . . . Victor, what's the word I'm looking for?" He shakes his head, as if trying to clear it. When he stumbles, Victor grabs his arm.

"Reputation."

"Lord no, not that."

"Maybe we should get back," Pavel suggests.

Maxim Andrevich turns and stares curiously at Victor, as if only now noticing him. "You're a good man, Victor. I've told you that, haven't I?"

"Yes."

"Well, it's true. Always looking out for me. That's rare these days."

"Someone has to," jokes Victor.

Maxim Andrevich nods. "Isn't that the truth." He wipes the toe of one shoe on the filthy blanket at their feet, lip curled distastefully. "We're over our heads this time, you know. The Zhdanovsky Steelworks. There isn't a chance in hell we'll finish those dormitories on schedule."

"Then we'll push the schedule back," Victor says.

"I've tried to. I've been on the telephone for the last two days trying to talk some sense into Solovev." He turns to Pavel. "Our director of operations. The man's an absolute horror. Which is to say, he has our balls in a vise. He's convinced we have to have the dormitories open by November so they can move the workers in. If that factory isn't putting out steel by December twenty-first, Victor, it isn't going to be pretty. His words."

Pavel asks, "Why is the twenty-first of December so important?"

"Stalin's sixtieth birthday," Victor says grimly.

"A present for the Boss." Maxim Andrevich pats his jacket pockets, pulls out a pack of cigarettes, then a gold lighter. "Anyway, Victor, for whatever it's worth, you have my full recommendation." He slaps the lighter shut. "Solovev asks, I'll tell him, 'There's your man, comrade. Victor Ivanevich. My right hand. No need to look any further for my replacement.' God knows you'll do a better job of it than I have. Of course you'd be a lunatic to take the position. Just ask the poor bastard I replaced, if you can find him." Maxim Andrevich blows a smoke ring toward the hole over their heads. "Not that Solovev will particularly want my opinion. He'll be too busy screaming."

After Maxim Andrevich has departed with his family, Victor stops by Pavel's room, where Pavel is packing for the drive back.

"That whole business this afternoon with my boss, I wouldn't make too much of it. He's been under a lot of pressure lately."

"Sounds like you both are."

A shrug. "He handles it his way. Not exactly the way I would, but then I'm not sitting where he is."

"This fellow Solovev, is he that bad?"

"Sometimes. Lately, yes." From downstairs comes Olga's voice, calling the boys inside. "Look, I'm not going to pretend I'm not worried. The Zhdanovsky Steelworks—it's a huge job. I'd be lying if I said I wasn't worried."

"What happens if it doesn't get finished in time?"

"It will."

"But what if it doesn't?"

A quick glance from the younger man, almost fierce. "I'm telling you, Pavel, we'll finish on time. Maxim Andrevich—he just gets like this. Especially when we're under a tight deadline and some screaming maniac like Solovev is breathing down his neck. He gets drunk, he blows off a little steam, the next day he's fine. Let's just drop it, all right?"

But Pavel cannot simply drop it. If anything, these last few years at the Lubyanka have taught him that one must always be attentive to signs: an angry word, an unintended gesture—the first faint milky cracks in the ice. He has seen what happens to people who failed to read the warnings, who refused to believe that the beautiful, bright world they inhabited could one day fall upon them like a hobnailed heel, crushing them into dust.

When Victor starts away, Pavel stops him.

"Will you do something for me, Victor? If—and I'm not saying it will—but *if* this project falls through and things begin to go badly for Maxim Andrevich, will you let me know? Please."

"Why?"

"Because I want to be able to help you, if I can. But you have to tell me, Victor. Do you understand? You can't wait for the other shoe to drop." *Because by then it might be too late. For you, for your family.* "Will you do that for me, please? As a friend."

"All right, Pavel."

The drive home is a somber affair—even the children, sunburnt, worn out, are quiet, as if Victor's pensive mood has somehow infected them. Misha sits in Olga's lap in back beside Pavel's mother, resting his head on Olga's chest. At the train station near their flat, as dusk descends, Victor gets out and pulls Pavel's suitcase from the trunk. "Interesting weekend," Victor says, then coughs. The borrowed Opel rattles beside them. Pavel offers his hand.

"Thank you for letting me come."

"We're glad you could."

"If you need anything," Pavel says, "you know where to find me."

"Yes." Victor's eyes drop. "Well. I better get the car back." He pats Pavel on the shoulder, then walks around to the driver's door.

At his mother's window Pavel taps the glass. She turns, smiling up at him, and mouths, *I love you.* "I love you, too," Pavel tells her, then lifts his suitcase and starts for the station.

# 22

Just over a week later, on Tuesday afternoon, Kutyrev is called upstairs to Fourth Section's main offices. From the agitated look on the junior officer's face when he returns twenty minutes later, Pavel can tell something has happened.

"I need you to get Babel's file together. Everything we have."

"Why, what's going on?"

"I don't know. Some sort of stink about a letter Babel wrote yesterday." Kutyrev pulls a folded handkerchief from his pocket, wipes nervously at his mouth. "To Beria, can you believe it? Major Radlov is pretty worked up about it."

No wonder he would be, if Beria has become involved. People's Commissar for Internal Affairs. Stalin's advisor and confidant. What was it Radlov told him? *Everything flows upward.* And downward too, it would appear.

"They should be sending down the authorization within the next fifteen minutes," Kutyrev says.

Strangely Babel's box feels heavier than usual when Pavel retrieves it, but then perhaps that is only the weakness in his chest, which is already leaching down into his vitals, into his legs. Two stories, which anyone closely checking the manifest against Babel's confiscated manuscripts will miss. *We seem to have a discrepancy here, Pavel Vasilievich. Why do you suppose that is?*

*I don't know.*

*You wouldn't be trying to make trouble for us, would you? Do you know what happens to people who make things difficult for us?*

*You torture them. You murder them.*

*What an imagination you have, Pavel Vasilievich. Now, where on earth did you get that idea?*

Ten minutes later the evidence-request form arrives. *Investigation File 419. Babel, I. Emmanuelovich.* All archived documents pertaining to Babel's case are to be immediately forwarded to one Boris Rodos, signatory.

Upstairs, in Fourth Section's spartan main office, the receptionist on duty, a middle-aged woman in black horn-rimmed glasses talking rapidly into a telephone, waves Pavel impatiently toward a chair. From the adjoining offices spills the fierce rattle of typewriters, voices. Finally the receptionist covers the telephone's mouthpiece with her hand. "Yes?"

"Boris Rodos."

The receptionist places the telephone to her ear, listens, replies briskly, "I understand," then again cups a hand over the mouthpiece. "Down the hall. Go out, turn right. Second-to-the-last office on your left."

The office to which she has directed him, Pavel discovers, is the very office Kutyrev sent him to back in July in order to interview Babel. The little table still stands by the window overlooking the inner prison, though the tea set and samovar are nowhere to be seen. On it instead are stacks of bound folders like those Pavel has brought. Files. Evidence.

"Just set them down anywhere," says Rodos. A blunt-faced man, he is sitting behind the desk, a file open before him, writing steadily. He does not look up.

Pavel puts Babel's manuscripts on the floor next to the little table. He turns to leave.

"Wait," Rodos says peremptorily, holding up one hand, on which a heavy gold wedding band gleams. The slow, deliberate scratching of his pen fills the office. With the morning light upon him Pavel can see the officer's white scalp through his oiled black hair where a comb has left a row of tiny furrows. A holstered pistol, the standard Tokarev TT, hangs from the coat-rack in the corner, along with Rodos's blue uniform cap. After a full minute the hand drops. "You are?"

"Pavel Dubrov."

"Dubrov. How come I've never seen you around?"

"I work downstairs. In Fourth Section's special archives."

"Doing what?"

*Cleaning up after you,* thinks Pavel. "I'm the archivist."

"Right. Our librarian. So." Rodos straightens in his chair. "Archivist. What's in the box?"

"Isaac Babel's manuscripts."

The weakness has climbed into Pavel's throat. He looks away, out the window. Across the courtyard the sunlight advances, sliding down the dark iron shutters of the inner prison. Rodos, rising from his chair, touches the cardboard box Pavel has brought him with the tip of his polished boot, nudging it.

"Our little scribbler. Writes one letter and suddenly the shit is flying."

"I thought," says Pavel, "the investigation was finished."

"It will be." Rodos returns to his desk. "Here." He plucks a piece of paper from an open folder, hands it over. A typed carbon copy, Pavel sees. Babel's letter to Beria.

*Citizen People's Commissar. During my interrogation, possessed solely by the desire to purge myself and repent, I have recounted my crimes, without any pity for myself. I also want to settle accounts for the other side of my existence, my literary work, which went on, hidden from the outside world, painfully and with interruptions, but unceasingly. I am appealing to you, Citizen People's Commissar, let me put the manuscripts confiscated from me in order.*

"What do you suppose he's up to?" asks Rodos.

The same thing I am up to, Pavel thinks, handing the letter back. Babel is trying to save himself in the only way possible now, by salvaging his stories. The carbon from Rodos's copy of the letter has blackened the tips of Pavel's fingers.

"I don't know."

"I'll tell you one thing," Rodos says, "our scribbler's out of his fucking mind if he thinks this stunt will work. He can write all the letters he wants, it won't make any difference in the end." He holds Babel's letter up, gestures with it toward the pistol hanging on the coatrack. "You ever see a piece of paper stop one of these?"

Even from here Pavel can smell the oil in the officer's hair.

"No," Pavel says.

"Neither have I."

# 23

That night, as Pavel is just beginning to nod off on the sofa, there is a knock at the front door.

"Did I wake you?" asks Natalya.

"Not at all."

Downstairs, in her bedroom, they undress as long-married couples undress, without heat. Sitting on the edge of her bed, she takes him in her hand, then her mouth. Lightly Pavel traces the bony ridge of her shoulder with his fingers, then stretches out beside her on the narrow bed. Immediately Natalya rolls onto her side so that her back is to him. When he slips into her, she presses her hand flat against the wall, bracing herself. He can hear her breathing through her teeth.

Afterward, as Pavel lies there spent, Natalya leaves the room and returns with a damp towel, which she drops onto his stomach. "I have some wine, if you'd like," she says. The offer, like the towel, is hospitable in a practical sort of way, if devoid of tenderness. "Could we drink in here?" he asks.

"If you'd like."

She returns with the wine and glasses, undressed still. For a brief moment, with the curtain pulled aside, the length of her body is ringed in light. Not a bad body, Pavel would admit, given her age. Certainly he is no prize himself. Perhaps one ought to abandon such considerations—beauty, tenderness—as a refugee in war might tip a cherished but unwieldy wardrobe from the back of the cart.

"Would you like a chair?" Natalya asks. "I was going to get myself one from the kitchen."

"The bed's fine," says Pavel.

"I'll be right back."

What is it she wants from him? What, wonders Pavel, does he have that anyone—especially a woman—might want? Certainly not romance: She is old enough to know better, she has seen too much of life to come to him, of all people, seeking love.

Again the curtain is drawn back. Along with the chair she has brought a candle, guttering in a little bowl, which she hands Pavel. He places the candle on the nightstand, settles himself. He is struck by the ease with which he has slipped into his role of the casual lover.

Sitting, Natalya crosses her long legs.

"I was just thinking about Marfa. You used to be able to set your clock by her. Every night she'd be out with that dog."

"I imagine I must be something of a letdown."

"He's lucky he's still drawing breath. The city gasses dogs like him all the time. Anyway," says Natalya, "Marfa didn't have anything else in her life. *He* was her life. I used to think, Good Lord, what if he gets sick, or run over? She'll go to pieces. She would have, too. You can't build any kind of life on a dog. They're too temporary."

"People come and go, too," says Pavel—the words are out of his mouth before he even realizes it. Elena, Natalya's daughters—what trace have they left behind? Would it be better to live life without becoming tied to others? Is that Natalya's solution? A life built on misprinted cookbooks, discards bound for the pulp mill.

"Yes. They do."

"Did you know her husband?" Pavel asks.

"Anton Dmitryevich? A little. He was an official of some sort with the water department. A womanizer, as well. I remember when he bought her that dog—out of guilt apparently. It was just a puppy, no bigger than your fist. Used to vomit in his slippers. He was always threatening to drown it in the river."

"Where is Anton Dmitryevich now?"

"Dead. He had a heart attack in some restaurant. With one of his mistresses." Natalya shrugs. "Funny, isn't it? Here the dog ends up outliving him. I'm sure Anton Dmitryevich never saw *that* coming."

"I'm sure he didn't."

"Who knows? We could end up in a war again. The little mutt might outlive all of us."

The flickering candle casts Natalya's shadow across the curtain behind her. "Do you think the Germans will stop once they've taken Warsaw?" she asks Pavel.

"If the British and French have their way, they will. Hitler won't have any choice."

"What if Hitler decides to go east?"

East, into the Soviet Union. "Then we will end up in a war," Pavel says. "God help us."

"Of course, we do have the Non-Aggression Agreement." *Our deal with the devil.* Or perhaps more accurately: *A deal among devils.*

"Yes."

Natalya regards him a moment. Then she reaches over and pulls open the nightstand, withdraws an old cigar box, which she sets on her lap. In it, beneath a pile of loose tobacco, are her squares of scavenged rolling papers, cut from books. In the candlelight she rolls herself a cigarette.

"Do you think they'll stop?" Pavel asks.

"No."

Pavel watches Natalya light her cigarette, the flaring match briefly illuminating the little room like a tiny white star. For a few seconds its orange afterimage lingers on his eyes.

"Would you try to get out of Moscow?" he asks.

"Without permission?" Natalya sighs smoke through her nose. "How long do you think it would take before the police showed up at my door?"

"You have connections."

"Not those kind. You've seen what my so-called connections amount to. A basement full of old books and magazines nobody in their right mind would want. Internal passports, residency permits—that's a bit over my head."

"But if you could get out. Would you?"

"And go where?"

"East."

Natalya flicks the ash from her cigarette into the bowl sitting on the nightstand. "Home, you mean," she says. A tinge of bitterness has crept into her voice.

"You must have family back there."

"Buried, yes. If that's what you mean."

Pavel says, "No," then falls silent. After a time he says, "What about your husband's family?"

"They want nothing to do with me."

"Why?"

"Because of my daughters."

The wine, the flickering candle, Natalya's voice—the effect is almost hypnotic. Pavel can feel himself growing drowsy. "I have a picture," says Natalya suddenly. She rises and crosses the room to the dresser. From a drawer she removes an envelope, yellowed with age. She hands it to him.

Inside Pavel finds only a single photograph, a studio portrait, glued to a scallop-edged square of pale green cardboard: a little girl of perhaps six, pretty in the delicately solemn way of dark-eyed children. Behind her, sitting against a rumpled backdrop painted to suggest trees, a pockmarked young man in a high-collared tunic gazes out unsmilingly. The lost husband.

"Where was this taken?"

"Vladivostok. We were all supposed to go into the city that day. But then my younger daughter came down with a cold, so I had to stay with her." Natalya reaches for more wine.

Pavel tilts the photograph toward the flickering candlelight.

"What were your daughters' names?"

"Anna. That's her there. And Nadezhda, after my mother."

Her daughters, my wife. They have led us into each other's arms, Pavel realizes.

"She's a pretty girl. She looks like you."

"That's what people used to say."

Carefully Pavel slips the photograph back into its envelope.

"What about Nadezhda? Do you have any pictures of her?"

"No. Just the one of Anna."

Natalya returns the envelope to its drawer, then announces that she must be up early the next morning. The message is clear: He has overstayed his welcome. Drawing on a robe, she gathers their glasses, leaves him alone to get dressed. Minutes later, buttoning his shirt, Pavel hears her shut the bathroom door, then the hollow sound of water splashing: She is filling the tub. Washing herself clean of me, Pavel cannot help but think. Passing the bathroom he hesitates, then touches the door. "Good night." But Natalya does not answer.

# 24

On Sunday, two days after his hearing before the Party membership committee, Semyon telephones from his office at the university with the news that he has decided to take Pavel up on his advice, at least partially so. He is sending Vera away to the country—"for a bit of a rest," as Semyon puts it. Wisely he does not say where.

"By herself?"

"With friends of friends, you might say." Semyon adds, "I still haven't told her about my hearing. Or about tomorrow, for that matter." His meeting with Boyarska, he means. "I told her I'd be along as soon as the semester breaks for holiday."

"You have to tell her."

"She won't leave if I tell her. You know that." Semyon is quiet a moment. "I've written her a letter explaining everything. As much as all this can be explained. I want you to mail it to her for me. If anything happens."

"You don't have to do this," Pavel says.

"Of course I do."

In the silence that follows, a barely audible static washes

intermittently over the line. A bad connection, a loose wire somewhere in the network.

"I assume your hearing went"—a wave of bleak weariness breaks over Pavel: He touches his eyes—"as expected."

"As expected. Turns out one of the committee members is a former student of mine. He seemed terribly uncomfortable about the whole business, had to make a big show of being especially nasty to me. For the record, I'm sure. Iron conscience, mercilessness before the enemy. Particularly," Semyon continues, "if the enemy once treated you decently. Just the sort of sneering little coward who does all his shooting from behind a desk. No doubt he'll go far."

"Did they at least let you speak?"

"I started to—I'd prepared a statement—but then that fellow interrupted me. Said they weren't interested in listening to my lies. Every time I opened my mouth he jumped in swinging. The next thing I knew, the committee was delivering its decision. So much for my statement."

Pavel says, "I'm sorry." Then, even though there is no hope of Semyon changing his mind, "You can still leave."

"No."

Pavel does not know what else to say. The windy static washing over the line has tunneled its way into his ear and scoured his brain, leaving him speechless. Even if he could find the words, they would fall unheard as into a chasm, tumbling down into a white wintry silence as immutable as that field where Elena died.

"It's probably better," Semyon says, "if we don't see each other for a while."

Pavel's ear has begun to ache from pressing the telephone so tightly against it. As though, he thinks, in catching Semyon's every word, he could somehow save them forever.

# 25

All at once, it seems, the nights grow cold. The trees outside Pavel's flat flare brilliant scarlet and orange. In Lenin Hills, the leaves begin falling, scattering out over the river in great billowing yellow curtains, floating away. For four days straight a nearly constant wind blows across Dzerzhinsky Square, carrying a stinging grit Pavel later washes from his hair. High atop Bolshoi Theater the rearing stone horses appear ready to leap into space, as if the wind moaning through their legs has whipped them into a panic.

That Friday Pavel finds Semyon's letter in his mailbox. The sealed envelope inside, which he does not open, is addressed to a flat in Gorky, a city some four hundred kilometers east of Moscow. *Friends of friends.* Far enough away, Pavel hopes. That night Pavel hides the letter in the basement wall with Babel's stories.

All week he has fought off the impulse to telephone Semyon. Still, Pavel is unable to stop replaying their last conversation; he has not reconciled himself to even a temporary separation. A terrible foreboding haunts him.

On Sunday Pavel finally gives in. From a pay phone near his flat he has an operator put him through to Semyon's number. After eleven rings the operator comes back onto the line: "Your party isn't picking up. Will you continue waiting?"

"I'll wait," Pavel says.

But there is no answer. Nor is there any answer over the next two days. Until finally, late Wednesday night, the very day Warsaw surrenders to Germany, the telephone is picked up.

"Semyon?"

A man's voice calmly asks, "Who is calling, please?"

Pavel returns the telephone to its cradle.

After that he does not dare telephone again. Pavel is not sure which he fears more: that the call could somehow be traced back to him or that he will find out Semyon is truly gone. At times he is almost able to believe Semyon has gotten safely away, though in his heart he knows better.

On the last day of September, Pavel crosses the city by tram. He is surprised to discover that the covered tram shelter near Semyon's building still bears its faded posters mocking Hitler. History, he thinks, has left this lonely, lost district behind.

He walks the three blocks to Semyon's building. In the courtyard a flushed-looking man in a filthy suit jacket is scattering bits of bread from a paper sack while a squirrel looks on warily from a linden branch overhead.

On the door to Semyon's flat, a dollop of red wax. From it dangles a lead-weighted string, left behind by the arresting officers as much to seal the door as to warn away the curious. Touching the waxen seal, Pavel feels the dread he has carried with him all these weeks, and perhaps longer, darken into deep anger, like a photograph fed into a fire.

Outside, the squirrel man is just pouring the last crumbs of bread onto the pavement.

"Where may I find the manager?" Pavel asks him.

He is led across the courtyard and down a set of damp stone steps. Pavel pounds on the door, waits. He can smell the alcohol radiating from the squirrel man, sharp as turpentine.

The door swings open. An old man with lank hair brushed across his skull blinks at them cautiously from the gloom of his flat. "Yes? What is it?"

"Are you the building manager?"

"Yes."

"Semyon Borisovich Sorokin. I need you to let me into his flat."

The old man stares. "On whose authority?"

The rage that has been simmering in Pavel suddenly boils over. "Do you really want to know that?" he says coldly, taking a step toward the building manager, who flinches. "Because I can just as easily summon a car to come get us, if you'd prefer. Do you know the sort of car I mean, old man? Shall I show you on whose authority I am here?" Behind them, with a half-strangled sob of terror, the squirrel man stumbles up the slick stairs.

From a hook beside the door the building manager pulls a ragged sweater. "I have to get my keys," he says shakily. Good, Pavel thinks: Let him choke a little on his fear. The more afraid he is, the less likely the old man will challenge him.

"Hurry."

They cross the empty courtyard. High on its whip-thin branch the squirrel chirps at them angrily. Over the rooftops the wind washes eastward, the clouds race across the sky.

The building manager hesitates at Semyon's door, his eyes dropping to the wax seal. The skin on his face and hands is so pale as to be all but transparent. Cave dwellers—isn't that what

Semyon called the generations to come? Certainly that is where we already are, Pavel thinks.

He rips free the weighted string, and the seal falls to the floor.

"Open it."

The tumblers click, the heavy door swings open. Averting his gaze, the building manager steps aside to let Pavel past.

"You may lock up after I'm finished," Pavel says, dismissing him.

"Of course."

The moment Pavel crosses the threshold and shuts the door behind him, his anger drains away.

A storm, he thinks dazedly. Books lie scattered on the rug beside the bookcase, some with their bindings torn loose. *A Sportsman's Notebook, The Brothers Karamazov, A Hero of Our Time.* The lid of the tall black upright stands open, a muddy shoeprint mars the piano bench. A trail of trampled photographs, wrenched from their shattered frames, leads to Semyon and Vera's tiny bedroom, where the dresser and wardrobe hang open. The mattress has been pulled halfway from the bed, the linen stripped. More books, more photographs. On the floor, a heap of shirts still on their hangers, neckties, shoes. Finally, from one of the drawers pulled from the dresser, personal letters, hastily read through and tossed aside. A life laid bare. Pavel kneels to pick them up.

*2 January 1925*

*Dear Vera,*

*I wish with all my heart that we could have spent yesterday together, though I understand perfectly well your wanting to be with your family during the holidays, just as I know you understand my need to work. Ah, the life of a probationary associate professor. So happy New Year, my beautiful new wife! I have been to the mailbox twice already this afternoon hoping for a letter from you. It is beautiful here today, very clear. As soon as I post this I will walk down to Chistyye Prudy and watch the ice-skaters on the pond, and imagine that you are with me, as I am with you.*

*I embrace you,*
*Semyon*

If only he could somehow speak to Semyon one more time, Pavel would tell his old friend he was right. Everything must be remembered. A letter, an icy lake, the skaters' clear, joyous laughter ringing in the air.

# 26

The next two weeks pass for Pavel in a fog. Every night he sits up as late as possible listening to the radio, drinking himself into a stupor, all in the hope of putting off sleep. Often when he wakes the next morning it is with some disturbing, half-forgotten dream still ringing through him, like the sound of weeping reverberating through a wall. He eats without appetite, bathes and dresses himself and makes his way to work, mechanically, one day folding itself into another. The margins of his everyday existence recede until life is just manageable, the same as it was those first months after Elena died. Only now, every time he steps into the Lubyanka, a shadow falls over his heart. The moaning elevator, the jangle of keys in the corridor, the wall of manuscripts behind his desk. He has hidden the letters he found in Semyon's flat in the basement wall with Babel's stories, though he has yet to mail Semyon's sealed letter. For Vera's sake, he tells himself. Let her go on believing for now that Semyon will join her soon, let her have that hope.

Semyon has not been taken to the Lubyanka—Pavel has been able to learn that much, if nothing more. "We don't have a file on any Semyon Borisovich Sorokin," an officer snaps at him when Pavel telephones the admissions department. "Check over at Lefortovo or Butyrka. They've been busy lately, I hear."

"I've tried. They won't tell me anything."

"Then you'll have to put in a request through the proper channels."

But that is further than Pavel is willing to go. He is afraid the request could lead back to him. He has already put himself at risk by visiting Semyon's flat.

Then, that Wednesday, Victor telephones. "It's your mother, Pavel. She's had a little accident. Don't worry, she's fine now," Victor adds quickly. "She just twisted her ankle. Still, it's probably better if you come out."

A tumble: That is what his mother calls it. "Those stairs must have been wet," she complains. She is in her room with Olga, sitting up in bed with the injured foot elevated on a pillow. "Really, I'm fine, Pasha. Embarrassed but fine."

Olga says, "There's nothing to be embarrassed about."

"Well, I am. Children fall down stairs. Drunks fall down stairs."

"I'm just glad you're all right," Pavel tells her. But his mother's haggard appearance, her tousled gray hair, frighten him. Worse still, he detects a carefully veiled wariness in her gaze. Something more is behind her accident than a simple fall, something he has not been told. Later, when Victor walks him back to the station, the story emerges. "She was in the wrong building," Victor explains.

"What do you mean?"

"When she fell. She was across the plaza in Unit 4. A friend of mine, Vlad, happens to live over there, thank God. He found her on the stairs and helped her home." Victor looks at the black line of trees beyond the railroad embankment, where the lowering sun has just vanished. "She told him she'd knocked on our door, on 310, but that another family was living there. Vlad said she was frantic."

"My God."

The cold wind touches Pavel's face. They pass the open market. In the twilight the air is blue. A pair of workmen burning brush behind the station stand leaning on their rakes, watching the fire.

"I think your mother ought to see that doctor again," Victor says after a time.

"Yes."

They have reached the station entrance. Behind them a woman is calling out to customers in a throaty singsong: "Beautiful daisies, beautiful roses, buy one for your sweetheart!" One of the workmen jabs at the burning pile with his rake, sending sparks swirling up into the darkness. Pavel reaches out and grasps Victor's coat sleeve, as if the sidewalk has suddenly tilted under him, as if he is the one falling now. He tries to speak but the words will not come. "I know," Victor tells him gently. He lays his hand over Pavel's, squeezes. "She will be all right, I'm sure. You'll see."

That Saturday he meets his mother and Olga in the echoing lobby at Kiev Station. Bundled in a coat and headscarf, his mother clutches her purse close against her side. Outside Pavel hails a taxi, tells the driver, "Eleven Yauzskaya."

As before, all the seats in the waiting room of the neurology department are taken. "Why don't we wait outside in the hallway," Pavel suggests. "They'll call us when it's time."

The smell of carbolic permeates the long corridor. An orderly passes pushing an empty wheelchair, humming under his breath.

After a few minutes Olga produces a smallish green pear from her purse, which she proceeds to cut into thirds with a tiny paring knife. "I have soda crackers, too, if anyone wants one."

Pavel accepts his portion of pear, thanking her. He is glad Olga has come along. Were it not for her he seriously doubts his mother would have agreed to another examination.

"You're not eating?" he asks his mother.

"No."

"There's a bakery across the street. I could run down and pick something up for you."

"No, thank you."

"What about some water?" asks Olga.

"What I would like," his mother says evenly, "is for everyone to stop treating me like I'm made of glass. I'm not hungry, I don't want any water. I don't mind that we have to wait—I've spent half my life waiting on lines, one more isn't going to kill me. Stop babying me. If I want anything I'll get it myself."

An old man shuffles from the waiting room, escorted by a bullnecked, middle-aged man who stares stiffly ahead. The old man's entire body is shaking—badly so, buffeted by some invisible force, some wind unfelt by those around him. Slowly the two men make their way down the corridor toward the elevator.

"Do you want me to go in with you?" Pavel asks.

"I'd rather go by myself." His mother turns, studying him a moment. Her expression softens. "I'm not afraid, Pasha. I don't want you to be either."

But he is afraid. He has lost too much already, he is terrified of losing her. "I'm trying," Pavel says.

"I know you are, darling."

Forty minutes later a nurse finally calls her name. "Are you sure you don't want someone to go in with you?" asks Olga. His mother shakes her head. She reaches for Pavel's hand. When the nurse calls her name again, his mother lets go and steps forward. "I'm Anna Dubrova." "Come with me, please. The doctor will see you now." His mother takes another step, then stops. "Should I bring my purse or leave it with my son?"

"Better if you leave it with your son," the nurse tells her.

An hour later, stepping outside, Pavel sees that it has rained, though the clouds have already cleared. Beside the hospital entrance a pigeon furiously splashing in a puddle goes still when they pass, iridescent feathers puffed. "I want to walk a bit," Pavel's mother announces shakily. She has yet to tell them about Dr. Hirsch's diagnosis—she has said almost nothing since emerging from her examination. Nevertheless, the way she is holding herself now, as if it hurts her to breathe, as if she has been struck in the chest, alarms Pavel. Her gray hair, loosened from her headscarf, hangs over her eyes. When Pavel reaches to take her arm, he feels her collapse a little against him.

"We'll go slow, all right?" Olga says gently. "If you get tired, we can take the tram."

The kiosks along Yauzskaya Street are doing brisk business. Cigarettes, film magazines. Cheap paperback novels: *How the Steel Was Tempered, Ivan Lapshin.* When Pavel's mother tires, they steer themselves toward a crowded tram stop, where Olga unwraps a small wax-paper packet of soda crackers. Surprisingly, his mother accepts a few, eats, if absently. Watching her, Pavel is suddenly overcome by an urge to throw his arms around her and weep. Instead, with an almost impatient gesture, he brushes the crumbs from her coat. "Finally," someone announces. The tram is slowly approaching their stop.

"I'm never going back to that place, Pasha," his mother says.

"That was the last time."

"What did Dr. Hirsch say?" asks Pavel. When his mother shakes her head and looks away, the fear that has been gnawing at him becomes too much. "Tell me!" he says sharply.

His mother flinches slightly but says nothing.

Olga puts her hand on his arm. "Pavel, please." *Go easy on her,* the look on her face says. *Let her tell you in her own time. Be patient.*

The tram arrives and disgorges a stream of passengers out the back door even as new passengers pour in up front. They must press themselves so tightly together they can barely move. Olga, separated from them, raises her hand to let Pavel and his mother know where she is. The tram starts forward. His mother's headscarf brushes against Pavel's chin, he can feel her breathing against him. After a time she turns and looks up at him.

"He thinks I may have a tumor, Pasha. On my brain." She touches her forehead. "Here."

"Is he certain?"

"No. Not without going into my skull and looking around." She shudders slightly. "He says all my symptoms point to a tumor."

"What about treatment? What did Dr. Hirsch say about that?" Pavel is too stunned to do more than respond—he is still struggling to absorb what his mother is telling him.

"We'll see," his mother says.

"What does that mean?"

The tram has stopped. They are being pushed back by a wave of boarding passengers, though there is nowhere really they can go. "What exactly does that mean, Mama?" Pavel asks more sharply than he intends to, raising his voice. Outside a hand smacks the window and stays there a second, palm flat, whitened against the glass. Then they are moving again.

"Don't shout at me, Pasha."

"Are you saying we should just wait? And do nothing?"

"Yes."

He stares at her, horror-stricken.

"What do you want me to tell you?" his mother asks. "You asked me what the doctor said, so I'm telling you. Short of cutting open my skull—which I'm not about to let anyone do—all I can do is wait."

"I don't believe that," Pavel says. "There has to be something we can do."

"This isn't about what you believe, Pasha. Listen to me. What are my options? Let this doctor drill into my skull? And if he does find something there, what then? He'll have to cut out part of my brain. So I can live out the rest of my life with the mental capacity of an infant?"

"Is that what Dr. Hirsch told you?"

"He said there's always that risk, yes. People come out of these operations, Pasha, they're changed. They can't speak, they can't read. They can't recognize faces. They're alive but their minds are gone."

"But they're alive."

"Yes," his mother says, "but they're not who they were before."

Their stop is approaching. Pushing toward the rear exit, Pavel stumbles, falling against the bodies pressing him in. He sinks to one knee, and for a moment simply stays there, unable to will himself to stand. *Incurable*—the word beats uselessly in his head. Above him a few of the passengers glance down, their faces showing indifference or concern or simple confusion. Pavel struggles to his feet and begins shouldering his way through. "Please," he says over and over.

"Easy, brother," someone says near his ear.

"I'm sorry, I have to get out, please."

Then he is out, on the street again, his mother and Olga beside him. The tram rolls on.

From here it is only another ten minutes more by bus to Kiev Station. All the while they are waiting for the bus Pavel is silent, turning over what his mother has told him, what she is asking him to do: resign himself. But how can he resign himself to her doing nothing? If there is any chance of his mother being helped, even if it means an operation, Pavel can't help but cling to that. Otherwise what does the future hold out for her but diminishment and loss? A day, one day, when his mother will no longer recognize him, will no longer remember their lives together. Two deaths then: her past, his. If that is what she is asking him to accept, then she is asking too much.

But what if his mother is right? A slip of the hand, the slightest mistake—she could be gone in an instant. A stranger to herself and to Pavel.

At Kiev Station the last call for their train echoes away. All down the concrete platform, past the immense strutted roof arching overhead, they must weave through crowds. At the head of the long line of blue carriages the enormous diesel engines thrum and vibrate, so that the whole length of the train, even the air, shivers. From the platform, after his mother and Olga board, Pavel watches them find their seats and settle themselves. When the train pulls away he walks slowly along with it, with his mother looking out at him, the reflected faces of the people on the platform slipping over the glass, until the platform ends.

# 27

By November the reorganization of the archives is nearly ready to start its final phase—the wall of manuscripts is to be returned, neatly and in due order, to the stacks. Each author, each numbered manuscript duly logged in some master evidence manifest to be filed away upstairs in Fourth Section and promptly forgotten. What happens then Kutyrev will not say. The young officer has noticeably avoided the subject altogether. Though it is only a matter of time before the burning of manuscripts begins in earnest.

Then, on Monday, Pavel arrives to discover the archives still dark. Thirty minutes later Kutyrev plods in grimly with mud on his boots and slumps in his chair without removing his overcoat. After a time he touches the rim of his left nostril, then the right, then coughs noisily, spitting into the metal wastebasket beside his desk. When he turns Pavel sees that the left side of his face is dull red. A bruise is coming up under Kutyrev's eye.

"What the hell happened to you?"

Kutyrev sniffs. "I had a little accident going in swimming. Slipped on a rock, smashed my face." He touches the bridge of his nose now. "Does my nose look crooked to you?"

"A bit, maybe."

"I already broke it once, when I was little. My cousin Lev kicked a door shut in my face. Now that hurt. Worse than this, I'll tell you."

"You think you broke it again?"

Kutyrev says almost contemplatively, "I could have, yes." Then, rousing himself, he adds, "I'll need you to go down to the incinerator this morning." He stands, and slips off his overcoat.

"How many boxes?"

"Just one for now."

For now. But only for now. Pavel imagines a day, years from this morning, when he will return with his metal cart from the incinerator and find no more boxes waiting: no stories, no novels or plays, no poems. Just empty shelves. The end of history.

For an hour or so they work without speaking, sorting boxes. Before long, though, Pavel notices Kutyrev's usual tireless pace lagging. Repeatedly the junior officer is seized by fits of ragged, painful coughing, which leave him breathless, stooped over. His left eye, blood-red, swells grossly until it closes altogether. By ten o'clock Kutyrev's suffering is too much even for him to conceal.

"Why don't you go home," Pavel says.

"I'm fine."

Later, watching Kutyrev shredding a cigarette, the thought occurs to Pavel that this pathetic display is in part for his benefit; that in his suffering Kutyrev is trying to set himself up as an example of stoicism in the face of—what? Affliction? Pain? *You see,* the young lieutenant seems to be saying, *this is how a true citizen of the Soviet republic behaves.* If that is the lesson, then the lesson is wasted.

The next morning Kutyrev's condition has only worsened. Hunched at his desk, feverous, the young lieutenant barely acknowledges Pavel's arrival. As Pavel hangs his coat Kutyrev suddenly doubles over and coughs explosively, holding a handkerchief to his mouth. Afterward, leaning back heavily, Kutyrev groans in pain. So you are human after all, Pavel thinks.

"You're looking well today," he tells Kutyrev.

"I'll be all right once I'm moving. I just need to get myself moving."

But he does not move.

"Have you considered the possibility," Pavel asks finally, "that you may have been knocked unconscious when you fell and hit your face on that rock yesterday?"

"So what?"

"So were you in the water at all? Because if you were, even for a few seconds, you may have water in your lungs. Water in your lungs could lead to infection, which could lead to pneumonia. And from the way you sound, you're already well on your way."

"You don't know what you're talking about."

"I know enough to know you're sick. Listen to yourself. It's like your lungs are about to tear loose. You need bed rest. If you don't take care of this now you're going to end up in the hospital."

"You'd like to see that, wouldn't you?"

Pavel stands, exasperated. "Suit yourself." He starts for the stacks.

"I'm not going to any hospital," Kutyrev calls after him.

By noon Kutyrev is so sick he has abandoned all pretense of working. When he is not coughing he simply sits, racked by chills, elbows propped on his desk, gazing bleakly into the stacks. With his badly blackened eye, his swollen, bruised cheek, he could well be mistaken for a prisoner, were it not for his uniform. "I think," Kutyrev at last announces, "I might go home a little early." He lumbers to his feet, reaching out for his chair to brace himself. It is clear to Pavel he will not make it out of the building by himself, let alone home.

Pavel hands Kutyrev his heavy overcoat, then retrieves his own lighter brown wool coat from the coatrack.

"What are you doing?"

"Taking you home."

"I don't want your help," Kutyrev says.

"What are you going to do, stand around for God knows how long in your condition waiting at some bus stop? In this weather? Be sensible. Let me help you."

"Why?"

Why would *you* help *me*? That is the deeper meaning behind Kutyrev's question. Because you need my help, Pavel thinks. Because you are human.

"Put your coat on," he says.

On the elevator up, and again as they are standing in front of the Lubyanka, Kutyrev is seized by a coughing spell that leaves him gasping for air. Pavel takes the junior lieutenant by the arm, holding him up. A light sleet is falling, the hailstones bouncing on the sidewalk around their feet. With his free hand Pavel signals a circling taxi over, and they climb in.

"Ten Sokolnicheskaya Street." Kutyrev's voice barely registers above the wipers scraping back and forth. The dense, sour smell of old cigarettes permeates the taxi; the backseat is blistered with cigarette burns. Out Pavel's side, on its island at the center of the square, ice is collecting on the shoulders of the statue of Iron Felix.

The sleet turns to snow, beating softly against the windshield. Occasionally Kutyrev tells the driver where to turn; otherwise no words are exchanged. Ten minutes into their drive the roads grow patchy, then patchier still: There are potholes so deep the driver must carefully maneuver around them. At one intersection, where an old truck has spilled its load of scrap metal, they must double back to find an alternate route. An abandoned factory looms, its dead stack rusted like that of some ancient trawler.

Finally Kutyrev announces, "Stop." The driver pulls to the curb.

A warren of towering buildings, probably erected a decade ago and diligently neglected ever since, stretches before them. The sidewalks have been torn up, they must trudge through ice-crusted mud, past piles of broken concrete, in order to reach Kutyrev's building. Beside them a trench has been hacked from the earth. "The new sewer," Kutyrev says feebly. The mounds of dirt along the trench edge are covered with sparse yellow grass. Pavel wonders how long these pits have sat here since they were first dug. He suspects that six months or a year from now he would find them still waiting to be filled.

Inside, Pavel trails Kutyrev up narrow stairs lit only by a single snow-covered skylight high above them. A tiny piece of the skylight has been broken out, letting in a little snow that sifts down the stairwell. On the third floor they stop for a few minutes to let Kutyrev rest, their breaths pluming in the icy air. "How much farther?" asks Pavel.

"Three more."

"Can you make it?"

"I'll make it."

Slowly they finish their climb. At the end of the dim sixth-floor hallway Kutyrev, discovering his flat locked, knocks listlessly on the flimsy door. A moment later a little girl answers, frowning with disapproval. She is perhaps eight, a spray of freckles across her pert nose, blondish-red hair tied with frayed green ribbon into two uneven pigtails. An old, oversize sweater hangs nearly to her knees, its sleeves rolled past her knobby wrists.

"You're going to wake the baby," she scolds Kutyrev, who pushes past her without a word.

The little girl regards Pavel curiously. "Hello," she says. She calls softly after Kutyrev, "I carried Valentina Antonievna's bag home for her from the market. She promised me a peppermint."

Again the little girl looks at Pavel.

"You have to take your shoes off."

"That's all right," says Pavel, "I'm not coming in."

Nevertheless the little girl reaches for his arm and pulls him inside. "I'm not supposed to leave the door open because of the cold," she explains.

The air in the flat has the slightly acrid edge of the furnace—Pavel can taste it on his tongue. Still, after the day's damp cold it is a welcome. "Just for a minute," he tells the little girl.

In the kitchen with Kutyrev are two young women—Kutyrev's wife and the mother of the little girl, Pavel surmises. For her part, Kutyrev's wife, Valentina, is every bit as homely as her picture, with her bulbous nose, blotchy complexion, and weak chin, though there is nothing stern or even unfriendly in the expression with which she greets Pavel now, no trace of the hard-jawed socialist hausfrau he expected. Another surprise awaits him: She is pregnant—immensely so. She smiles pleasantly up from her chair. "Hello."

Kutyrev says, "Pavel Vasilievich—" He looks down, embarrassed. "He brought me home."

"Will you sit down, Pavel Vasilievich?" Valentina asks. "Would you like some tea?"

"Thank you, no. I should probably get going."

Sick as he is, Kutyrev has not sat down yet. He is standing beside his wife, his hand on her shoulder. He asks her now, "What happened today at market, Valya? Did you tire yourself out again? I've told you you have to take it easy."

"I was all right. Tanya helped me."

"Can I have my peppermint now?" the little girls asks.

"Shut up," the other woman sighs. Like Valentina, she is in her mid-twenties, sharply thin and pale, with the same freckles across her nose as her daughter. She absently worries a dish towel in her large white hands, the backs of which are criss-crossed with scars. "Stop being a pest, Tanya," she tells her daughter evenly. "I hear one more thing about candy and I'll beat you bloody." The threat, spoken without heat, nevertheless instantly silences the little girl, whose face assumes a carefully blank expression. From another room, suddenly, rises the soft muffled sob of a baby.

"I'll get him," the little girl volunteers.

"It was nice meeting you," Pavel tells Kutyrev's wife.

"And you."

Kutyrev, still avoiding Pavel's eyes, merely nods. His embarrassment has made him resentful. Not the man of iron after all, but simply, irrefutably, a man of flesh and feeling: a husband, soon a father. It has been an afternoon of new perspectives. Pavel realizes suddenly that he is still capable of being surprised, of being caught short by life.

The little girl returns carrying a towheaded toddler half her size, a boy, who regards them all sleepily, quiet now. "There's my heart," says the young woman, holding out her scarred hands. The little girl passes the child to her. And for a moment, watching the young woman holding her son, Pavel finds himself reluctant to leave.

"Thank you for seeing Misha home," Valentina says.

At first the name throws Pavel. Kutyrev, he realizes. She means Kutyrev. Misha.

# 28

Late next afternoon, as suddenly as Elena was taken away, she is restored to him. Simonov telephones. The paperwork regarding Elena's remains, which has all these months languished in bureaucratic limbo, has finally been returned from the district office. Her ashes have been officially released.

"I'm only sorry it took so long," Simonov says. "Unfortunately our district office moves at its own pace."

What Simonov might more accurately say is that Pavel has been waiting nearly a year for some official to scratch his signature on one form or another.

"I understand, you're angry—" Simonov begins.

"I'm not angry." Pavel breathes out. Of course he is angry, but more than that, he is profoundly tired. "I'm just ready to have this behind me, is all. I just want to bring my wife home."

Simonov is quiet. "Yes, well," he says finally. "As far as arrangements go, I should be able to have everything taken care of in a day or two. Then there's the matter of transport back to Moscow."

"I'll come get her myself."

"Of course there's no need—"

"I want to," Pavel says.

"Of course," says Simonov. "In that case, I'd be happy to meet you at the station in Tula."

And the cousins responsible for his wife's accident? It occurs to Pavel that the subject has yet to arise. Does this mean the case against them has been resolved? But then Pavel discovers he is not really interested in the cousins and their case anymore, if he ever was. Having reached this point, he has no desire whatsoever for revenge.

"And what of my wife's bag?"

"Not yet released. Don't worry, I don't expect any problems," Simonov assures him. "But if there are, I have a number of contacts with the authorities here."

"I'll wire you as soon as I know when I'm coming."

So that's it. A five-minute telephone call. Elena is to be returned to him. And afterward, when her remains are properly interred—will he simply go on with his life as he has this past year? Even as that life has become intolerable to him. He looks up at the photographs of Elena on the bookshelf and thinks, Come back to me. This Elena, he means. The Elena that lives in his memories of her. In a rush he realizes how grateful he is to have that, at least.

In Yalta, a block's walk from the shabby hotel where they always stayed, was a café called the Sun Dial, and on those warm nights when the Gypsy jazz band played up on the café's tiny wooden stage, Elena would pull Pavel from his chair, out onto the crowded dance floor. The floor shook so badly Pavel joked it was going to collapse, but Elena didn't seem to care. When he held her close he could feel the heat of her sun-browned skin through her dress, feel her heart beating strong and quick. Most nights they hurried back to their hotel room, where Pavel opened the balcony door so they could hear the waves breaking along the seawall as they made love. In the morning they woke to the sound of those waves, washed themselves in the white enamel basin on the bureau, then walked down to the beach, Elena carrying their bathing suits and a book or two in a little striped cloth bag.

All gone now.

One by one, Pavel examines each photograph, then takes Marfa Borisova's dog out. It is snowing. The pug, turned loose, stays close by, as if wary of letting Pavel out of its sight. "Go on now." Pavel waves the dog away. The naked branches of the trees rattle in the wind. Snow swirls through the islands of orange lamplight along the street. Behind him a door bangs heavily, and Pavel turns: A woman has emerged from his building and is hurrying away down the sidewalk. It is Natalya—though the image that superimposes itself over her retreating figure is Elena, suitcases in hand, rushing off to catch her train. Leaving him.

All at once Pavel is weeping. He covers his face with his hands.

# 29

A box of manuscripts arrives from Fourth Section. After signing for it, Pavel checks the evidence manifest against the box's contents: forty-seven handwritten, heavily edited poems, three thick journals full of notes and observations, a running diary of sorts, across the creased black cardboard covers of which the writer has scrawled *1933–35, 1936–38, 1939.* The final entry into the journal for 1939 is barely two weeks old.

> Lunched with Fedya today. As always, he is full of plans for the coming winter, nine-tenths of which he will never start. His sons have been stationed in Poland ever since the partitioning with Germany, he shows me the letters they write home, which he admits he carries everywhere with him. He is terrified for them, and rightly so. Poor man.

Anatoly Gurov. A minor poet, scratching along in his quiet way—certainly Pavel has never heard of him. But then the archives are full of so-called lesser writers like Gurov, whose words may be known to only a few dozen readers, if that. These poems and journals may represent the entirety of Gurov's literary output. Reading through them, Pavel is repeatedly struck by their unexpected beauty.

> At Yuri's flat, all his lovely unsold paintings leaning three-deep along the peeling wall. Yuri munching the bread I brought him, the paint on his hand seeping into the bread.
>
> Spent four hours this morning working on my poem, and all I have to show for it are six lines. Six lines! Oranges in a basket. My daughter's laugh as I lowered her into the warm tub, the water shining on her skin.

A window, Pavel thinks. An entire world.

This makes the second box of manuscripts Pavel has received from Fourth Section since helping Kutyrev home. In the three days the junior officer has been out sick Pavel has not once visited the incinerator. For now the archives are safe.

But for how long? Eventually Kutyrev will return, and the burning will begin again. With every manuscript he destroys, Pavel can feel a little more of his soul being chipped away. He has ceased imagining a future for himself—six months, a year: a darkness. If he is unable to get free of the Lubyanka once and for all, by this time next year there will be nothing left of him.

That same evening Natalya knocks on his door. "Some fellow was by looking for you earlier," she says.

"For me?" Pavel tries to keep his voice neutral. "Did he leave his name?"

"No."

"Was he alone?"

"As far as I could tell."

For a moment she meets his eyes but says nothing. Since that night at her flat there has been an unspoken, if sometimes cautious, intimacy between them.

"They found Elena," Pavel says now. But then Elena was never truly missing, he thinks. Isn't that what Simonov said? Simply a matter of paperwork.

"That's good. It's what you've been waiting for." She reaches out and squeezes his arm, once, briefly. "I'm happy for you."

There is little to do after she has gone but wait. He is not going to run. If he is to be arrested, let them arrest him here. He will immediately confess to whatever crime they charge him with, however far-fetched or ludicrous: He will abase himself, he will grovel, he will beg. Because if he tries to resist, if his captors detect even the slightest resistance, they will simply torture him until he confesses, however long that takes, and in the end all Pavel's silence will have been for nothing.

And Babel's manuscript? They will have that too. One can hold out only so long, the human heart can withstand only so much battering. If they keep him awake for days on end, if they beat him long enough, if they smash out his teeth and break his nose and then his fingers, one by one, or worse, threaten to break his mother's fingers before sending her off to the death camps of Kolyma—then it is only a matter of time before Pavel tells them exactly where Babel's manuscript is hidden. And then that too will have been for nothing.

In the kitchen he pours himself a glass of whiskey. There is only a little remaining in the bottle, bought, like all his whiskey, at the Lubyanka special commissary. Marfa Borisova's pug has followed him, hoping for food. What will become of it if he is arrested? "You and Natalya will just have to make friends," Pavel says now. The dog tilts its head. The urge to throw his glass at the wall wells up in Pavel, but then just as quickly recedes.

Resigned, he packs a small suitcase—sweaters, woolen socks, a pair of heavy trousers: winter clothes. If he is arrested, he will need them. Then he returns to the living room.

He should write his mother—Natalya will see she gets the letter. He sits down at the table, pen in hand, but the words are slow coming. He has never had a gift for writing, only a deep admiration for others who did. Finally he manages a few lines:

*I'm not sure where I'll be when you receive this. What's important is that you look after yourself as best you can. That's all that matters to me now.*

He addresses the envelope, and is about to take it downstairs when the knock comes. Marfa Borisova's dog scrambles to the door, barking. Heart pounding, Pavel slips the letter into the copy of Chekhov's stories and returns the book to its shelf. He shoos the pug away before opening the door.

"I hope," Victor says, "you don't mind my not calling first."

Pavel exhales shakily, unable even to speak. His tongue has dried in his mouth.

"Are you all right, Pavel?"

"It's nothing," Pavel says. "Come in."

Inside, Victor removes his shoes—expensive leather dress shoes, gray with mud and salt. Clumps of ice cake the cuffs of his trousers, but already the snow is melting on his hat and coat.

"I was by earlier," Victor explains. The flat's warmth has brought a flush to his cheeks.

"Has something happened to my mother?"

"No, nothing."

Victor smiles uneasily, glancing into the living room, as if he half-suspects they are not alone. This is the first time he has been in Pavel's flat. A pink ring marks Victor's forehead where his hat pressed; his hair is matted. For a moment neither man speaks, both perhaps waiting for the other to break the silence.

"I'll go get you some dry socks," Pavel says.

"Thank you."

When Pavel returns with a towel and a pair of his wool socks, he finds Victor in the living room, petting Marfa Borisova's dog. With a shock he realizes Victor has been crying, though Victor hurries to hide it now, wiping at his eyes. "Are you all right?" Pavel asks. Victor nods. "Oh, sure." He smiles wanly. "You have a nice place here. I'm surprised they let you keep it all to yourself."

"Just my luck." Pavel tosses the socks to Victor. "If I sent you home with frostbitten feet, Olga would never forgive me." He forces himself to return Victor's smile.

In the kitchen Pavel places the teapot on the stove. "Is that Donskoy Monastery?" Victor asks from the doorway. He is gazing out the window, where the snow is beginning to taper off.

"Yes."

"I've never seen it before. When I was in school, we read about how the city moved all the cemeteries out here during the Black Death. They used to burn the houses of the people who'd died to stop the plague from spreading. Did you know that?"

"No," Pavel says. Then: "Has something happened, Victor?"

"I think Maxim Andrevich was arrested today."

"You think? You're not sure?"

"I don't know. An NKVD investigator named Mirovsky telephoned our office this morning and asked if Maxim Andrevich would meet with him tomorrow. Half hour later Mirovsky calls back and says he has time today to meet. He was very polite. Offered to send a car round.

"What's strange, the car showed up right after that," Victor says shakily. "So they must have already been on their way. Maxim Andrevich said Mirovsky told him it shouldn't take more than an hour or two to clear matters up. Said I should expect him back in the office no later than one o'clock."

"But he didn't come back."

"I waited all afternoon. They've made some sort of mistake. The Zhdanovsky project—I know we're behind schedule, but that's only because the schedule was unrealistic. If anyone's to blame, it's Solovev, not Maxim Andrevich."

The teapot begins to whistle shrilly, and Victor winces. Yet Pavel feels strangely becalmed. He turns off the burner and sets the murmuring teapot aside.

"Will you tell them that, Pavel? Please."

"Tell them what?"

"That it's not Maxim Andrevich's fault."

"And after I tell them," Pavel asks, "what do you expect will happen?"

"They'll let him go. They have to."

Pavel shakes his head. "No, Victor."

"But he hasn't done anything wrong!"

"These men who arrested your boss, they don't care if he's innocent or not. As long as Maxim Andrevich confesses, they have their case. They'll charge him with sabotaging the Zhdanovsky project, or spying, or they'll simply call him a counterrevolutionary. A Trotskyite. Whatever they come up with, he'll confess to it."

Victor has gone pale.

"They'll want a list of names. Accomplices. As many names as Maxim Andrevich can produce." Pavel allows his words to settle a long second or two before continuing. "Who do you suppose will be on that list?"

"He wouldn't do that."

"He will." Pavel remembers that afternoon he happened upon Maxim Andrevich's young daughter petting the dog, the sunlight on her arm. He feels suddenly sickened, as though he has had a hand in her grief. "He won't be able to help himself."

"I don't believe you."

But he does believe him—that is why he has come here. Not to save Maxim Andrevich but to save himself. Even if Victor hasn't entirely convinced himself of the threat hanging over him—not only over him but his family as well—he is fast on his way.

"You're his immediate assistant, Victor. Soon they'll have the names of everyone in your office—that is, if they don't already have them. You, the people working under you. Everyone. Right down the line. That's how it happens." A plague, Pavel thinks, spreading from house to house, sweeping away everything.

"You could tell them I'm innocent."

"It wouldn't matter. Even if I were one of them—which I'm not, Victor: They tolerate me only because in their eyes I barely exist—but even if I were, it wouldn't make any difference. They have no loyalty, even to their own kind. Better someone else take a bullet than me or my family—that's what they think. Just like everyone else. You read the newspapers, you listen to the radio. What do you think has been happening in Russia? Have you forgotten where you live?"

Pavel stops. He has already said enough to seal his own fate—more than enough. He could just as easily be pulled beneath the waves already washing over Maxim Andrevich. No longer is he the calm observer leading poor Victor along—instinctively Pavel turns to the window, scanning the narrow street below. The few cars parked along the curb are covered in snow, empty. It is nearly eight o'clock. Too early, he surmises. But then the hour is theirs for the choosing, they could already be on their way.

It is Friday. If Maxim Andrevich is immediately interrogated, it will only be a matter of days before he breaks. If he even resists, which he may not. But chances are they'll let Maxim Andrevich sit stewing in a cell for several days, perhaps even as long as a week. They will keep him waiting until he is nearly out of his mind with worrying, and then one night a guard will roughly awaken Maxim Andrevich and drag him blinking from his cell, he will be dropped into a chair in some bright office. *Why are you here, citizen?* A beginning, an end, all in the same bottomless question.

"Listen to me, Victor. It might be days from now, it might be a week—they'll come after you. Or they'll simply call you up one day and ask you to drop by their office, like they did with Maxim Andrevich. And because you haven't done anything wrong, you'll go. What you don't understand, Victor, is that moment—when they have you in front of them—is the moment your innocence becomes irrelevant. Words like 'innocence' and 'guilt'—they're for the people outside the prisons."

Victor begins backing out of the kitchen. "I have to go home," he stammers.

"But when those same people disappear, everyone pretends nothing's happened." Pavel has followed Victor into the living room. "My best friend, Victor. They arrested him, too, you know. He just vanished." Pavel's voice breaks with emotion. "And for what? For teaching literature?"

Victor starts for the front door.

"I don't want that to happen to you and your family. Please. Let me help you."

"I have to go home."

*They will kill you*, Pavel nearly tells Victor. But Victor already understands. That is why he is so desperate now to be home with his family.

"At least let me go to the station with you, Victor."

Victor grimly pulls on his ruined shoes. "I'll manage," he says.

Watching him, Pavel thinks, How quickly everything changes! It seems like only yesterday they were watching Victor's boys race each other across that field. Marfa Borisova's pug has followed them to the door. Victor notices it, and for a moment his hands go still.

"Do you know where to catch the bus?" Pavel asks.

"I think I remember."

Pavel pulls his coat from the row of pegs, takes up the dog's leather lead. "We'll walk down with you."

# 30

The telephone awakens him—it is nearly two in the morning. Pavel stumbles blindly through the dark flat to answer it.

"Yes?"

It is Victor. "I've been thinking about what you said." He falls silent. He has not mentioned names, he is already being careful. "Will you help me?"

"If I can, yes." Pavel takes a breath, then adds: "Don't go to your office."

"All right."

"I'll come out to see you this afternoon, we'll talk then. Can you meet me on the platform? Say, two-thirty? I'd come earlier, but I have to take care of something first."

A half dozen dirty children are throwing rocks at one another beside the pit lining the path to Kutyrev's building.

"Kill the Nazis!"

Pavel recognizes the little girl from Kutyrev's flat, and calls her over. "Do you remember me? I brought Mikhail Yegorovitch home last week."

Her nose and cheeks are red with cold. A rusty streak stains her skirt and thick white stockings where the iron pipe she is holding has brushed against her.

"We're playing war."

"I see that. Whose side are you on?"

A shrug: *Does it matter?* "Kolya keeps shooting all our prisoners." She gestures with the pipe at one of the older children, a sharp-faced boy in a black ushanka with the earflaps hanging down. "But they still run away. They don't know they're dead."

"Good for them," says Pavel.

At Kutyrev's flat, his pregnant wife, Valentina, opens the door. She seems unsurprised to see Pavel.

"How are you feeling?" he asks her.

"You're the third person to ask me that this morning," Valentina says good-naturedly. "You should see how Misha keeps after me, always telling me to sit down."

"How is he?"

"Better. I think his chest is finally beginning to clear, thank God." She smiles. A faint shadow of hair darkens her upper lip. She is absently rubbing her enormous belly, her chapped hands making slow circles. A delicate pattern of tiny embroidered trumpet flowers climbs the open neck of the maternity dress she is wearing. "He's awake, if you want to see him."

"Please."

She has him wait outside the bedroom door. "Pavel Vasilievich is here to see you," Pavel hears her telling Kutyrev. "Who?" "Pavel Vasilievich." A murmur. "I don't know," Valentina says impatiently. There is a silence, then finally the door opens. "Go right in. I'll be in the kitchen, if you need anything."

Propped on a pile of pillows, unshaven, Kutyrev regards him miserably. A glass of water rests on the tiny bedside table next to a wadded handkerchief. "What are you doing here?"

The week has whittled Kutyrev down considerably. A sickly pallor tinges his skin, his black hair sticks out on one side almost comically, as if he has just awakened.

"You've lost weight," Pavel says.

"What do you want?"

"Just to ask you a question. Then I'll go."

He can hear Kutyrev breathing, a wet click with each inhalation. The smell of sweat and unwashed sheets is nearly overwhelming.

"Do you remember me asking once what you thought you would do after the archives were organized?" Pavel pauses. "You said you would move on."

Kutyrev glowers at him. "You came all the way out here to tell me something I already know?"

"I came here to ask what you think *I* will do. Afterward."

"What are you talking about?"

"You told me to be careful," Pavel says.

He catches a flicker of unease in Kutyrev's eyes.

Pavel says, "Something's going to happen to me, isn't it? Soon. Did one of your connections tell you that?"

"It's none of my business," Kutyrev mutters.

"I'm asking you. Please, Mikhail. Will I be allowed to move on as well?"

It is the first time Pavel has ever addressed Kutyrev by his Christian name. "And do what?" asks Kutyrev finally, and Pavel sees all at once that there is no bitterness or hostility behind his question, only a kind of weary resignation. The young officer reaches for the handkerchief and coughs fiercely into it, face crumpling with pain. The bed shakes, springs squeaking. Pavel hesitates, then reaches for the glass of water and waits for Kutyrev's coughing spell to end. "Here." Kutyrev wipes the spittle from his mouth, then gulps the water down, sagging against the pillows. A full minute passes before he speaks again—adequate time for Pavel to understand that whatever their differences, he can no longer despise Kutyrev, now that he has glimpsed the man beneath the armor.

"Did you think you were special, Pavel Vasilievich?" Kutyrev asks. "You think you're any different from the next person?"

"No."

"Then, what did you expect?"

"I wanted to look after my mother. Read my books," Pavel says. "Just live. That's all. The same as you."

Kutyrev gazes at him. The look on his waxen face—a mixture of dismay and pity—is answer enough for Pavel. "Don't ever visit me at my home again," Kutyrev says. "Do you hear me? Ever."

"Don't worry. I won't."

He finds Kutyrev's wife alone in the kitchen, thanks her. "Of course," Valentina says. She is pressing her hand to her abdomen, searching for the baby there, unselfconscious. "She's been kicking me all morning, the little busybody. She's restless. I think she knows her time is getting close."

"How do you know it's a girl?"

Valentina's eyes slide away, embarrassed.

"You'll laugh at me if I tell you."

"No, I won't. I promise."

"She talks to me in my sleep." Valentina looks at him now, and smiles. "You believe me?"

"I believe you," Pavel says.

# 31

Stepping off the train at his mother's stop, Pavel scans the Birulevo station platform for Victor, then checks his watch. Two-twenty. He walks to the wooden bench at the far end of the concrete platform, sits. The sun, bright this afternoon, warms his face. The train pulls away. Arrayed along the station wall are identical posters of Stalin in military cap and overcoat, surrounded by a sea of adoring faces. *The Collective Decides Everything*. In the lower-left corner of the scene a throng of marchers no bigger than Stalin's boot strides joyously forward, red banners raised. A few of the posters have already begun to peel away from the wall.

Fifteen minutes later Victor has still not arrived. I will give him until three o'clock, Pavel tells himself. If by then Victor has not shown up, chances are he has decided against this meeting or is already in NKVD custody. If he has been arrested, then he is beyond help.

A paper cup at the edge of the platform rolls back and forth on its rim.

*Please,* Pavel finds himself silently praying, *don't let me be too late.*

A few minutes after that Victor appears.

"Sorry I'm late." Victor sits down beside him. "To be honest, I almost didn't come." He exhales nervously, glancing over his shoulder at the station door.

"How are you holding up?" Pavel asks.

Victor shrugs. "I feel like shit. Considering I haven't slept in over twenty-four hours, I suppose that's normal."

The paper cup has disappeared. A moment later Pavel catches sight of it tumbling in the wind over the tracks, then down the gravel embankment, a spot of white against thornbushes.

"You're going to need money," Pavel says. "I'll give you what I have. If you have any other friends you can borrow from—and I mean close friends, people you trust—do it. Quickly. Get as much as you can. They'll ask what it's for, so you'll have to make up a believable story."

"And what am I supposed to do with this money?"

"You pack up your family and you leave."

"Just like that?"

"Yes."

"And go where, Pavel?"

"East, if you can. You'll want to stay away from Moscow or any big city where you'll have to register with the district office of internal affairs. The NKVD closely monitors those offices. It will be safer for you in the smaller towns and villages." Safer but not safe—they both understand this. Nowhere in the Soviet Union is entirely safe for Victor and his family now. "If you can stay with relatives, all the better. They'll be able to hide you."

"Won't the NKVD look for us there?"

"If they look for you, maybe. Generally they just count on people being where they're supposed to be. I mean, why run if you're innocent, right? They rely on that sort of thinking. They won't tear their hair out hunting you down, Victor. They'll just put your file aside and move on to someone else. Someone easier."

Victor rubs his face with his hands. He reaches into his coat and removes a pack of cigarettes, Primas, turning away from the wind to light up. "I've always thought I'd like to visit America," he says, sitting back against the bench. From his expression it is unclear whether or not he is joking.

"You wouldn't actually try to get out of the country, would you?"

"I may be desperate, Pavel. I'm not insane."

"You do read about people buying passports on the black market," Pavel says carefully. Passports, forged residency permits: new identities. A new life. Perhaps it is not too much to hope for. "Anyway, it's one possibility."

Victor tips his cigarette dismissively. "A *slim* possibility."

Better, Pavel is tempted to tell him, than what you face if you stay. A cold cell, a quick trial before a military troika. At least this way you try and save yourself. At least this way you have a chance.

"I need you to take my mother with you," Pavel says.

"What are you talking about?"

"I think I'm going to be arrested, Victor. I don't want her to be alone."

"Then come with us," Victor says. "Pavel, you have to."

"I can't."

At the far edge of the snowfield, where the woods begin, a bundled figure steps out into the sunlight, following a rough path of footprints through the snow.

"What I said about them putting your file aside and forgetting about it," Pavel tells Victor, "I don't expect they would do that with me. I think they'd make a point of tracking me down. Wherever I went."

# 32

The night before his mother is to leave, Pavel knocks on Natalya's door. For once he is empty-handed—he has brought no wine, no whiskey: He has only himself to offer. Natalya gazes for a long moment into his face, as if deciding whether or not to let him in. "It's late, Pavel," she says.

"I know. I wanted to see you."

"When do you go to Tula?"

"Tuesday."

Natalya nods. Pavel senses a wariness in her this evening. And he has no interest in dragging any more misfortune into her life. "I'm sorry," he says. "You're right. It is late. I'll leave."

"No, don't."

He follows her to her bedroom, where Natalya lets fall the heavy curtain across the doorway. In the darkness Pavel pulls her tightly to him, their mouths finding each other. He can taste the smoke from her cigarettes on her teeth, her tongue, bittersweet. Her hands work rapidly at his belt, then his trouser buttons.

Afterward, as if picking up the thread of an earlier conversation, Natalya asks, "What are you going to do about the dog?"

Her question stops him short. "I hadn't given it much thought." Lately he has not thought about much of anything except his mother, of her leaving. Ever since his meeting yesterday with Victor, Pavel has brooded over what he is going to tell her: what he will say, what he will never be able to say.

"I'll look after it, if you want," offers Natalya.

"You don't mind?"

"It's only for a few days. I think we can avoid killing each other for that long."

*I could keep going*—the thought comes to Pavel without warning. He could leave everything behind.

In the darkness he feels her hand touch his shoulder.

"Are you worried?"

"About what?" asks Pavel.

"I don't know. This whole business with Simonov."

"In a way it doesn't quite seem real."

"What do you mean?"

"Like Elena could come back tomorrow. Like she's still alive." After a time Pavel adds, "Or it's like she never existed. It feels like that sometimes, too. I mean, people talk about the burden of memory, but what about how vulnerable our memories are? How insubstantial. Everything I remember about Elena—the way she used to look at me, her voice. What happens to all that?" *When I'm gone,* he does not say.

Natalya's hand has gone still on his shoulder. Any moment, he is sure, she will withdraw into herself, signaling it is time for him to leave. But then, unexpectedly, Natalya speaks.

"My husband always believed we would see our daughters again. That picture you saw of Anna. He left that for me. Do you want to know why?"

"Why?"

"Because he understood I would need it. A picture. And he

needed nothing. For him every day of his life was one less day he would have to wait, one day closer to Anna and Nadezhda. He thought they were waiting for him. With God."

After a time Pavel asks, "What happened to him?"

"Nikolai? He went back East eventually. For a few years I'd get long letters from him, about nothing in particular really—his job, old friends of ours. I think he was drunk when he wrote them. The terrible thing is that he never mentioned Anna and Nadezhda. Not once. He talked about everything except them. As if they'd never been born. After a while the letters just stopped coming."

"Did you ever write back?"

"I didn't see the point." Then Natalya says, "I didn't hate him, Pavel, if that's what you think. I never hated him. Even after what he did to me. To my face."

She sits up, then reaches over Pavel. He hears the drawer on her nightstand open, and a moment later a match flares. Pavel looks up at her face, the long scar illuminated by the flickering match as she lights a cigarette. For a few seconds the shabby little room coalesces around them, then recedes again into darkness.

"He beat you."

"Just the one time," Natalya says. "We were on the train to Moscow. He just—I don't know—attacked me. One moment we're sitting there, the next I'm on the floor, and Nikolai's standing over me, screaming. Kicking me. I blacked out. Woke up in hospital. Naturally they'd put us off the train."

"Why in God's name would he attack you?"

"Why do you think? He blamed me for what happened to Anna and Nadezhda. Nikolai wasn't there, you see. He was off sick with pneumonia at the village clinic—he almost didn't make it himself. But I was there. I was their mother. And I was supposed to protect them. And I couldn't."

"What happened to your daughters, Natalya?"

Natalya sighs. "They died, Pavel. That's all that matters."

"Do you believe you'll see them again?"

A silence. Then, softly, "No." He hears Natalya draw a sharp short breath, almost a gasp. "I don't." She begins to sob.

He has only reopened old wounds long healed over. Pavel imagines what it must have been like on that train all those years ago, the crazed husband raining blow after blow onto the grief-ravaged face of his young wife while the other passengers looked on in stunned horror. Had such a scene occurred before him, how would he have reacted? Would he have moved to stop Nikolai? Would he have done anything?

Sitting up, Pavel pulls Natalya to him.

# 33

In Monday's *Pravda* there is little word of the looming war. Toward the back of the newspaper, Pavel finds a single, cursory article about Soviet troop movements just north of Leningrad, along the border with Finland. The same border Molotov has repeatedly requested be pushed back "a few dozen kilometers." In response to which the Finns have likewise mobilized their army.

A trail of muddy melted snow stretches into Kiev Station. The commuter train from Birulevo is due shortly, so Pavel heads out to the crowded platform to wait. A steady snow is falling beyond the high steel ribs of the station roof. An elderly porter in felt boots slips on the icy concrete and overturns a luggage cart. The crowd continues flowing around him.

When the train from Birulevo pulls in, Pavel helps Victor carry their bags into the station while his mother and Olga follow with the boys. As soon as everyone is settled, Victor and Olga walk over and join the line fanned before the ticket counter.

What have they told his mother? That they are going on holiday, like their last trip to the country? As if feeling his thoughts turn toward her, she looks at Pavel now, and smiles. "What?"

"Nothing."

The light from the chandeliers overhead pools in her glasses. Her small battered suitcase, held shut with a leather strap, sits between them. "Thank you for coming to see us off," she says. "It's sweet of you, Pasha. Although you certainly didn't have to." Beside her on the bench Victor's boys are coloring in one of Andrei's school cahiers.

"I wanted to." He hesitates. "Anyway, how are you feeling?"

"Like myself."

"Meaning?"

"Meaning I've decided I'm not going to discuss how I feel, good or bad." His mother says this without rancor. Nevertheless he recognizes the tone: determined, set. "I'm sick of constantly thinking about how I feel from the moment I open my eyes in the morning. I just want to enjoy the day, Pasha." She touches Misha's head, brushing the fine dark hair by his ear with her fingers. "What's that you're drawing?" she asks the boy, who accepts her caresses as a matter of course. "Is that our train, darling? Is that us on the train?"

"Yes," says Misha solemnly.

He will never see his mother again. For days Pavel has pushed the thought away, but now it returns with all the force of a blow. In a matter of hours, with Moscow behind her and this new, unmapped life begun, she will be well on her way to becoming what Elena has become for him, and Semyon. Memory. A ghost. Pavel thinks: And what will I be to her, what will I become? As the days grow into weeks, the months into years. As his mother's mind succumbs to darkness, and one by one the memories flicker out. A life cut loose from its own contracting history. He is that history now. Unearthing his picture one day, will she ask,

"Who is this?" "That's Pavel, love," Olga will tell her. "Your Pasha." The lost son.

Victor and Olga return with the tickets.

"Here, why don't we let Pavel Vasilievich and his mother have a bit of time together," Olga tells Andrei and Misha. "We'll go see our train, how's that?"

After they are gone Pavel's mother says, "You seem distracted, Pasha. Is everything all right?"

"No."

His mother's expression turns cautiously puzzled.

"It's important you listen to me now." Pavel takes his mother's hand in both of his. "Something's happened, Mama. Victor's boss—" Pavel lowers his voice, even though there is little chance of their being overheard. "He was arrested Friday. If Victor stays here, he probably will be, too. That's why he has to get his family away from Moscow."

"My God."

"They need your help, Mama. *I* need you to help them." Pavel reaches into his coat and removes a sealed envelope, which he passes to his mother. "Put this somewhere safe."

"What is it?"

"Money."

His mother turns the envelope over in her hands. "When will I see you again, Pasha?" she asks finally.

"When it's safe for me to visit." The lie sickens Pavel, but he hasn't the heart to tell his mother the truth. "Until then, you're not to write me. Do you understand? No letters, no telegrams. No telephone calls. Anything that can be traced back to you."

His mother shoves the envelope back into his hands.

"I'm not going," she tells Pavel, her voice cracking. "I'll stay with you."

"You can't."

His mother stares at him. "Why can't I?"

A family has taken the opposite bench, dropping their suitcases. They are plump, red-cheeked, robust—father, mother, adolescent son. As soon as they are seated the woman spreads an embroidered linen napkin beside her, produces from her bag sausage, black bread, mineral water, and lastly a pair of bananas, a rarity in Moscow for many years. An aura of warmth and well-being isolates them, even amid the shouts and noise of the bustling station.

"Why can't I stay with you, Pasha?"

"Please, Mama. Lower your voice."

"Then answer me."

*I can't answer you.* And perhaps his mother is able to read his thoughts, as the hurt on her face quickly fades and is replaced by a kind of wary comprehension. Pavel reaches for her then, hugging her to him, his mouth near her ear. "It's better this way," he whispers.

Victor and Olga return with the children. By now the family opposite them has finished their meal: The napkin with its border of blue flowers has vanished, the empty bottles have been thrown away, along with the bright banana peels. The luminous bubble of simple familial bliss, which only moments ago surrounded them, has evaporated.

Andrei asks, "Is it time yet, Papa?"

"Almost."

One after another, trains are called: arrivals, departures, the announcements echoing over them.

Finally Victor stands. "Will you walk us to our train, Pavel Vasilievich?"

"Are we going now?" asks Andrei.

"We're going," Victor tells him.

Outside a fringe of untrampled snow lines both sides of the

long gray platform. The hiss and throb of the waiting trains melts into the general murmur of voices. Following his mother through the crowd, Pavel finds himself unable to look away from the faces of the people streaming by—so many faces. So many memories. His mother stops suddenly, holding Misha close by her side, then turns. And it is her face Pavel now cannot look away from, his mother's face—like Elena, like Semyon—he would have live in him forever. *Pasha,* she says: Pavel can see his name on her lips, but he cannot hear her. Around them the crowd pours past.

# 34

Hours after he wires Simonov his travel itinerary, a reply arrives. *Will expect you tomorrow.* In a way this single simple line is the confirmation Pavel has been awaiting ever since Elena vanished from his life. "So that's it, then," Natalya says when Pavel tells her.

"That's it."

Late that night he is once again at Kiev Station. Less than a day has passed since he saw his mother off, and yet Pavel imagines that he has entered another station entirely. At this hour no crowds jostle along the platform, and the noise and activity have been supplanted by a deep, unhurried calm. Ticket in hand, Pavel climbs onto the train. In his berth, he locks the door and lies down on the bed until he feels the train moving. The station slides away, the lights of Moscow recede. After a while Pavel goes out into the corridor to look for the conductor, whom he finds sitting on a cot in an alcove, in his socks, reading.

"I was hoping I might buy some beer."

Opening a closet, the conductor sorts through a stack of crates. "How many bottles?"

"Two should do. And an opener, if you have one."

The beer is warm, bitter. In the end Pavel drinks only one bottle, then undresses and crawls into bed, slipping between the cold sheets. Sometime later in the night, half-asleep, he hears the doorknob to his compartment rattle. "Who's there?" Pavel calls, but no answer comes. Dressed again, Pavel pulls open the door to find the corridor empty. A ghost, he thinks.

"I wouldn't worry," the conductor says when Pavel reports the incident to him—once again Pavel has interrupted his reading. "Probably someone got the wrong compartment. Middle of the night, people getting up to piss." He shrugs. *What do you expect? These things happen.* Something in the conductor's expression suggests that there is little in the world that surprises him anymore. He is holding the book to his chest, as if to hide its cover.

"Do you ever sleep?" asks Pavel.

"Not if I can help it."

Pavel awakens once again before dawn. The train has stopped. Outside, the moon pours its brilliant blue light down over snowfields stretching away to the horizon; the shadows of clouds are sliding slowly across the snow. Wind presses against the window—Pavel can feel it pushing against the icy glass when he lays his hand there.

# 35

A schoolmaster, Pavel thinks. That is what Simonov immediately reminds him of, with his worn but neat wool suit and wire-rimmed spectacles, his crisp earnestness: a doting young schoolmaster, exiled to the provinces. He is not at all the pallid drone Pavel expected—nor is Tula itself quite the industrial pit he pictured. Wide, clean, well-paved streets lined with shops—tailors, shoemakers, teahouses—run down to the river, dark still with the dawn. "Actually it can be lovely here in the summer," Simonov tells him. "My wife and I, we'll sometimes bring our daughter down for the day. The swimming is quite good."

The smell of corrosion and oil permeates the clerk's car, a salt-splashed GAZ that has long since seen better days. The seats are split, faded. A spidery crack climbs a corner of the windshield; the steering wheel shudders under Simonov's hands. "How much of a ride do we have?" asks Pavel. The long night has left his nerves raw.

"A few hours. We should be there before noon. Have you eaten?"

"No, but I'm fine."

Once they are clear of the city, the countryside opens up, flattening. A wide, rutted track of packed snow stretches ahead. In the middle distance a train labors along in silence, trailing a neat runnel of brown smoke. The interior of the car, already cold, seems to grow colder, the windows fogging with their breaths.

"Sorry. The heat has a tendency to quit," Simonov explains. He leans forward to wipe a circle clear in the windshield with his sleeve.

For a time they drive in silence, the car swaying and slipping over the packed snow.

"I assume," Simonov says carefully, "you'll want to get back to Tula as quickly as possible."

"If I can, yes."

Simonov nods. "Will you have time to eat, do you think? My wife was hoping you might do us the honor of having lunch with us at our home." He glances at Pavel. "Nothing fancy, of course!" he hastens to add, as if already sensing Pavel's reluctance. "Just a simple hot meal." He lifts a hand from the steering wheel, and then, unsure what to do with himself, lowers it again. "Whatever you prefer."

"I'm afraid I wouldn't be very good company," Pavel says.

"It was just a thought."

A ragged collective farm looms—long low metal sheds, gray-weathered outbuildings, a gutted tractor rusting among rotting tires and discarded equipment. A man bundled up to his eyes in rags plods stiffly across the mud-scalloped yard, a bucket swinging at his side. "Are there other collectives nearby?" asks Pavel.

"A handful."

Pavel turns to look back at the man in rags, just in time to see him slip from sight. "Isn't that where they worked? The men who sabotaged my wife's train. On one of the collectives. Didn't you tell me that?"

Simonov is again wiping the cracked windshield clear.

"Yes." He taps the speedometer with a finger. "I think it's gone as well," he says.

"Do you know their names?"

"Filipov. Ilya and Ruslan Filipov. I didn't know them—personally, I mean—but you'd hear about them getting into trouble from time to time. They had a bit of a reputation." Simonov sighs. "Anyway, that's behind us now."

"How so?"

"Perhaps you'd better talk to the police."

"I'm asking you. Were they convicted?"

"They were found guilty, yes." Simonov clears his throat uncomfortably. "They ended up confessing. To everything. Once they did, the case against them more or less sorted itself out."

"They were shot, weren't they?" Pavel says.

Simonov nods once, barely dipping his chin. The car drifts, tires rumbling against the hard ruts.

Simonov says, "We've put it behind us."

"Yes." Then: "Do you think they did it?"

"They confessed."

"That wasn't my question. I asked if you thought they were guilty."

The question hangs in the air. Simonov looks over, and all at once Pavel sees the anguish in his face. *What does any of that matter now? They're dead. Leave it alone.* The clerk turns back to the road ahead, tugging at the wheel.

Tamoy's morgue is confined to a collection of wooden buildings at the edge of town. A gate stands open onto the muddy courtyard, in the center of which sits a single boxy lorry foursquare in the bright midday sun. Simonov parks crookedly in front of one of the buildings. "I have some paperwork you'll need to sign. It shouldn't take long."

Inside, a young man in tattered coveralls is slopping white paint on the wall of the small office with a rag tied to a stick. "The speedometer on the car's not working, Dmitry," Simonov tells him. "Will you go take a look at it?" Without a word the young man leans the dripping rag over the dented paint bucket and leaves. "I'll just crack the window a little," Simonov says.

Pavel glances through the doorway in the half-painted wall, into what appears to be a storage room. His gaze fixes on a row of simple wooden shelves set against the back wall. On all but two of the shelves are black metal boxes. "These boxes," Pavel says, "what's in them?"

Behind him, straining at the window, Simonov says wonderingly, "He's painted the damned thing shut."

"What is in these metal boxes?"

Simonov appears at his side. "Those are remains. We keep them here—those that aren't claimed—for a month or so. Of course, with your wife's case an exception was made." The clerk touches his arm tentatively. "Perhaps you'd like to get started on the paperwork."

Pavel does not move. So this is where Elena has been all this time.

"What happens if no one claims them?"

"We have a place set aside. In back of the compound."

"A common grave."

Simonov fingers the bridge of his eyeglasses. "A site, yes."

Pavel is tempted to ask the clerk to take him there—he doubts Simonov would refuse him, a man who has come hundreds of miles to retrieve his dead wife; a man who has suffered so long. To think: All these months of unanswered waiting, and where has it brought him? To a provincial office reeking of paint, to this storage room, these shelves. Until this very moment he has somehow believed that Elena could come back to him. When his knees weaken Pavel reaches out and braces himself against the doorframe, breathing through his mouth.

"You should sit down."

"I'll be all right," Pavel says.

A set of release forms awaits his signature. "Just a moment." Simonov slips into the storage room. Seated at the clerk's desk, Pavel signs his name over and over, mechanically, until Simonov returns. The clerk has a metal box in his hands: The lid has been secured with a neatly knotted length of twine, like a gift, from which an identification tag dangles. *Dubrova E. Antonievna.*

Pavel remembers the morning he and Elena married. A civil ceremony, with his mother as witness. Afterward, as the three of them walked to Red Square, they passed a tiny church, and Elena asked if they might stop. "Just for a few minutes." Inside, the gilt-paneled walls had been stripped to the raw plaster, and most of the icons were gone, but a row of tall thin candles smoked near the entrance. A few elderly men and women prayed softly in the dim amber light while the young priest sitting by the narrow window looked on sleepily. On a bier beside him lay an ancient-looking coffin with glass set in its lid, and Pavel and his mother and Elena each took their turn looking through the dusty glass at the body in the coffin, the church's shrouded, shrunken patron saint. A piece of lacy yellowed silk was draped over the saint's head, so that all Pavel could see was the shadowy impression of the face beneath. "How long has he been here?" his mother asked the young priest, who answered solemnly, "One hundred and seventeen years. Since our founding." In Red Square later Pavel's mother pointed her camera at them, and just before she snapped her picture Elena unexpectedly turned and kissed Pavel, with tears of happiness in her eyes, and her hair smelled like that church, smoky and bittersweet. Then the camera clicked and they moved on.

"This isn't my wife," Pavel tells Simonov. "This isn't Elena."

"You have my deepest condolences."

From another room Simonov retrieves Elena's belongings: a suitcase, a single blue leather bag. "If you'll just sign for them, I'll have Dmitry bring them out to the car," says Simonov. "Then we can be on our way."

"No," Pavel says. "I'll carry them myself."

# 36

Pavel finds Babel's manuscripts awaiting him on his desk at the Lubyanka. The accompanying form, dated two days ago—20 November 1939—bears Rodos's signature, beside which the investigator has scratched: *Hold*.

Hold.

How strange, Pavel thinks, laying his hand upon the box of bound folders: that there is no end to how far one may fall. Now, instead of adding Babel's files to Kutyrev's wall, he picks up the manuscripts and carries them into the nearly empty stacks. Overhead the bulb burns silently in its wire cage. He returns to the wall of boxes, lifts another set of manuscripts, carries it back. Then he lifts another. This is what he has stayed behind to finish.

A gesture, the hand held up before the gun's barrel, through which the bullet will pass as easily as through paper. That is what Denegin was up to, hiding his treasures in plain sight. Eventually Kutyrev will return, and as soon as the shock has subsided the junior lieutenant will once more plunge into the archive stacks. In a matter of months this small sabotage—this reprieve—will be undone.

Nevertheless, Pavel works all morning and into the afternoon, gradually whittling away at the wall of manuscripts, carrying them back into the archive stacks. He removes the manifests from every box of manuscripts—he will burn these later. Chaos: That is what Kutyrev will find waiting for him; months of meticulous work undone in a matter of hours, all of which will have be to started over again, from the beginning. By two o'clock Pavel's arms and back are so tired he must stop and rest for minutes at a time. He does not sit: He is afraid if he does he will not be able to get up again. Pavel is leaning against a shelf with his eyes closed when the telephone on his desk rings.

Sevarov says, "The major would like to see you."

The gloss of buoyant civility present in his previous meetings with Radlov is absent. The table overlooking Dzerzhinsky Square is covered not with serving dishes and cups but with folders—prisoners' folders, file after file. Radlov, sitting behind his desk, waves Pavel wearily toward an empty chair.

"How goes the reorganization?"

"It's nearly finished," says Pavel.

Radlov studies him a moment. "I understand your colleague had some sort of mishap. He's been out since last week, yes?"

"Yes."

"That's unfortunate." The officer flicks the pen on his desk blotter, sending it spinning. "I'm sure you'll manage for the time being. As long as you understand that I want this finished. We need to move on."

Move on. You and I will never move on, Pavel thinks. What we have done here, together, in this building—it will follow us to the end of our days.

Pavel says, "The last time I was here you were reading Gogol. Did you ever finish?"

"Gogol."

"You said you understood why Gogol killed himself. That you'd discovered his motivation just from reading his stories. What was that motivation?"

Radlov gazes at him curiously—he cannot seem to make up his mind whether to be angry or amused. He shrugs. "He was disgusted."

"With what?"

"His fellow man."

"No, Comrade Major. A priest, Father Matthew Konstantinovsky, had told Gogol that literature was sinful, and that he must stop writing. For Gogol, this meant the same as not living. Nonetheless, he renounced literature, in the hope of saving his eternal soul. He burned the book he had spent years writing, which was the second volume of *Dead Souls*. Then he stopped eating." Pavel asks, "Do you think this Matthew Konstantinovsky was haunted afterward by what he'd done?"

Radlov sits back in his chair, wonderstruck. "Are you quite finished with your lecture?" he asks finally. "Or is there more?"

"No more," says Pavel. "I'm done."

# 37

Pavel searches Kutyrev's desk until he finds the proper form, which he fills out, as required, in triplicate on the archives' clattering typewriter. He forges Kutyrev's crabbed signature on the final line, then summons a messenger. Afterward he returns to his work of tearing down the wall of manuscripts.

He hasn't much time now. Days, perhaps a week if he is lucky. He had seen the look on Radlov's face earlier. There is still so much to be done.

Thirty minutes later, Pavel telephones the guard on duty, who informs him the prisoners are having their afternoon exercise up on the roof. "They should be finished soon."

"Would it be possible for me to go up?"

"What, now? Can't it wait?"

"No," Pavel says. "Probably not." He can sense the guard's reluctance—as a matter of protocol or simple laziness, there is no telling which. "It will only take a few minutes."

Finally the guard says, "Bring your coat."

"My coat?"

"It gets cold up there."

* * *

Pavel has never been up onto the Lubyanka's roof. A wall of perhaps five meters shuts out the surrounding city, though the sounds of traffic in Dzerzhinsky Square can be heard. As the guard latches the gate behind him, Pavel scans the faces of the half dozen or so prisoners milling about beneath the ever-watchful eye of a tower guard, until he spots Babel.

"Do you remember me?"

Babel turns. He has gotten his glasses back, Pavel sees. His face is thinner, almost gaunt now, the cheeks sunken and hollow, covered by a scraggly beard. His coat hangs loosely on him. He appears at once both older and younger, if such a thing is possible—two men, two souls coexisting behind the same exhausted face. For a few seconds he peers searchingly at Pavel.

"The teacher."

"Yes," Pavel says.

A bird—a sparrow—swoops over the wall like a leaf caught in the wind's grip, then darts toward the funnel of smoke pouring from the incinerator chimney at the corner of the roof.

"They returned your glasses."

"For now."

Pavel nods. The plumes of their breaths drift out, disappear.

"I saw your letter," he tells Babel now. "The one you wrote to Beria, asking for your manuscripts back."

"He never answered." Babel shrugs. "Not that I really expected he would." He shoves his hands into his pockets. "I was so close to finishing them."

All this time Babel's expression has remained carefully masked. Now a flicker of despair touches his eyes, and he looks quickly away.

"At least they gave me my glasses back," he says after a time. "Something else, too." His clenched fist emerges from his coat pocket, knuckles red with cold. For a moment Pavel thinks Babel is going to strike him, but then the fist opens, revealing a handkerchief.

"My wife," says Babel. "They let her send them to me a few weeks ago. Handkerchiefs, clean clothes."

The hand closes, vanishing again into Babel's coat. "Have you brought me another story?" he asks Pavel.

"Not today."

"Pity."

The wind, strengthening suddenly, moans along the top of the wall. The guard in the watchtower turns his back to it.

"I wanted you to know that I did my best to look after your stories," Pavel says. "I only wish I'd been able to do more."

"What's going to happen to them?"

He has no answer. The two stories that Pavel has stolen—there is no way of knowing they will not eventually be discovered, and so destroyed. Or if not discovered, then simply, irrevocably lost, in that basement wall beneath his building.

The wind dies. For a moment even the noise from the square fades, first to a whisper, then altogether.

"I'm sorry," Pavel says.

Babel regards him steadily. Then, from his coat pocket, he pulls the handkerchief again. "Wipe your face. You've dust on your cheek."

"I don't want to get your handkerchief dirty."

"I have more."

Pavel accepts the folded handkerchief. He can smell the perfume on it. Babel's wife—she must have sprinkled the handkerchiefs with perfume before sending them along. A thread connecting them across distance and time, a memento of their lives together. Memory.

"Thank you," Pavel says, his voice shaking. When he reaches to return the handkerchief Babel waves him off.

"That is for the tea."

When he returns home late that night, Pavel finds a postcard waiting for him in his mailbox. *You are in my heart and in my dreams. Love.* It is unsigned. Ryazan, the postmark reads. He closes his eyes, holding the postcard to them, imagining his mother's hand touching him. He dares not keep the postcard, lest it be discovered later. He will have to hide it, too—like Babel's stories, like the photographs of Semyon and Vera. That is what this age demands: One must conceal every treasure. In this way his heart is no different from that basement wall.

Upstairs Marfa Borisova's pug meets him at the door, yelping with pleasure, eager to be outside. Pavel takes up its lead. "Good dog," he says softly, following the pug down the dark stairs. "Hurry now."

Afterward he knocks on Natalya's door. He is filthy still, he realizes: He has not even washed the dust from his hands.

"Water not working?" asks Natalya wryly.

"I was hoping I might use yours," Pavel tells her.

In the tiny bathroom Pavel fills the tub with water so hot it almost hurts, then slowly lowers himself into it. As he scrubs himself clean with a soapy rag, the water turning gray, Natalya comes and sits on the rounded edge of the claw-footed tub. "You look tired," she says finally. "I am," says Pavel. Later in her room when they make love Natalya caresses his hips, his back. Pavel has become familiar with her body, as he imagines she has become familiar with his. Again and again he traces a finger across her cheek, her mouth, feeling the soft ridge of scar, her breath on his hand. Remember this, he tells himself. All of it.

Later still, when he thinks she is asleep, Pavel dresses. It is after midnight. As he is buttoning his shirt Natalya asks quietly, "Where are you going?"

"I forgot to do something," Pavel tells her.

He slips into the basement. The darkness closes around him, but he does not turn on the light at first. Instead he pushes away every thought but one, letting it fill him even as Pavel in his exhaustion feels himself fading, as though his body were dissolving, the darkness flooding his veins.

*I read the book to the end and got out of bed. The fog came close to the window, the world was hidden from me. My heart contracted as the foreboding of some essential truth touched me with light fingers.*

From Maupassant's hand to Babel's, from Babel's to his. They are part of him now, every word.

Pavel pulls everything he has hidden from the wall: the photographs and love letters rescued from Semyon's flat, Semyon's sealed letter to Vera, and lastly, Babel's stories. Behind him the boiler clicks on, igniting with a soft *whoof.* He sets the letters to one side, then carefully returns the rest along with his mother's postcard, plugging the hole with the brick.

Natalya has waited up for him.

"Do you have an envelope?" he asks her.

He opens Semyon's letter, transfers it and the love letters to the new envelope, seals it again. "Gorky," Natalya says when he hands the envelope to her. "Who do you know in Gorky?"

"An old friend. Would you mail it for me?"

"Of course."

Pavel kisses her.

"Will I see you tomorrow?" asks Natalya.

Pavel does not answer. He kisses her again, holding her tight to him. Only then does he leave.

Upstairs Elena's suitcase and blue bag still sit in the entranceway closet, along with the small suitcase of warm clothes he has packed for himself. As for Elena's ashes—he has made arrangements to have them interred at the village cemetery in Birulevo, not far from his mother's old flat. Tomorrow he will take them there on the train, but for now the box sits on the bookshelf. He hopes there is time enough for him to finish this one last thing.

Will he hear the car that comes for him?

Pavel looks out the window at the street, but it is empty. He imagines that morning in May when they arrested Babel, the crunch of tires on the driveway, then footsteps, approaching. Babel, roused from sleep, rising from his bed to stand at the window. The dark trees, the immense, starless sky—all still. The very edge of the hidden world. His breath on the glass.

ACKNOWLEDGMENTS

I would like to thank the following individuals and institutions, both here in the U.S. and abroad, for their generous support and encouragement. Susan Kamil. Noah Eaker. Peter Ho Davies. Nicholas Delbanco. Eileen Pollack. Nancy Reisman. Amy Williams. The Avery Hopwood and Jule Hopwood Writing Awards Program. The Fred R. Meijer Fellowship in Creative Writing. In Moscow, Vladislav Yashkov and Hugh Winn. The Andrei Sakharov Foundation. And finally, for sharing your stories with me: Yevgeny Borisovich Bronshtein, Peter Demant, Lev Mendelevich Gurvich, Paulina Stepanovna Myasnikova, and Marina Nikanorovna Okrugina.

## A NOTE ON THE AUTHOR

Travis Holland holds an MFA from the University of Michigan, where he was a recipient of Hopwood Awards for short fiction and the novel. His stories have appeared in *Ploughshares, Glimmer Train, Five Points*, and *The Quarterly*.

## A NOTE ON THE TYPE

The text of this book is set in Bembo. This type was first used in 1495 by the Venetian printer Aldus Manutius for Cardinal Bembo's *De Aetna*, and was cut for Manutius by Francesco Griffo. It was one of the types used by Claude Garamond (1480-1561) as a model for his *Romain de L'Université*, and so it was the forerunner of what became standard European type for the following two centuries. Its modern form follows the original types and was designed for Monotype in 1929.